STRANGE THINGS DONE

As winter closes in and the roads snow over in Dawson City, Yukon, newly arrived journalist Jo Silver investigates the dubious suicide of a local politician and quickly discovers that not everything in the sleepy tourist town is what it seems. Before long, the RCMP have begun treating the death as a possible murder and Jo as the prime suspect.

Strange Things Done is a top-notch thriller—a tense and stylish crime novel that explores the double themes of trust and betrayal.

D0103851

STRANGE THINGS DONE

ELLE WILD

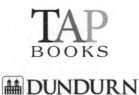

TAP
BOOKS

DUNDURN

Copyright © Elle Wild 2016

All rights reserved. No part of this publication may be reproduced, stored in a retrieval system, or transmitted in any form or by any means, electronic or mechanical, photocopying, recording, or otherwise (except for brief passages for purposes of review) without the prior permission of TAP Books Inc. Permission to photocopy should be requested from Access Copyright.

All characters in this work are fictitious. Any resemblance to real persons, living or dead, is purely coincidental.

Editor: Diane Young
Design: Jennifer Gallinger
Cover Design: Sarah Beaudin
Cover Image: Aurora Borealis by Rafal Konieczny; Ice by Jared Erondu
Printer: Webcom

Library and Archives Canada Cataloguing in Publication

Wild, Elle, author
    Strange things done / Elle Wild.

Issued in print and electronic formats.
ISBN 978-1-4597-3380-0 (paperback).--ISBN 978-1-4597-3381-7 (pdf).--
ISBN 978-1-4597-3382-4 (epub)

    I. Title.

PS8645.I4135S77 2016   C813'.6   C2015-908783-X
                                           C2015-908784-8

1 2 3 4 5   20 19 18 17 16

 Conseil des Arts   Canada Council   ONTARIO ARTS COUNCIL
du Canada   for the Arts   CONSEIL DES ARTS DE L'ONTARIO
                                                       an Ontario government agency
                                                       un organisme du gouvernement de l'Ontario

We acknowledge the support of the **Canada Council for the Arts** and the **Ontario Arts Council** for our publishing program. We also acknowledge the financial support of the **Government of Canada** through the **Canada Book Fund** and **Livres Canada Books**, and the **Government of Ontario** through the **Ontario Book Publishing Tax Credit** and the **Ontario Media Development Corporation**.

Care has been taken to trace the ownership of copyrighted materials used in this book. The author and the publisher welcome any information enabling them to rectify any references or credits in subsequent editions.

— *J. Kirk Howard, President*

The song lyrics to "Frozen Town" in Chapters 14 and 20 are reproduced by the kind permission of Dave Quanbury and Brandy Zdan.

The lines from "Thirteen Ways of Looking at a Blackbird" from *The Collected Poems of Wallace Stevens by Wallace Stevens*, copyright © 1954 by Wallace Stevens and copyright renewed 1982 by Holly Stevens. Used by permission of Alfred A. Knopf, an imprint of the Knopf Doubleday Publishing Group, a division of Penguin Random House LLC. All rights reserved.

The publisher is not responsible for websites or their content unless they are owned by the publisher.

Printed and bound in Canada.

TAP Books Inc.
3 Church Street, Suite 500
Toronto, Ontario, Canada
M5E 1M2

For Mr. Wild and Max Wild.
And for Sally Whitehead.

Prologue

The pattern of her demise became suddenly clear, as though a dark kaleidoscope had just been turned. Everything snapped into focus then: the sharpness of the stars, the bowed outlines of trees, the expression on his face.

A blast of arctic air hit her with such force that it made her gasp and take a step back, breaking a crisp skin of snow. He moved forward, her partner in the same terrible dance. The air between them was charged, and out of the corner of her vision she saw something flash, as though the intent written on his face had become a tangible, physical force. She turned to flee into the shadows of the forest, but he caught the sleeve of her parka, then grabbed her by the throat. Impossible to twist away, though she railed and shoved. He swung her hard and the kaleidoscope turned again—filling her with a bright shower of sparks and then blackness.

———∞∞∞———

Gradually she heard a distant clamour and something being dragged; that something was her. But what really bothered her was the bone-aching cold.

She opened her eyes and found herself staring up at tangle of stars. She marvelled for a moment at the emerald hue of the sky. How did she get here? Where was she going? The stars looked jittery. Not quite right. She felt like some lost explorer, painfully scanning from the Great Bear to Polaris, as though mapping the night sky would help pinpoint her location. But the stars would not stay still and it hurt to look at them. She turned her head away and saw instead the jagged silhouette of trees flashing past in jerky stops and starts. Snow and ice scraped against her cheek.

She felt herself lifted into the air and seated on something. A fence, perhaps. For one teetery moment, she balanced there, her arms hung loosely around someone's shoulders like a sleepy child. Somewhere below her, the roaring grew louder. She was dimly aware of a tilting feeling, the needling scent of pine, and that she was slipping backwards. She lifted her head and their eyes met, a fleeting exchange filled with mutual surprise, and she remembered everything.

She tumbled backwards, kicking and clawing at the emptiness as she fell. Her panicked hands reached out to the swirling mass of northern lights above her, an undulating pattern that formed a last wordless message while the river below rushed up to meet her.

1

Jo Silver heard the throng of reporters before she saw them: a cacophony of questions and her name shouted abrasively.

"Josephine! Over here! Jo!"

She cursed under her breath, but kept her head down as they swarmed, jostling and squawking like the seagulls that battled for scraps in the city's bloated dumpsters.

"Jo, what do you think of the public's scrutiny of the media in the wake of …?"

She focused on navigating the wet concrete stairs down from the Vancouver Sun.

"Jo! What about the media's moral obligation to protect the public's safety?"

Jo wondered who had talked. Was it her source? Or was it someone associated with the department? Either way, the fallout would be the same.

"Josephine, is it true that the VPD paid you to kill the story?"

She hurried from the base of the building to an adjacent parking lot, watching the water bleed into the toes of her black canvas sneakers.

"Josephine! Do you know the true identity of the Surrey Strangler?"

She calculated the distance to her car. Twenty feet? Thirty?
"Is the Sun going to keep you on?"
Cold rain trickled down the back of her neck and traced the top of her spine. Almost to the car. Almost safe. And there it was. The question she'd been dreading.
"Josephine! How does it feel to be responsible for the death of another human being?"

Jo jolted awake. The dream was always the same in tone, if not in content. Accusation. Anger. Guilt. Her present surroundings were only vaguely familiar … *Dawson City*, she thought. She'd been in this "city"—if you could call it that—for a week now. She'd rented a room from a dancer named Sally LeBlanc, her new housemate. That much she remembered, but her recollection of entering the room any time recently was dim.

Jo lay on the bed in the darkness and breathed deeply, taking in the dry, dusty air, feeling the cold permeate layers of bedding. The scent of smoke from the bar lingered on her hair. The skin on her face felt like it was stretched to the point of breaking, same as the rest of her. Brittle. She listened to a heater working overtime, thinning out the air even more. Her tongue was coated in a layer of something thick and sour, and her head throbbed. *Had that been the pounding sound?* The pillowcase smelled of mold and nicotine. She wished she'd had the foresight to leave a glass of water on the bedside table last night.

Last night …

There was a thudding sound again, a fist on wood. Someone was at the door. Someone wanted in.

Her memory of the previous night was hazy after a certain point. They'd been drinking something Sally ordered … Canadian Ice: peppermint schnapps and Yukon Jack. (She felt her insides roil at the very thought.) They'd argued and Sally had stormed off in a clatter of high heels. Alone at the bar, Jo had quietly observed the woolly strangers around her, searching for some hidden connection with another person, finding nothing. The dark winter months had stretched out before her then. She'd toyed momentarily with the idea of leaving on the next flight out. Last chance before freeze-up: when the Yukon River froze and the ferry to the west was dry-docked. Then the Top of the World Highway to Alaska would close, the airport would follow suit, and the Klondike Highway—the only route out via the south—would begin to snow in. She'd shivered and pushed the thought away. A winter in Dawson might be punishing, but it was at least a chance to start over.

Jo had known she was in trouble when the first slap of cold air hit her in the parking lot and she still didn't feel sober. The stars had looked messy as she'd squinted at them, and she'd fought the urge to rearrange them. Then she'd felt a gentle hand on her elbow.

"Hey," he'd said, "you okay?" It was his eyes that had startled her: the shifting colours of water, framed in laugh lines. He'd looked concerned, despite his smile. There was an intensity about him that was disarming, but also promising. Jo's timing had always been lousy.

She'd turned away. "Fine."

"You're Josephine, aren't you?"

"Just Jo."

"Well, Just Jo." He'd said his name, but she was distracted. His dark hair was long, almost down to his shoulders, and there was a hint of fire in the suggestion of a beard. He had a Celtic look about him. She was willing to bet he'd had freckles as a kid. He'd removed his glove to shake her hand, so she'd done the same, and felt an electric jolt when their skin met. She'd shoved her mittens back on and thrust fists back into pockets while he'd layered on thick gloves. *What had he said his name was? Burn? Burnie?*

Then Jo had remembered reading something about him during her first couple of days in Dawson. *Byrne.* "You're the artist, right?"

"Yeah. Maybe you should let me paint you sometime," he'd said. "Is that a line?"

"Most definitely. I'm a carver." Said with a smile.

Jo had seen his carvings around Dawson: smooth, elegant lines, hewn from wood and antler and bone. Many of the statues were snarling wolves or the stray huskies that loped through town with heads lowered and tails down, sniffing the bones of buildings abandoned since the Gold Rush. Dawson City was a ghost town, with snow drifting along the wooden boardwalks instead of tumbleweed.

Whether or not the offer of a ride had been entirely innocent was difficult to say, but something about the man was like a flaming hearth in a snowstorm. The heat generated by his touch had coursed through the rest of her body.

Again the banging sound. "Go away!" Jo called out, her voice hoarse. It was probably Sally. Jo couldn't remember if Sally had come home last night. Maybe she'd forgotten her keys.

Had anyone seen Jo leave Gertie's with the sculptor? There'd been that woman in the red parka. Byrne had just opened the passenger door to his pickup when a figure descended the front steps of the bar and disappeared into the shadows of parked trucks.

"Christopher!" The woman's voice had been shrill. Byrne had slammed the passenger door, but Jo had still been able to hear snippets of their dispute. Their faces through the thick frost on the window had looked distorted and eerie, the woman's red parka bleeding through the cracked ice.

"It's none of your business, Marlo."

"There are some things that I make my business, Christopher. I've been watching you. I know where you go!"

The woman had followed him to the driver's side. In the cab, he'd thrust the key violently into the ignition and let the engine idle for a moment as she shouted at him and banged on the glass. "Don't think I'm going to keep your dirty little secret! I'll tell! I'll tell *her!*"

Then the giant pines were moving. Jo remembered the icy feel of the seatbelt under numb fingers. Byrne had fumbled with the radio dial until something soft was playing, guitar strings pleading in time with the insistent scratch of wipers against windshield. Jo had the dim recollection of driving somewhere with Byrne, and also of him being at Sally's house. He might have helped Jo into bed. *Oh no ...* Then her memory ended.

Someone hammered at the door again, in time with the thudding in her head. They weren't going away, then.

Jo leaned on one elbow and felt for the switch on the lamp next to the bed. The light blinded her momentarily. She squinted at the bedside clock; it was just after seven. *A wholly uncivilized hour.* Next to the clock: an old photo of her father and his terrier, Pepper Spray, a paperback copy of *The Name of the Rose*, and a pair of prescription glasses.

The windows were framed with velvet curtains, not fully drawn, exposing a thin line of black glass. Still dark outside. The room was small, but lushly decorated in hues of bright pink and blood red that made Jo think of a Western frontier bordello. A bearded face on the wall watched her with beady eyes: the stuffed head of a mountain goat, which resembled either Pan himself or some kind of sacrifice to the god of pleasure in his honour.

Jo pulled back the musty blankets to reveal that she was still wearing the same clothes she'd worn to Diamond Tooth Gertie's. Minus her jeans. She caught sight of herself in a gold-rimmed mirror on the far wall. Her dark, unruly hair was tied back in a painfully tight ponytail, and her face—pale at the best of times—looked downright ashen. She looked older than her twenty-five years. *Some days it's best not to look.*

There was a plastic bucket next to the bed.

"Oh God," she said, to no one in particular, though it sounded as if she were addressing the goat. She had just remembered that it was her first day of work in her new post: editor of the *Dawson Daily*. She leaned over and unceremoniously dry heaved into the bucket.

Jo managed to pull her jeans back on, navigate the stairs, and find the front door, while only bumping into one item of furniture in the dark living room on the way. She considered this to be a victory of sorts. "Coming!" she called out, irritated as much by another knock as by life in general. She'd planned to set her alarm for 6:30 a.m., but had either bungled it or forgotten. "Keep your pants on!" She kicked away a stray pair of Sally's stilettos that were blocking the door and opened it to find a uniformed officer. His dark eyes expressed surprise. He blinked.

"Josephine Silver?" His tone was serious. Jo felt a rush of confusion. Surely he must want her housemate? Or did he have some connection to her father at the VPD? Strange hour for a welcoming committee …

"Jo. Yes," she said.

"Sergeant Cariboo, Dawson RCMP." He flashed the badge.

Jo caught herself thinking that he was young to have made sergeant, still this side of thirty.

"I'm sorry to bother you, Ms. Silver, but I need to ask you a few questions."

"Me? Now?"

"I'm afraid so." Cariboo had a lean and lanky look about him that made Jo think, "hungry." He also had an undeniable boyish appeal. *Too clean cut, though. And a uniform*

"Come in," she said.

Jo felt around the wall in the kitchen until she found a light switch, then immediately regretted it. Sally was not the type to tidy up. The sheer scale of disorder in the two-bedroom Victorian house was overwhelming. A faucet above a sink full of moldering, unwashed dishes tapped out a methodical rhythm. On a table in the living room, an emerald bottle of absinthe dripped onto the stained carpet, gluing a hot pink feather boa in place. Jo led Cariboo through to the living room. The floors were uneven, or maybe it was just that she felt off balance; it was difficult to tell for sure. She made a quick mental list of things that needed to find another place to exist: an antique sewing machine accompanied by scraps of fur and sequined material (apparently abandoned in midproject), more dirty dishes, a discarded can-can costume, and bits of laundry—of dubious cleanliness. The pièce de résistance: a rifle leaning precariously in one corner of the living room. *Hope to God she's got a licence for that.*

The sergeant glanced at the gun only fleetingly, accepting a seat on an overstuffed Victorian armchair once Jo had swept a pile of laundry onto the floor. "Is there anything wrong?" she said. "Is Frank okay?"

The officer pulled out a notepad. The knuckles on his right hand were bandaged. "Frank?"

"My father." She felt her throat constrict.

"It's not a family matter, Ms. Silver. I'm sure your father is fine. Can you tell me where you were last night between the hours of midnight and 5 a.m.?"

Jo swallowed. She wished for a glass of water, an idea that was both appealing and repulsive at once.

"Ma'am?"

"Am I in some kind of trouble?"

"Just a routine investigation at this point, but I do need you to answer the question."

"What kind of an investigation?"

Sergeant Cariboo straightened up in the chair, as though squaring off for a fight. "I'm not at liberty to discuss the investigation. Please. Answer the question."

"Hang on a second, Sergeant ... Cariboo, is it?"

"Yes."

"I'm pretty familiar with police procedure, and I know that I don't have to participate in the interview unless I want to. And I'm not feeling especially helpful at the moment. So if you want to interview me, you're going to have to tell me what this is all about."

Cariboo gave her a long, appraising look. He pushed himself farther back in the chair, as though shifting gears. "We've found a body in the river."

"Whose body?" Jo leaned forward.

Cariboo said, "My turn. Where were you last night?"

"I was at Diamond Tooth Gertie's last night. The gambling hall?"

"Yup," he said. "Until what time?"

"Whose body?" Jo folded her arms over her chest. There were times when it was handy to have been raised by a police officer. Of course, that sad fact had also been her undoing.

Cariboo looked conflicted. He raked one hand through his thick, black hair. Jo tried not to think about what pressures he might be under. She guessed by his surname that he was First Nations and wondered then whether he had a point to prove—and a small, underqualified team to prove it with—but she filed the thought away. She didn't want to empathize with him. Not this time.

"I'm not at liberty to discuss it with you," Cariboo said. "Besides, we haven't made a positive identification yet."

"Well, what's this got to do with me?"

"What time did you leave Gertie's last night?"

"I'm not sure … I didn't look at my watch when I left."

"Did you leave before closing?"

"Why would the RCMP want to question me? What is this, some kind of small-town 'pin-it-on-the-outsider' act?"

Cariboo's expression softened a little. "Look. I'm sorry to have to start your day like this. Your first day, right?"

Jo nodded, giving him nothing.

"We just have to rule some things out. Trace this person's movements in her last hours. In all probability, this is just a stupid accident. It happens. Sometimes people drink too much, and things happen."

Trace her movements in her last hours. Another dead woman. And it sounded as though the RCMP already knew where Jo had been last night and had some reason to speak with her specifically. She forced herself to breathe deeply. "What kind of things? Has anything like this happened before?"

"Oh …" Cariboo squirmed in the chair a little. The Victorian wingback looked too formal for him. "I couldn't say specifically, but we do respond to a high number of alcohol-related incidents. Big part of policing in the North." Something about his demeanour had changed. He looked unduly embarrassed.

"Have you led a murder investigation before?"

Cariboo's lips parted slightly and he made a soft sound, like air leaving a balloon. "Nobody's talking about murder."

"But you haven't ruled it out yet?"

Cariboo considered her for a moment. There was a long pause, during which Jo was dimly aware of the nagging cold and the raucous laughter of a distant raven.

"Look," he said with a sigh, scratching his head. "Let's help each other here. I'll make this as quick and easy for you as possible, and you tell me about last night. You were seen leaving the bar with a local named Christopher Byrne. Can you confirm that?"

She wanted to tell Cariboo that the last time she'd helped police in a murder investigation, a woman had died as a result. Instead she said, "Why do I need to confirm it if you already have a witness who's confirmed it? I'm under no legal obligation to answer any of your questions."

"Look, you're a journalist, so you'll need information about things from the police from time to time. Right now I need information. Do we have an understanding?"

"No, Sergeant, we do not." Jo had stood her ground with veteran officers who were far more intimidating than Cariboo. The sergeant had a melancholy aura about him that made him seem—not fragile exactly—but somehow damaged.

"I see …" Cariboo frowned and scribbled something in his notepad. He thought for a moment before returning her gaze with a new intensity. "Are you worried people will find out that Byrne stayed the night?" There was something about the tone of his voice, some effort to make the question seem more matter-of-fact than it really was.

"He did *not* stay the night. He just gave me a ride home."

"What time did he drop you back here?"

"I'm not sure."

"Did you sleep with him?" Cariboo gave her a sharp look.

"Is this still part of the investigation, or are you just trying to determine whether I'm available?"

"Part of the investigation." Cariboo looked down, where his gaze found the pile of laundry that Jo had toppled, including a bright orange thong. Flustered, he looked away. Jo was relieved to see that the undergarments on the floor were not her own.

"Then no." *At least, I don't think I did.* As if on cue, the raven made a guttural sound.

"Did you stop anywhere on the way back from Gertie's?" Cariboo was searching her face.

"No." Jo said, and then thought about it. She remembered the cab of Christopher Byrne's truck. The strip of duct tape marking a tear in the cold leather seats. The feathery patterns of ice on the windows. Byrne's face in profile: tousled dark hair, high cheek-bones, and a coppery shadow across his jawline. The windshield wipers beating a slow tempo—a drowsy metronome. She'd closed her eyes, just for a moment … then … had she fallen asleep?

"Are you absolutely certain of that?" Cariboo glanced up from the notebook.

"Why does it matter?" Because it did matter. She could tell.

"Do you remember?"

"Yes." But she didn't. Not entirely. *Stars. There were a thousand stars in the sky at one point. The dark shapes of trees through the window. No houses. Not downtown then.*

"Think very carefully, Ms. Silver, because if I find out that you're lying …"

"I'm not lying," Jo bristled at the accusation. Lying was something you didn't do in her family. She learned very quickly never to lie to a police officer. *Unless you lie very well.* Frank hated being lied to by his own family: he had enough of lies at work. Jo had always prided herself on being honest. *I should never have killed that story.* "I'm not lying," she said again, with more force than she felt. "However, my memory of the evening is a little foggy."

"How much did you have to drink last night?"

"Enough that I am not feeling especially perky this morning."

"I see." He rested his notebook and pen in his lap for a moment, giving her a look. "One last thing. Did you meet anyone in the parking lot as you left?"

"Yes. There was a woman there."

"A woman?" His tone was hopeful.

"Yes, she came out of the casino just behind us. Mr. Byrne might have called her Marta ... or Marla ... Something like that, I think."

"What did she look like?"

"Long hair. Brunette. Red parka. Jeans maybe? Very angry."

"What was she angry about?" He leaned forward in the chair, his movements tight.

"I dunno. I couldn't hear very well once Byrne shut my door because they were both outside. It sounded as though she'd been following him and was upset about something."

"You have no idea what?"

Jo shook her head. She knew she could give the sergeant a little more, but something held her back. In part it was the past, but it was more than that, too. Maybe she wanted to know more about Byrne before she sold him down the river. Or perhaps, if she were honest with herself, there was something else at work.

Cariboo was watching her closely. "If you remember anything else about last night, anything at all, please get in touch with me." He pulled out his card and handed it to her, stiffly. The atmosphere in the room had changed. "And a word of warning, Ms. Silver." Cariboo's eyes were so dark they were almost black. "If I were you, I'd be more careful about who I associate with in Dawson."

Jo held his look. "And if I were you, Sergeant, I'd be more careful when I was shaving." She nodded to the bandages over his knuckles.

His eyebrows raised in surprise and some emotion twisted at his mouth, but he made no response.

A sobering blast of Yukon air followed in the wake of Sergeant Cariboo's departure through the front door. Jo briefly considered another unsatisfactory retching session, but opted instead to call her father, a choice she only narrowly preferred. She hated to ask anyone for help. Ever. But Frank would be able to tell her how to handle Cariboo and his questions. When she pulled out her cellular, however, the phone bore a bleak "No Service" message. Jo frowned. She'd forgotten about that, too. *It's flipping 2004. The world is wired, and Dawson City can't even get cellular service.*

She tried not to think about the body in the river for a moment, or how she was going to make it through her first day at the *Daily*. She knew she was going to have to forgo her morning shower and get right to work, making her introductions at the *Daily* as brief as possible. But first, she needed to hydrate.

A quick inspection of the kitchen revealed that every glass in the house needed washing, so she snapped on a stained rubber kitchen glove and washed one. The water from the kitchen tap had a mysterious murky quality to it. As she took another sip, she felt her stomach turn. *To hell with it.* She emptied the rest of the water into the sink and annexed a bottle of gin from the bar instead. She poured liberally, then opened the freezer door of the refrigerator to look for ice, revealing a landscape of Tupperware and steaks labelled "moose." An ice-cube tray had frozen to the appliance.

Sally shuffled into the kitchen, wearing a leopard print bathrobe and blinking like some nocturnal creature. "There's an ice pick in the top drawer."

"Good to know if I need to leave town in a hurry," Jo said.

"You'd better not, if I heard correctly." Her housemate's blonde hair stood up at odd angles and there were dark circles below her eyes.

This was a different Sally than Jo had first been presented with: the one with the carefully pencilled lips and brows, the modern Marlene Dietrich. With her make-up on, Sally could pass for being still in her twenties, perhaps only a little older than Jo. At a generous guess, she was about five and a half feet tall—if you counted her customary six-inch heels. But now, without her make-up and stilettos, Sally looked small, thin-lipped, and cynical. Jo decided that she liked this Sally better.

"*Shame*less eavesdropping!" Jo said.

Sally's voice was quiet but cutting. "I am a little worried you may not last the winter." The look she gave Jo had a seriousness about it, like a scientist assessing the results of an experiment gone horribly wrong.

Jo took a sip from the glass. The soapy gin had a pleasantly antiseptic flavour. "What's it to you?"

"Your rent money." Sally put her hands on her hips, blocking the doorframe.

"What do you need it for? You've got a job."

"The tourists are leaving, if you haven't noticed. Gertie's will close soon." Her lips formed a firm line.

Jo had the distinct impression that Sally was leaving something unsaid. Normally Jo would have pressed further, but as she'd just been caught red-handed drinking Sally's booze, she let it go for the time being. "About last night ..."

"Yeeesss ..." Sally smiled, and Jo noticed that one side of her mouth lifted more than the other, giving the impression that even she didn't quite believe the smile.

"You don't happen to know ... what time I got home ...?"

"No, dear. But I did see Christopher Byrne's truck parked out front, as bold as daylight when I came in. And the door to your ... *boudoir* ... was closed."

"Ah."

Sally cocked an eyebrow, sizing Jo up. "By the way dear, don't let all the attention go to your head. I mean, you're cute and all, but Dawson is a pretty small dating pool, especially in the winter, and you're fresh meat. Everyone has already slept with anyone they're interested in sleeping with."

"Did I ...?"

Sally wore a quizzical expression, a cat with her paw on the tail of some small creature. "I haven't the slightest, darling. I didn't talk to Chris."

"Oh."

"Of course, it's everyone else you have to worry about in this town. Particularly anyone else who saw you getting into the cab of his truck."

Jo felt her stomach lurch again.

2

Jo Silver closed her eyes tightly. It felt as though a meaty taiko master were using her head as a drum. When she opened them again, the *Dawson Daily* was still a tiny, one-room office. Stacks of newspapers the colour of tobacco-stained teeth lined every available counter space, making her feel decidedly queasy. Fortunately (for her head), the room was dim, illuminated by a metal desk light and a dented floor lamp. The windows of the *Dawson Daily* were still coldly black.

"Whose body?" Doug Browning, outgoing editor of the *Daily*, blinked behind 1970s aviator-style prescription frames. The glasses seemed to magnify his pale eyes, hedged by bushy, apologetic eyebrows. His long, blonde hair was pulled back in a ponytail, and his greying goatee accented his face like an excla-mation point. Jo found herself betting that he owned, or had once owned, a VW camper van.

Jo cleared her throat. "He wouldn't say."

When Doug had shaken Jo's hand, he'd said, "I'm, uh, man I'm sorry about what happened in Vancouver, eh?" His soft, earnest tone of voice had caused Jo to break eye contact. "An emo-tional bleeder," her mother would have said in one of her snap judgements. Not someone who would survive life in a hospital emergency ward. Jo generally wasn't good with Doug Browning's brand of touchy-feely softness. At least she would only be working with Doug for a week, until she officially took over as editor.

Doug was swinging back and forth in a peeling, faux-leather swivel chair: a pendulum that measured discomfort. Jo wondered whether she was the source of his unease, or whether it was the news that Jo had just conveyed. Probably Doug had realized that he would know the deceased Dawsonite, which might explain his look of alarm. Still, there was something about his reaction that expressed shock, but not surprise, a fact that Jo decided to file away for later.

Doug licked his lips. "Ah. What part of the river, did Johnny say?"

"Johnny?"

"Sergeant Cariboo," Doug said, tugging at a stray bit of wool on his curling sweater.

"Ah. No, he didn't say." Jo was already zipping her parka back up. "What's he like?"

"Who? Johnny?"

"Yeah."

"Different."

"Meaning?" Jo had left her black toque on, hoping that it might stifle the scent of stale smoke in her hair. It didn't seem to be working.

"Different from when he was a kid. Everyone thought he'd be a rock star. He was that good."

"What happened?"

"His old man had a gig one night. Uh, he was a musician, too, you see. Taught Johnny to play guitar. Anyway, James—his old man—went out in a snowstorm after the gig. Never made it home."

"Oh no," she said.

"Yeah. Johnny had to support his family. He started working the front desk at the Dawson RCMP office one summer and has been there ever since. Smart kid, at least."

"I see." Jo looked at her boots for a moment, thinking about her old guitar, about strumming it on the back porch. She'd never been all that good, but she'd once dreamed of writing for *Rolling Stone*. "Well. Better get out there. Any tips?"

"Yeah, don't eat yellow snow." Doug sniggered.

Jo shot him a look that she hoped would read as, "*Seriously?*"

"Okay, um, you could talk to people at the Riverside Café on Front Street. I think it's still open. Or try the Snake Pit—that's the pub in the basement of the Westminster Hotel. Pink building on Third. Locals go there for a little somethin' in their coffee to start the day right." A litany of weary smile lines framed his eyes.

"But the sun's not even up yet. I don't think …"

"Nine. The Pit opens at 9 a.m."

"What!"

"That's the North for you."

"Well, I guess it does have its merits," Jo said, turning to leave. "I'll meet the others when I get back."

"Oh, about the others …"

There was something in the way he said it that made her turn around. "Yes?" she said. Wary. As if on cue, a papery, scurrying sound emanated from a crate next to Doug's desk. Curious, Jo moved forward for a look, causing a flurry of activity inside the box. A sticker that read "The medium is the message" had been affixed to the lid.

"That's Marshall," Doug said. "He's in charge of newspaper disposal and recycling."

Jo leaned closer. Inside the crate, a plump, gold-coloured guinea pig perched on his haunches, sniffing the air and worrying

his hands. One beady eye appraised Jo, the other was conspic-
uously missing.

"What happened to him?"

"I rescued him from a … well, a classroom bully who thought
it would be funny to put a pencil in his eye."

"Omigod … Poor little fella." Jo reached out to pet him. Marshall
trembled suspiciously, flaring his nostrils. "What classroom?"

Doug's shoulders lifted, as though expecting something
heavy to be placed there. "Didn't I mention that?"

"What?"

"Well … everyone in Dawson kind of leads a double life. Has
to, to make ends meet, in, uh, all honesty." His mouth did something funny on the word "honesty," as though he had trouble
with the shape of it.

Jo studied Doug's face, the solemn creases of his forehead,
feeling somewhat apprehensive about the direction the conversation was taking. Whatever detail he had omitted in their
conversations about the position, Jo felt it hadn't been an accidental oversight.

"I teach school by day and run the paper by night. But it's
all good, right?" Doug brushed self-consciously at a smudge of
chalk on the cuff of his cardigan.

"Oh. I mean, the salary is not sizeable, but surely …?"

"This is the first year the salary for this position has been sup-
plemented by the KLA. That's the Klondike Literary Association.
Prior to that, the salary was based entirely on ad revenue, after
the hard costs of running the paper were covered."

"I see," Jo said. "But you didn't wish to stay on, then? Now
that there's been a salary increase? I mean, you could have …"

"No." He said it firmly, as though trying to persuade himself.
"I need to … I would like to be gone by freeze-up. I'm taking an
early retirement."

Jo found herself wanting to ask how this was possible, but thought the question would come off as being too personal. "Well, what about the other staff? I mean, there are other names credited on your site. Why make an outside hire?" Jo was now genuinely alarmed by Doug's revelations.

"I contribute additional articles, when I can. You know, under pen names."

Jo stared at him. She had the sense that something in her universe had just subtly shifted. She had believed that the *Daily* was made up of a team of writers, and that she would be managing them. There were no other writers on staff. At all. Just Jo.

"For this week, I can meet you here shortly after 3:30 every day, when school lets out. I'm just over at Robert Service Elementary on Third, next to the Westmark Inn."

"By the Snake Pit?"

"Yes."

"Convenient."

Doug gave her a look to see if she was kidding. She wasn't.

"RSE is a great little school. Yellow clapboard building. You can't miss it. Also houses the town library." His eyes crinkled a little. "You can come by at recess if you need anything. I'll give you a schedule." Somewhere a heater clicked on, whining under the strain of its workload.

Jo struggled to find a response that didn't ring shrilly in accusation. The sound of the heater mocked her, imitating her own laborious mental machinations.

"Try and get some good photos out there," he said. "Of the body, I mean."

"I'm sure the RCMP will have the scene under some kind of lockdown by now. The place will be cordoned off. Forensic team, divers … you know."

"Hmm. Wouldn't be too sure about that. Johnny's only got four guys—mostly newbies doing time in Dawson until they can get enough experience under their belts to be transferred south." He shrugged. "Anyway. I'd go with you, but ..." He patted her lightly on the shoulder. "I'll review your work every evening, just for this first week ..."

"I don't need my work reviewed."

"... just to give you some suggestions. Pointers. We go to print on Fridays."

"But you *are* called the *Dawson Daily*?"

"We were daily—at the turn of the last century. Bit of a population decline after the Gold Rush. So ... uh ..." He fumbled with some paperwork on his desk. "Any questions?"

Jo swallowed. Her mouth felt dry. "Have you got a map of town?"

Doug pointed to a framed map on the wall behind her, drawn in black ink, with a violin and bow in the top right quadrant marking north. The map made the town appear even more cornered, with an angry river circling the south and western shores and dark mountains walling off the north and east—the Klondike Highway the only thin ribbon of escape to the south between river and mountains. A campground and hostel in West Dawson, on the western shore of the Yukon River, was misspelled with an "i," so that it read "hostil" instead of "hostel." Areas outside of town disappeared into sketchy nothingness.

"And Jo?"

"Yes?" Jo already had one hand on the door handle.

"Remember, I'm still the editor for one more week, so everything goes through me. It's still, you know, my story." His eyes locked with hers. She thought about telling him where he could put his story, but after all, he would be gone in a week. Besides, until she knew for sure that there was a story, beyond someone drinking too much and falling into the river, it could all be wasted energy. Jo allowed Doug to mistake silence for agreement as she closed the door behind her.

⸺◌⸺

Jo eyed the dark, churning surface of the Yukon River, imagining just how glacial it would be if she were suddenly pitched from the deck of Dawson's rustic ferry. The width of the river from Dawson proper to West Dawson was probably half a mile, but it looked tumultuous. Jo tried not to think about the thousands of gold prospectors who had gambled their lives to risk these waters in 1896, arriving on roughly hewn rafts or overburdened paddle steamers. How many had lost the bet? Dawson had a long history of being the last refuge of the desperate. *Still is*, she thought. She was living proof.

Jo took a sip of lukewarm coffee and Baileys out of a chipped mug that read, "THE PIT." No takeout cups in Dawson—she'd been given a loaner. Jo wasn't in the habit of drinking in the morning, or even during the day, but just this once she indulged. *Hair of the dog.* She knew she'd been drinking too much since things had gone wrong for her in Vancouver. Frank had always said that alcohol wasn't a good coping strategy. *Pot. Kettle.*

Jo hadn't needed to hang around long at The Pit. By the time the doors to "The Pink Palace" had opened at nine, everyone in town knew that a paranoid, cave-dwelling recluse by the name of Caveman Cal had found a body, which had washed up just outside his makeshift abode on the western shore.

The sun was just beginning to lift its head, burning the belly of distant cloud and sending a long claw of light across the surface of slate waters like a beckoning finger.

The ferryman misunderstood her solemn appraisal of the river. "Pretty, eh?" He was not much taller than Jo and a good forty years older. He wore a broad grin that made his face crinkle, though his raisin eyes assessed her with a certain shrewdness.

"Pretty cold," Jo sort of agreed. "Haven't they ever considered building a bridge?"

The man slapped his knee as though she'd just told the best pub joke in town. "A bridge over the Yukon River!" He continued chuckling, shaking his head. "Where'd be the fun in that, eh?"

"Public transportation should be fun?"

Still smiling, he said, "Lady, you don't know Dawson. If there's no challenge to a thing, it doesn't belong here. Folks live in West Dawson for the sport of it. To survive after freeze-up, once they're cut off from town. They hunt off the land and boil ice for water. Bridge! Ha. Good one."

"Oh."

"You'll see." He gave Jo a look that said he already knew who she was. "One winter and you'll be a sourdough, too."

"Sourdough ...?"

"A survivor. Tough enough to survive, eh?"

Jo hoped the man was right. Then she hoped she wouldn't have to find out. "But why *sourdough*?"

"The first settlers here, the miners, made sourdough bread instead of regular bread because they found that even freezing doesn't kill sourdough starter." When he laughed, the sound was a long, rasping smoker's cough that made her wince.

"Ah. So when life gives you lemons ..."

He shook his head and looked away, squinting into the distance at something upriver that Jo couldn't see. "No. You don't *make* sourdough. You become it."

They were nearing a flat stretch of shoreline where two flags mired in stone and snow signalled the docking area. Next to the landing, a Zodiac marked "RCMP" had been dragged up onto a bare stretch of gravelly shoreline. The boat was a cheerful banana-yellow, a hot, tropical colour that seemed at odds with the austere and shadowy surroundings. Further down the rocky line of beach, a throng of black figures were milling about.

"So, what's going on over there? Have you heard?" Jo asked.

The ferryman frowned. "Find out soon enough."

Jo lifted her face against the wind.

⸺∞⸺

Jo had her camera ready as they docked. The wind off the river was biting, carrying with it the scent of winter, pine, and mud. Many of the inhabitants of Dawson had already migrated to join a ragtag collection of neighbours on the northwestern shore, huddled together with their collars raised against the cold. Jo snapped a quick picture of the crowd, then shoved her way forward, muttering "Sorry ... excuse me ... press!" when she deemed it necessary. A handful of RCMP officers had already cordoned off a section of the shoreline and were in the final throes of erecting a tent over the area. The officers pushed the crowd back as Jo pressed forward.

Then she saw the body, face down in a small cove in the Yukon River. The corpse had lodged or been dragged mostly ashore, but the long, dark hair was still partially submerged and strangely beautiful as it writhed like seaweed in the water. The back of the head, though, was ruined in a way that forced Jo to look away. The woman was wearing the same quilted red parka as the woman last night. Jo took a deep breath of bracing air.

Next to the body, a young officer in hip waders was taking photographs. He was approached in long strides by Sergeant

Cariboo. "Reid, what's taking so long? Get her out of there and into the tent." Cariboo eyed his wristwatch.

"Sorry, Johnny. Had to wait for the light. Wanted to make sure we git it right."

Cariboo glanced at the sky, where the salmon glow of dawn was still breaking through ribs of cloud, though it was now well after nine. He turned toward the crowd and caught Jo's eye. A flash of recognition played across his features, followed swiftly by something else. Annoyance, perhaps.

"Sergeant Cariboo," Jo said. "Could I have a word on behalf of the *Daily*?"

He moved forward, hands out like stop signs. "We have no comment at this time. Please step back." He added more gently, "You shouldn't be here, Josephine."

"Jo. Was it an accident?"

Sergeant Cariboo blatantly ignored her, turning back to his team as though he hadn't heard the question. "Scott, what's our ETA on the coroner?"

Scott, gangly and still in his twenties, wore an expression that Jo interpreted as "eager to please." He responded quickly with, "He's got a three-hour drive from Mayo. At least, that's three hours in good weather. We called him just after six."

"Good. Should be here any time." Sergeant Cariboo nodded, his brow furrowed.

Scott studied the sky with a look of apprehension. "Unless the weather turns."

"Hurry up with that tent in the meantime."

Scott nodded and scurried away.

There were five officers present, including Cariboo, but there didn't appear to be a forensic team. While Jo had waited for the ferry, she'd seen the RCMP Zodiac—still just a dark shape on the water—bumping up and down the river. Cariboo had no men to spare, yet he'd made time to leave the site to question her.

The tent flapped angrily in the wind and the cold metal-on-metal sound of a mallet striking pegs rang out like bullets, startling a conspiracy of ravens, their shrieks echoing across the landscape. "Okay, boys. Let's get her in." Cariboo looked grim.

Silence fell over the crowd as the body was painstakingly rolled over by two officers in hip waders. Then, people began to whisper. Despite the swollen face, gashes, and bruises, Jo recognized the woman instantly. The crowd murmured, and someone whispered the name "Marlo." The battered head flopped back as the body was lifted, obscuring the face once again. Water drained out of the red jacket, quilted with pockets like a flotation device.

Jo raised the camera to get a shot for the *Daily*, but when she looked through the lens at the broken figure and saw the blue marks at the throat, her mind focused elsewhere. She saw the face of another woman with long, chestnut hair, as her photograph had appeared in the *Vancouver Sun*. Smiling and unknowable. Jo had never seen the woman alive, she had only seen the smoking wreckage of her car after police had asked Jo not to print a particular story. Hands shaking, she lowered the camera.

3

The morning that a body was found in the Yukon River, the town was alive with the business of preparing for winter. The sound of hammers reverberated through the crisp air as windows were boarded up. "Closed for Season" signs were posted along Front, Dawson's main street. The hotels remained open, with admittedly few occupants, but many of the shops and restaurants shut. Jo was disappointed to find that Wild & Woolly, "Purveyors of Fine Winter Clothing," had already closed. A particularly cosy-looking pair of fur-lined North Face boots taunted her through the window, while the reflection of a departing tour bus passed behind her. The reverse rush: the rush to escape. Dawson's population dropped from 60,000 in the summer to just over 1,000 by freeze-up. Jo resisted to the urge to call out after the bus to stop it. Instead, she trudged toward the fire station.

The locals who were leaving waved goodbye to their neighbours from cars and RVs piled high with luggage, en route to warmer climates like Mexico or even Seattle. They called out email addresses and honked their horns as they left, all smiles. The backside of their vehicles disappeared into the distance, along with bumper stickers that read, "Live long and prosper."

Those who were staying leaned grimly into the wind, whispering to one another about the girl in the river.

In front of the station, a town crier wore a ruffled shirt, scarlet coat, and a tri-cornered hat with feather plumage. He was a tall man, but the greying beard and hunch in his shoulders spoke of surrender to some nebulous, greater force. He rang a gold bell as he called out in a dismal tone, "Hear ye, hear ye: meeting at city hall at eleven-thirty." As Jo drew closer, he put away the bell and held out his hat, reciting,

> *There are strange things done in the midnight sun*
> *By the men who moil for gold;*
> *The Arctic trails have their secret tales*
> *That would make your blood run cold;*
> *The northern lights have seen queer sights,*
> *But the queerest they ever did see*
> *Was that night on the marge of Lake Lebarge*
> *When I cremated Sam McGee.*

At first, Jo thought that the crier must have mistaken her for a last, fleeing tourist. Perhaps the man thought that hers would be the last coin to grace his hat until spring. Jo knew the poem, but wasn't fond of the fiery images that it brought to mind. She dropped a loonie into his hat just the same. The man mumbled a few words of appreciation. Then, as she began to walk away, he called out after her, "Heard you're dating Byrnie."

He knew exactly who she was.

Jo's shoulders tensed. Some sensible part of Jo's brain told her to shut up and keep walking, but instead she turned and said, "And I heard that Robert Service was particularly fond of sheep, so it must be true." She shrugged. "Probably why he had to leave Scotland for Canada."

The man's mouth made a circular shape as the hand holding his hat sagged pleasingly.

Yup. That's me. Making friends and influencing people. They're going to love me in this town.

∞∞∞

The fire station had two identities—like the city itself that was really a town. Jo was thankful to the ferry passenger who'd tipped her off, or she might never have found the city hall. The Gold Rush had ended so abruptly, the passenger said, that prospectors left town without taking their possessions with them, anxious to get out before a Yukon winter hit. The town's abandoned original structures had become living museums. Often a hand-shaped sign, cuffed with Victorian lace, would point the way to the "modern" version of the bank or post office or saloon: a doppelgänger nearby, still built in the same period style. Sometimes, though, a historical building's new owner had preserved only the original signage and not the contents of the place, so you might walk into a "Saddlery" only to discover you were in the liquor store. A happy accident, she thought.

As Jo hurried inside, she barely registered the small secondary sign on the fire station that read "Municipal Offices." It was rumoured that Sergeant Cariboo was going to make some kind of announcement about the investigation, and everyone in town was making the icy pilgrimage to hear it.

Jo was hoping to find Caveman Cal in attendance. She also hoped that Christopher Byrne might be inside. Perhaps Byrne would give her some clue as to what had happened last night … how long he'd stayed … and why Cariboo was asking pointed questions about the two of them.

In an austere room that smelled of wet wool and burning dust, an eclectic collection of straight-backed chairs had been lined up in neat rows facing the podium. Several heads turned to look at Jo as she slipped into the back row, and someone distinctly whispered the word "Byrne." Jo hoped the reference was made in the context of some public art display, but she had her doubts.

She scanned the room, but could find no evidence of Byrne. Nor could she see anyone who fit the description she'd been given for Cal Sanders, a.k.a. Caveman Cal: six-foot-something, black beard, floppy black hat. Jo wondered if Caveman might still be down at the RCMP office.

There was a certain nervous energy, bordering on excitement, in the air. People jumped at every little sound, spoke in hushed tones, and watched their neighbours carefully. Shopkeepers who were staying in the off-season had closed their stores so that they could come to the town meeting. Retirees had braved the cold and risked hazardous walkways—where an uncertain step could mean a broken bone and an airlift to the nearest (but not near at all) hospital in Whitehorse. In short, the day had all the makings of a holiday in a small community, with an added dash of big-city drama. An elderly woman in a crocheted shawl, all done up in shades of heather, was making the rounds with a tin of homemade cookies and squares.

The audience still wore their toques and heavy jackets as the mayor took the podium. Probably in his late forties, Peter Wright had a beard that was beginning to silver and a waistline that was heading south like the tourists, yet he had a definite charm about him. He had a ruddy, cheerful complexion and when he caught anyone's eye, his entire face smiled, projecting something that felt like mirth. A smattering of applause greeted his appearance.

Jo moved to the front of the room as he stepped up to the microphone, and in her peripheral vision caught the nudges and nods of the townspeople as she passed. Her mouth felt dry. She snapped a close shot of the mayor, and another of Sergeant Cariboo, who was waiting in the wings. He was wearing a blue uniform with a yellow stripe down the leg. Jo had half-expected the RCMP in Dawson to wear the red Mountie outfit that you see in postcards for tourists; part of her felt a little disappointed. Cariboo caught her eye as the shutter clicked, and he frowned. He bore a dark shadow of stubble that communicated a busy morning, and his eyes flashed. For a moment, Jo felt sorry for contributing to the strain of his day.

"Good morning," Peter said, his expression somehow achieving the appropriate balance of solemnity and congeniality. When his gaze met those in the audience, his warm smile was returned easily. "Well, it sounds as though last night was a bit of a doozy." A few people laughed, nodded, or muttered in low voices. Jo caught Cariboo looking at her, but he quickly glanced away. "Before we start our scheduled discussion, I know that many of you have come to hear news of our dear friend and Liberal MLA, Marlo McAdam, who, sadly, was found in the Yukon River this morning." Peter paused to allow a ripple of shock to pass through the audience. "For those of you who knew her, and I expect there are many here who did, I know how much she will be missed. We'll let you know about any service details as soon as we can, but in the meantime, we'll have a quick word from Johnny." Then Peter quickly added, as though correcting himself, "Sergeant Cariboo." Peter moved to one side and hung his head to look at the floor as Cariboo fumbled with the mic, creating a squall of feedback. Jo took another photo for good measure, causing Cariboo to shoot her a warning look.

"Yes, good morning." Cariboo cleared his throat and tugged at his collar. "At approximately five-thirty this morning, a local hunter discovered the body of Marlo McAdam in the Yukon River, just off the western shore. It appears she may have entered the water from one of the high points along the river, possibly Crocus Bluffs." A series of gasps and whispers followed this announcement, and a few people could be heard saying "*Suicide Bluffs*." Cariboo ignored the outburst and carried on. "Next of kin have been contacted, and we are conducting a routine investigation into her death. Now, the coroner has examined the … Ms. McAdam … and has ruled that the cause of death is inconclusive. So there's no need for anyone to panic. Ms. McAdam will be flown to Vancouver for an autopsy."

The room hummed with speculation and gossip. Sergeant Cariboo raised his hands to quiet the crowd. "At this point, we are treating the discovery as an accidental death. However, we will be speaking with certain members of the community. If anyone has information regarding Marlo's death, about her state of mind, or about her whereabouts after she left Diamond Tooth Gertie's last night, we would like to hear from you."

Jo's hand shot up. "Sergeant Cariboo!"

Cariboo frowned as his eyes found Jo. Before he had time to say that he wasn't taking questions, Jo asked, "Is there a possibility of foul play here?" Heads turned in her direction, and she felt suddenly self-conscious about the bluish circles that she knew were under her eyes and the unwashed hair that framed her face under her toque. Jo suspected that she might be emitting the scent of stale gin and cigarette smoke. This was turning out to be one hell of a first day at work.

"I'm sorry, we're not fielding questions from the press, Ms. Silver." Cariboo's dark eyes narrowed at Jo. "I can tell you, however, that we don't have any concerns for public safety at this time, and that the investigation is going well. Ms. McAdam was wearing an Arctic Armour parka, which many of you will be familiar with if you do any ice fishing. Fortunately, the coat kept her afloat, so we were able to find her quickly."

Yeah, lucky, Jo thought, but she was picturing Marlo in the parking lot outside Gertie's, wearing that red parka. The rosy colour of her cheeks. "Are you able to tell which injuries were sustained before the fall, and which were sustained after?"

Cariboo held her look for a moment. "We'll know more once we have the full pathology report back from Vancouver, but we don't expect to find anything unusual, and we will keep the public informed if we have any concerns at that time. Thank you. That's all for now." Cariboo stepped away from the mic.

The mayor stepped forward, motioning to Jo in the audience. "Ladies and gentlemen, this is Josephine Silver, who will be taking over next week for Doug as editor of the *Daily*."

More heads turned to get a look at Jo. She moistened her lips and swallowed. A few people muttered something indecipherable, and she felt for the first time the full weight of the town's collective scrutiny. She hesitated just for a moment, and in that moment, caught sight of one woman whispering to another, her sharp eyes studying Jo as though she were an acrobat just about to lose her balance. Jo could suddenly feel all the electricity in the room—a hot static waiting to shock fingertips on doorknobs and make hair stand on end. A fiery, dangerous feeling of anticipation. Her face burned.

Jo was transported instantly back to the time when the story first broke in Vancouver, when she was unable to enter coffee shops or shopping centres or—worse—stand in line at the grocery store next to the racks of tabloids, where her face might be exhibited along with the candy bars and breath mints. She didn't blame them. Sometimes she wished they'd present her side of the story, but she also understood that the purpose of the media is to sell papers. Besides, she'd made the wrong choice. She should have published her story. It occurred to her again just how much that choice had shaped her life.

"Thank you, Sergeant Cariboo." The mayor's voice recalled Jo to the here and now. Cariboo seemed to survey the townspeople to gauge their reaction. *Or look for signs of guilt,* Jo thought.

"I'm sure that you'll keep us posted," Peter said, turning his attention back to the audience. "This would not be the first time someone has fallen into the river after a big night at Gertie's, I'm sure. Though we are deeply saddened."

"Is that true, Mayor Wright?" Jo called out. "Has anyone ever drowned in the river after a night at Gertie's?" A murmur from the audience. Some shook their heads.

"Er … I'm not sure. I will definitely get back to you, Jo. Will you be at the *Daily* this afternoon?"

"Mayor, if the party line is that Marlo McAdam had too much to drink at Gertie's, went for a midnight stroll, and fell into the river, could you answer one question for me?"

The mayor glanced at Sergeant Cariboo, who had started to leave, but now turned back, the irritation clear on his face.

"I'm sorry, Ms. Silver, but …" The mayor didn't have a chance to shut her down.

"What was she doing up on that cliff?"

A tsunami of shocked whispering rolled through the audience.

"Some people hike up there for the view," Peter said.

"After midnight?" Jo asked.

Another burst of hushed conversation. Someone giggled, a high-pitched, nervous sound. Peter looked like he was about to say something and then changed his mind. He held up his hands for silence. "Thank you, Ms. Silver, for raising excellent questions. I'm sure that Sergeant Cariboo and his colleagues will keep us informed as they find answers for us." Cariboo gave Jo a blistering look before leaving the room. "And speaking of questions," Peter continued, "Mabel will be coming around with an agenda for our meeting today."

The discussion resumed its scheduled course, tapering off into a debate about new helmet bylaws for Ski-Doos, the liability of aggressive husky owners, and whether or not Dawson would finally pave its streets. (It would not, as Dawson was dependent on tourist dollars and tourists wanted an authentic "Old West" town. Paved streets were not a part of the image.) As Jo had encountered neither Caveman Cal (paranoid recluse and finder of dead bodies) nor Byrne, she stood up to leave.

A few heads turned, but one person nearby held her attention. She had the face of an aging Hollywood screen-ninja: serene and confident, with a smile that spoke of secrets well kept. The woman in the luxurious fur opened her mouth to speak, but just then the mayor invited questions. She looked conflicted, but raised her hand. Something about her made Jo pause to listen.

The mayor scanned the audience for other hands before finally taking her question. "May?"

"Yes, Peter, speaking of tourist dollars, I was just wondering about the town's budget. How are the books this year?"

"I'm happy to report that we've got a balanced budget."

May smiled and her finely groomed eyebrows lifted, perhaps a little surprised, perhaps pleased, it was difficult to tell. A few members of the audience applauded, muffling the sound of the door closing behind Jo.

4

Jo happened to glance through the kitchen window of Sally's house on the way to the front door. Her housemate was standing at the counter, wearing a retro apron patterned with red cherries. Head down, threads of gold hair obscuring her eyes, she was spooning a powdery substance that resembled baking soda onto a little electronic scale. A series of canning labels were lined up like soldiers across the counter. Sally looked up as Jo passed the window, her lips forming a perfect, lipsticked "O." Evidently she hadn't been expecting Jo, who was supposed to be at work.

By the time Jo kicked off her rubber boots in the entryway and stepped into the kitchen, Sally had her pink mixer running at full tilt, ferociously blending some gooey concoction. Both the little scale and the canning labels had disappeared, but there was a bulge in the pocket of Sally's apron. A small spiral notebook lay open on the counter. Scrawling, enigmatic notes implied that some dark alchemy had just transpired. Jo was able to read, "two grams of natriumalginat," "spherification process," and "perhaps a chocolate coating?" before Sally followed the direction of her glance and casually slipped the notebook into her pocket too.

"Hey," said Jo. "Nice apron." She felt a little sheepish, given that they had not hit it off on their first meeting and then had argued about the cleanliness of their shared space. And now Jo needed a favour.

"Don't you love it? Made it myself." Sally held the frilly apron up at the corners, further emphasizing the contrast between her petite waist and generous hips.

"Whatchya making?" Jo asked.

Sally waved her hand nonchalantly. "Oh, a little smoothie. I'm on a health kick."

"You?" Jo wished she hadn't said it with such obvious disbelief.

"Yes. I find it quite tasty with vodka."

Jo snorted a little.

"Care to try?" Sally offered.

Jo looked dubiously at the lumpy mixture in Sally's bowl: it reminded her of the bubble tea sold in malls back in Vancouver and had a suspicious resemblance to fish eggs. "It's a little early for me."

"That's not what I heard," Sally said archly.

"Well …" Jo choked back a retort. "I didn't mean to disturb … whatever it is that you're doing. I just needed to ask a favour."

"Hmm?" Sally had a way of imbuing anything she said with additional meaning.

"I wondered whether I might borrow your truck."

"Sure." Sally's lips were pursed a little. "But it will cost you a bottle of iceberg gin." Now Sally warmed to a smile. "Keys are on the hook. Chains are on 'er. You crack her up, you die."

"I die, I'll be sure not to come back and tell you about it."

"Where are you going?"

"Just up the Dempster. Need to talk to Christopher Byrne. Do you know where his cabin is? Heard it's up there somewhere."

Something about Sally's composure seemed to slip. "Sure, everyone knows," she said. "I'll give you a map." She turned away quickly, under the pretense of looking for a map, fussing perhaps more than was necessary with the contents of a kitchen drawer.

After removing random bits of paper, numerous corkscrews, bear spray, and several dog-eared recipe books, she did eventually produce the map. "Here," she said, circling the location with a red pen.

"Can I ask you something?" Jo said.

Sally hesitated and narrowed her eyes. "You care too much."

"What?" Jo said.

"Yes. Dawson will be good for you. Loosen you up."

"I wasn't aware that I needed loosening."

"You do. You could also do with a bit of product. Tame the hair."

Jo put one hand self-consciously to the smoky bits of dark, wild hair escaping from her toque.

Sally gave her an appraising look. "Do you dance?"

"Sure, if someone points a gun at my feet."

"That could be arranged."

"No."

"You know, you have potential. I bet you clean up all right. What are you, a size six?"

"No."

"A four, then?"

"*No.*"

"Okay, okay," Sally shrugged. "Just a thought. You have to survive the winter too, you know."

"Don't worry, I will."

Sally looked skeptical. "You look pretty scrawny to me. You should always fatten up before a Yukon winter. I don't know what Doug was thinking when he recommended you as a housemate. I really don't." She added under her breath, "I owe him one." The way she said it, it didn't sound as though she'd be returning the favour with kindness. She began chucking things randomly back in the drawer, so that it failed to close at least once. "Oh, what did you want to ask me?" She squared her shoulders as she turned to face Jo.

"This morning, you said you saw me getting into Christopher Byrne's truck last night at Gertie's."

"Did I?" Sally said, as though she couldn't remember.

Jo raised an eyebrow. *Nice try, sister.* "Were you in the parking lot at the time then?"

"Nooo, I saw you leave together." Sally hesitated for just a fraction of a second. "Then I happened to look through the window and saw you ..." She turned her back on Jo, toward the dishes piled up in the sink. "Somewhere I have gloves for this sort of thing," she said, looking at the dishes.

"Why?"

"Hmm?" Sally began running the water, as if to drown out the question.

"Why would you watch us?"

"I was just curious." The pots and pans jangled, creating a sense of discomfort and unease in the room, or perhaps just heightening what each woman was already feeling. "I noticed Marlo following Chris around that night and saw her go out the door after the two of you. I do enjoy a good show." She smiled over her shoulder at Jo.

"Marlo was following Byrne that night? Why?"

"No idea." She turned away again under the guise of cleaning the counters, something that was rarely done by the look of things.

"Were you home when I got back?"

"You don't remember?" Sally stopped cleaning at this. She leaned on the counter and folded her arms across her chest.

"Honestly? No."

"I told you. You were already back when I got home. In your room. With the door shut. Why?"

"And you don't know what time you got home?"

"God only knows. And she isn't telling." She waved one gloved hand in the air.

"Do you know for a fact that Byrne was in my room?"

"His truck was out front."

"Yes, but did you actually see him? Or hear him?"

"No. Why?" Her green eyes narrowed.

"Just … something I'm thinking about."

After a second try, the engine of the old pink Chevy pickup hacked, rattled, and reluctantly started. Jo allowed Sally's truck to idle, flipping down the mirror over the driver's seat, fully expecting the dark circles under her eyes. What she was not expecting were the small, vintage photos that had been taped around the mirror like a Hollywood vanity. One caught Jo's attention. Jo tugged at the photograph to release it: a black-and-white snap of a handsome gambler wearing a white shirt, black waistcoat, and bow tie. Christopher Byrne. His hair was shorter then, though still a bit tousled in the front, in the style of a 1940s screen hero. He was posing with Sally. Jo returned the photo and snapped the mirror back in place before noticing the gauge was almost on empty. She left the truck running for a moment while she went back to ask what kind of fuel "Bettie" took.

Sally's back was turned away from the window when Jo walked by it this time. She was on the landline in the kitchen. Jo opened the front door quietly and stood in the boot room, one hand on the door handle, while Sally finished her conversation.

"Yes, of course. Who else would it be?" There was a note of annoyance in her voice. "She was just here. I don't think she remembers much. But she's certainly asking a lot of questions."

Sally listened for a moment. "Hel*lo*?" she said. There was a muf-
fled reply. "Uh-uh. I don't want to know all the gory details. But
she's on her way to your cabin now, so perhaps you should ask
her yourself." Another long silence. "I just want you to know that
in the time you've taken to formulate your response, I've painted
my nails, assisted a midwife in Uganda with the birthing of twins,
and brushed up on my knowledge of ancient Greek mythology. And now I must go. Toodles." Sally returned the receiver
and plucked the miniature scale out of her apron pocket. "Ah,
Molecular Gastronomy, prepare to pleasure me," she said, rifling
through a cluttered kitchen drawer to find a plastic syringe.

Jo closed the door quietly behind her.

5

Snow fell mutely over the log cabin in the woods. The icing on the roof made Jo think of a gingerbread house, lending an eerie fairy-tale quality to the hushed forest as she walked up the long lane.

A smoke-coloured husky appeared on the little porch, barking. One eye brown, the other the colour of ice. Byrne shushed the dog as he joined it on the front stoop, leaning against a cedar support beam. "Hello again," he called out. He was wearing a thick cable-knit sweater and a plaid shirt-jacket. Jo was immediately reminded of why she had taken the ride with him. Those eyes, not green and not blue, expressed some mutual understanding. A shared secret. There was an intelligence about him, and when he smiled he emanated a warmth that made everything else melt away. She liked him instantly. He made her want to laugh. "The kettle's not long boiled," he said. "Want to come in for a cuppa?"

A fire flickered and snapped in the woodstove, kicking out a pleasant wall of heat. The room had a definite rustic charm: one table, two chairs—each painted a different colour—some exposed shelves filled with Mason jars and cooking supplies, a wooden counter for food preparation, a bunch of pots and pans, a four-poster bed that looked hand-carved, and a tin horse trough that might have been used for bathing. There was no refrigerator, no oven, and no sink. The bookshelves, though, were crammed with dog-eared books and the walls were richly decorated with original art and carvings made from wood and antler or bone. Jo might not have agreed to come in if she had realized that she'd be in Byrne's bedroom as well as his kitchen, but it was too late.

"Nice place," she said. She cleared her throat. "I suppose you heard what happened?"

"Yes," he said, frowning. "Terrible thing. Please," he motioned to a chair, "have a seat. You must have had a shock. Coffee?"

"Umm … How much trouble would that be exactly?"

"None at all. I've already melted the snow."

"Then yes, thanks." Jo studied the angles of his face, which seemed just as artfully crafted as one of his pieces. "So, you melt snow for cooking." She looked around again. No outlets. An oil lamp on the bedside table. "No electricity?"

"Nope."

"Why would you buy a cabin with no electricity and no running water?"

"I didn't buy it. I built it. I went into the woods because I wished to live deliberately." The weight of his gaze was unnerving.

"Thoreau?"

"Yes." A copper kettle whistled. He filled a glass coffee press and placed it on the table with two mismatched mugs.

"The RCMP came to see me this morning." Jo watched the steam rising from the Bodum, writhing in the air.

"Johnny Cariboo?"

"Yes," she said. "He told me about the woman they found in the river. He wanted to know if I was with you last night."

"What did you tell him?"

"The truth, of course."

51

"Which is?"

"That I don't remember how I got home."

Byrne furrowed his brow. "You don't remember?"

She shook her head. "I remember you picking me up in the parking lot."

"I see," he said. "I'd hoped you'd remember more." He pushed the handle of the Bodum down, pressing the grinds to the bottom of the pot.

"Why? What happened last night?"

"Well …" He poured her a coffee, filling her head with the uplifting scent. "Sugar?"

"No thanks," she said.

"I gave you a ride home. And … well …"

"And? Did we …? Did anything …?" He raised an eyebrow, making her feel foolish. She rushed to finish what she had to say. "Only Sally told me that you were in my room …"

"No! No … Plenty of time for that." He hid his smile behind his coffee cup, and Jo felt a rush of heat. She looked away, but found herself looking at the bed, the thick fur throws there, and felt herself blush. She looked at the husky instead, who was beating his tail rhythmically on the wood floor. She took another sip of coffee, warming her hands on the mug.

"That's Nugget," he said, following her look.

"Cute."

"Thank you," he said, as if accepting the compliment for himself. There was laughter in his eyes.

Jo felt herself losing patience. She glanced at her watch. She was running out of time before she had to meet Doug. "Look, Sergeant Cariboo came straight to my place after finding the body because he thought you were with me. Why would he do that?"

Byrne shook his head, his expression harder now. "No idea. You'll have to ask him, I'm afraid."

"Did he interview you?"

"Yes. I spoke with him when I was in town this morning."

"Did you use me as an alibi?"

"Not exactly, because I don't think it's a murder investigation," Byrne said. "But yes, I said that we were together." The weight of his gaze was unnerving. *No wonder I let you take me home last night.*

"*Together*, together?" She crossed her arms tightly over her chest.

Byrne opened his mouth a little, then closed it tightly. "You don't remember anything at all." It was a statement, not a question. "Really, Ms. Silver. I am wounded." He didn't look wounded. He looked amused. "Perhaps we could do something to jog your memory." He leaned forward, and she wondered whether he was going to try to kiss her, and whether she wanted him to or not.

"Look, I have to be back at the office soon."

"At the *Daily*."

"Yeah. Could I use your phone? I need to let Doug know that I'll be back late. He's the editor."

"Yes, I know Doug. And I'd be happy to let you use my phone, only I haven't got one."

"Oh, right."

"And there's no cellular service in Dawson."

"But I heard Sally call you this morning."

He grinned. "She called me at the pub."

"Why? Why would she think you'd be there?"

"Because I often go there during the day. Have a coffee in the morning. Play Scrabble or cards with the guys. You know. Until my shift at Gertie's begins."

"You work at Gertie's?"

"Card dealer on the poker tables. Only in the tourist season, though. I try to save winter for art."

Jo looked around the room again. "Are all of these yours?" She raised her mug toward the twin shelves framing the bed, where elaborate carvings perched on or next to stacks of books.

"Uh-huh. I studied in the South for a bit. I mean, at the University of Northern BC."

"Still in the North."

"Not compared to Dawson. There's north and then there's North."

Jo had to smile. She stood to look at his work. Animals in fight-or-flight mode. She felt his eyes following her as she moved and felt self-conscious. "They're beautiful." She meant it. The curve of each line was achingly perfect.

"Thank you." When she glanced at him, he had a curious expression on his face.

She walked toward a rough tree stump in the corner, near the bed, where something had caught her eye. A sleek blackbird, wooden wings outstretched, the detail on the legs so fine that you could see every scale. The beak was open in midcry, chest thrust forward, and wings about to beat. His work expressed the power of the creature at a transformative moment. The fury of nature and the fragility. "I love this one. A raven?"

"Yes. It's a bit of a family reference. Byrne comes from the Irish name Ó Broin, from the first name Bran, which means 'raven.' Descendants of Bran related back to an ancient king of Leinster and his clan, whose motto in Latin was *Certavi et vici*. 'I have fought and conquered.' "

"Your work is really emotive."

"Thanks. It pays homage to Taggish mythology and the creatures of the North. But sometimes they don't like me stealing their stories. Cultural appropriation, I believe they call it."

"Well, it's lovely." *A man and a woman and a blackbird are one.* The words of a forgotten poem surfaced, unbidden. She said, "*I know noble accents / And lucid, inescapable rhythms ...*"

Byrne cocked his head. "Wallace Stevens?"

Jo wasn't listening. She was still struggling to remember. "Sorry?"

" 'Thirteen Ways of Looking at a Blackbird.' We talked about it last night ..."

"Did we? Look, I need to get going, but I'd really like a bit more detail about last night." When she turned away from his art and back toward him, he was suddenly very close to her. "Everything that happened," she said.

He put his hand on her chin and lifted her face. "Everything?"

"Yes," she said, conscious of their proximity to the bed.

"Okay," he said.

Jo decided not to tell him that she remembered seeing Marlo.

"I love the lines of your face." They stood there for a moment like that, him cupping her chin, the heat between their bodies a shared force. He was going to kiss her. Jo was sure of it now, and she wanted him to. Instead, he released her.

"We should get together when you have more time. What do you say to a reenactment tomorrow night? I'd say tonight, but I'm working. How's your head, by the way?"

"Poor," she said, truthfully, but her pulse was racing.

"I'm sorry to hear it." He walked her to the door.

Jo found herself reluctant to leave. She paused at the threshold. "One more thing, why would Sally call you? Why would she tell you that I was on my way over?"

"She's an old friend of mine," Byrne said, but he frowned.

Jo thought about this all the way back to Dawson.

6

Large photos flashed by on Doug's desktop computer, full of the cheerful woollen colours and patterns of the townspeople at sunrise. The way that people folded their arms and leaned in to one another, Jo could almost feel the icy breeze off the river again. Another shot showed the yellow RCMP Zodiac patrolling the shoreline; the next, the troubled expressions of Mayor Wright and Johnny Cariboo at the town meeting. Jo found her gaze lingering on Johnny Cariboo longer than it should. He had striking features, and there was a dark intensity about him that Jo appreciated. Something a bit melancholy. *Shame he's a uniform.*

"Photos aren't bad." Doug glanced at her, as though guessing what she was thinking. He was seated at his metal desk, framed against the backdrop of a huge poster that read, "We drive into the future using only our rearview mirror." The image pictured Marshall McLuhan, head on hand. "But, uh ..."

"But *what*?" Jo said, instantly regretting the sharp tone of her voice. The nagging questions about her missing memory had left her feeling on edge. She also wondered how trustworthy her new housemate might be, now that she knew Sally had warned Byrne about her impending visit. The drive back into town through blowing snow hadn't helped matters. Even with the chains on Sally's 1950s Chevy, Jo had thought she might not make it back. She could barely find the road.

"Firstly, we can't use the word 'suicide,'" Doug said.

"Context," Jo said, folding her arms. She was seated on a cold metal stool next to Doug, legs tightly crossed. "I didn't say that Marlo McAdam committed suicide. I merely said that Crocus Bluffs was the most likely place for the fall and that the place is known locally as 'Suicide Bluffs.'"

"But the link is obvious to the reader, and given Marlo's position in the community, it would be politically, uh … insensitive … to make that suggestion without more factual evidence." Doug looked away, back at the article on his desk.

"Oh, come on. There are only two choices. She jumped, or she was pushed."

"She could have fallen," Doug said.

Jo gave him a disbelieving look. "From the top of a cliff. In the middle of the night. Seems a little …"

"Secondly …"

"… convenient for an accident."

"We can't go to print ahead of schedule. Thursday night we print it, and Friday morning we deliver it."

"But … that's *four days* away … and this is the kind of story that could get you national readers if you run it first. The body of a prominent politician washes ashore in a town of thirteen hundred people …" Jo waved one hand, stirring the cold air.

"*Could*. If it were murder. Or a suicide. But chances are it was an accident," Doug said. "This isn't some big city in the South. We get the odd bit of domestic violence, but we haven't seen anything more serious in years. Well, except for that time Two-By-Four Tom put a bullet through another prospector's head. Very intense." Jo raised an eyebrow at Doug's choice of words, but the gesture appeared to be lost on him. "At any rate, we don't have the budget for additional print runs." He shoved his hands in his pockets. "We just don't. And, you know, I'm right in the middle of parent-teacher meetings."

Jo placed a hand over her lips, suppressing the urge to laugh. "If we can't go to print until Friday, we could at least dig a little deeper. Have something more than the nationals have by the time we do."

"Look, I'm not sure how to say this ..." Doug's watery blue eyes contained undercurrents of meaning. "I know you're looking for a chance to make a ... you know, a comeback with a big story, but ..."

"That's not fair. The public have a right to know if this is something more ominous than the RCMP are admitting. I mean, it's important to me to ..."

"It's just that I don't want us jumping to conclusions. I'm only the editor for one more week, and I knew Marlo, and if you want to talk about *fairness*, I want to be fair to her. We report the facts, and we don't speculate beyond them. This paper has always been about community service, and I want to make sure it stays that way. At least while I'm still here. So for my last edition, we're doing service to Marlo's memory."

"But ..."

"Look, you can talk to Caveman ... uh, his real name is Cal Sanders ... about the experience of finding Marlo's body. Geez, that must have been quite a shock."

"Yes."

Doug shook his head and looked stern again. "But let the RCMP do their work. I don't want us, you know, stepping on toes. And anything you write this week goes through me first. Cool?"

"Understood."

"Our professional reputation is on the line here. Goddamn it, how did Marshall get out again?"

Jo looked down, where Doug's attention was focused. The plump guinea pig waddled by, pausing to chew blandly on a scrap of newspaper.

Despite the plummeting temperatures outside, Diamond Tooth Gertie's Gambling Hall was warmed by the hot colours of lumberjack shirts and velvet curtains. A spirited fire snapped at a stone hearth. The crowd was much sparser than it had been the previous evening, though, and the mood very different. Full of misgiving. The special of the day looked disconcertingly bloody: cranberry wheat beer.

Although the cancan dancers appeared to have packed it in, Sally was still on stage, doing some kind of dance of the seven veils to a cover of "Trust in Me." She was on fire. The sequins on her tangerine-coloured costume caught the stage light, flaring in sudden sparks. The serpentine motion of the veils gradually exposed more sparkling skin, dusted in gold, and more goosebumps. The clientele were seated at round tables with red tablecloths, hunched over bottles of Yukon Gold or glass steins of ruby-hued ale. A few turned to look at Jo when she entered, their faces hard with suspicion, but most were mesmerized by the translucent fabric falling onto the stage and the shimmering flashes of skin. Jo scanned the room full of baseball hats and toques until she found the telltale floppy black hat that she was looking for: Caveman Cal. He was seated at the bar, with Christopher Byrne leaning next to him. They had their backs to her as she approached them, but Jo caught low snippets of conversation as she made her way over. Marlo was a popular topic of conversation.

The bartender was turned away, reaching for a new bottle as she said, "Froze my ass off this morning." She had a blended malt whisky voice and nicotine stains on her fingers. When the bartender launched the cap and handed a sweaty brown bottle to Caveman, Jo wondered how many times the woman had performed this ritual; the way she popped the caps off of beer bottles in one efficient, fluid motion communicated a kind of grace and artistry. The gold caps spun on the bar momentarily, winking at an inside joke or an empty promise. Fool's Gold.

"Yup. We should get the ice pool going, eh?" Caveman admired the amber bottle as he peeled the label. Shards of tawny light refracted in the smooth glass.

Jo got a good eyeful of Christopher Byrne just then. Somewhere in the back of her mind, the lyrics from a song snaked their way through her thoughts. Byrne was wearing a smart, collared shirt with a black waistcoat and bow tie—the dealer uniform for the card tables. He hadn't noticed Jo yet, so she allowed her gaze to linger, appreciating the strong lines of his profile and the way his dark, mahogany hair contrasted with the whiteness of his shirt.

"I bet the south lane was bumper to bumper today," he muttered.

"Might not be just the tourists escaping this season," Caveman said. "Might be one of the locals."

"Locals ..." Byrne said in a flat, measured tone, but there was a certain timbre to his voice.

"Now hang on a second ..." The bartender gave Caveman a warning look.

Byrne said, "You think it was one of us." Not a question.

Caveman countered, "*I* might think it was one of *them*. But it's just a matter of time before they start asking *you* questions, right Byrnie?" Caveman gave him a look that was difficult to interpret. He might have been teasing him. He might have been serious.

"Hey, you know where I was."

"Problem is, your alibi may not remember."

Suddenly self-conscious and about to turn away, Jo was caught in the all-knowing, all-telling beam of the bartender's gaze. "That's enough, guys. Your new girlfriend's here, Byrne," the bartender said, with only a corner of her mouth committing to a smile.

Byrne turned. He looked at Jo with such calm self-assurance that she thought there must have been some kind of misunderstanding; he looked as though he'd been expecting her, his expression one of bright playfulness. "All right, all right already!" he said. "I'll go out with you!"

"Sorry?" Jo felt her face turning the deep shade of a cancan dancer's skirts.

"You don't need to stalk me just to get a date. Geez!" Patrons seated along the bar turned to watch them, amused.

"You're mistaken. I'm here to talk to Mr. Sanders." Jo fought to suppress the irritation in her voice.

Byrne shrugged. "Are you sure about that?" He smiled easily. His tone implied that he was sure, even if she was not. Jo gave him a sour look. Byrne straightened. "Okay, I can take a hint. My shift is starting anyway." Then he leaned in and whispered, "I'm looking forward to the reenactment," his breath warm against her throat, "so I can show you what we did." As he leaned back out he added, loud enough for the bar to hear, "I'll pick you up at seven tomorrow." He turned abruptly and walked away, in the direction of the poker tables.

"What the hell is his problem?" Jo said to no one in particular.

"You," the bartender said, polishing a glass. Her face was closed, obscuring her meaning, but Caveman grinned into his beer before tipping it back.

The bartender slid a glass of merlot in front of Jo. "Oh, cheers," Jo said, wondering if she would be required to pay for the wine (since she hadn't actually ordered it). When she held up the drink, it caught in the light, reflecting the bar and everyone in it upside down, in a sea of red.

⤖

Jo and Caveman hunched over a table, conspiratorially. Caveman peeled the label on his Yukon Gold with long, dirty fingernails. He appeared to be in his early thirties, with a long, lean frame and an unkempt beard. His hands interested Jo. Not just the dirt, which communicated something about how he lived, but also the dexterity as he reached for a leather pouch full of brown, withered leaves and began hand-rolling a cigarette. Everything about him was sparse, efficient, and capable.

On the ferry back from West Dawson, Jo had asked around about Caveman. Everyone had a theory about him, as well as just about everyone else in town, if you cared to hear it (and even if you didn't). By all accounts, Cal Sanders, a.k.a. "Caveman Cal," former-city-hall-worker-cum-paranoid-cave-dweller, was—or had at one time been—privy to the town's secrets. Caveman survived off the land after freeze-up, when the ferry to West Dawson was docked. He spent the winter hand-building furniture, which he sold in town after thaw.

"Who told you where to find me?" He looked around the room, then pulled his wide-brimmed felt hat down over his eyes a little more.

Jo smiled. "Well, there aren't too many places that are still open. Everyone is here—I figured you'd be here too."

"Oh … yeah." He seemed uncertain about the truthfulness of her response. He raised his bottle to Jo and then took a big

62

swill. "So, what brings you to Dawson? Owe somebody money, like the rest of us?" He laughed.

"I'm the new editor at the *Daily*," Jo said and quickly changed the subject. "What's the story behind your name?"

Caveman licked the cigarette to seal it. "I took a bet to live in a cave for six weeks."

"Ah."

"I decided to stay." Caveman lit the cigarette, the end flaring warmly. "I live in one cave, keep my chickens in the other." He looked around warily, before exhaling a long blast of smoke and leaning in to whisper, "It's safer across the river. Harder for them to get me out there."

Jo leaned forward on her barstool. "Who?" On impulse, she fished for her notebook and pen in her bag, before remembering that Caveman had the reputation of being a bit of a nutter.

"Now they're trying to tax my cave. Property taxes on a fucking cave."

She leaned back a little.

Caveman held up a hand in protest. "Hey, before you tell me that I'm crazy, you should know that I've been right before about stuff that goes on in this town. What about the Meter Cheater, eh?"

"Who?"

"Peter the Meter Cheater." Caveman pointed across the room toward the roulette table, where Peter Wright was having quite a good chuckle about something, his broad cheeks flushed. "In the blue sweater," Caveman added.

"The *mayor*?"

"Yup. He did time for tax fraud. Used to be an accountant."

"Really?" Jo said, paying close attention to the bearded man at the roulette table across the room. Peter was heavily into his game. His eyes were fixed intently on the wheel as it spun, but when the silver ball rattled to a stop and the dealer raked in his money, he laughed loudly in an infectiously good-natured way. He was clearly the kind of person who knew how to enjoy himself. When Peter smiled, the faces around him lit up too.

"Sure," Caveman patted Jo on the arm, adding, "But that's small potatoes compared to other stuff that goes on in this town."

"Like what?" Jo's skin was getting prickly, the way it did when she was on the edge of a good story.

They were interrupted by the sound of electronic bells and an elderly lady squealing, "Woooohoooo! Grandma needs a new pair of North Face Chilkats!" Her lined face glowed along with the lights on the slot machine as it spit up its shiny contents.

Jo returned her attention back to Caveman. "Sorry, you were saying …?"

Caveman looked at her blankly. "What?"

"You were about to tell me something. About something going on in Dawson?"

Caveman's eyes narrowed. "Who do you work for?"

"I told you. The *Daily*."

Caveman shook his head. "No, I mean, who do you *really* work for, eh? Are you here about the mine?" He stood up, eyes wide, a hunted expression on his face.

"What? No! I told you, I'm the new editor at the *Daily*. I just wanted to ask you some questions about …"

"Because it's definitely not safe to talk about that here. Especially after Marlo …"

"Marlo what? Please. Sit down. Just for a minute."

Caveman sat back down, looking uneasy.

Jo lowered her voice and attempted to sound casual. "I heard you found the body." She sipped her wine.

"Yeah. Launched my canoe first thing to go hunting and almost ran into it." The brim of his hat cast a shadow across his features as he stroked his beard. "It was a warning, eh?"

"A warning? Why? From who?"

"Those arses at city hall, that's who. Want me to know they mean business about taxing my cave." He folded his arms, one hand pulling nervously at a loose thread on his bulky sweater.

"What? But that doesn't make any sense."

"All I know is, I git up in the morning and the*rrrr*e it is." His voice rose, mirroring his surprise.

"What did you do?"

Caveman took a swill of Gold. "Paddled over there to tell Cariboo. He's the head honcho with the RCMP, eh? Those guys, they had the police boat up and down the river looking for the murder scene."

"They used the word 'murder'?"

"Yeah."

Jo felt something inside her slide a little, like a picture that had been hung straight and was now slightly askew. She tried to keep her voice calm, and steered her mind away from the past. Away from Vancouver. "The RCMP told the *Daily* they were operating on the assumption that Marlo McAdam's death was an accident," Jo said.

"Yup. What they said." Caveman's expression said that the police couldn't, or shouldn't, be believed. As though Jo needed a reminder.

"*Damn* it." *Assholes.* This time would be different. She wasn't about to keep the RCMP's dirty secrets; if there was a killer on the loose in Dawson, the public was going to hear about it this time. "Did they find anything?"

"Nah. Too much fresh snow."

"What about forensics? They got a forensics unit up here?"

Caveman chuckled. "You're kidding me, right? They got, what, five guys? Most of 'em junior—up here to get experience—and one Ski-Doo between the lot of 'em. God help us all if we ever have, you know, a serious problem up here after freeze-up."

Jo shook her head, entertained for a moment by imagining what her father and his cronies would have to say about this, huddled around some crappy, east-end bar after the dogwatch shift. "Any idea who might have wanted Marlo McAdam dead?"

"Marlo was a politician." Caveman said, and his lip curled a little.

"So she was unpopular?"

"No, everyone pretty much liked her. She was good people. Honest. Which is rare in the Yukon, especially for a politician, eh? You know what they say: 'Yukon, I con, we all con.'" He laughed dryly and took a long pull on the cigarette.

Jo leaned forward in her chair. "I couldn't help but overhear earlier that you thought the police might ask Christopher Byrne questions about Marlo's death."

"Maybe. Okay, probably." He glanced over to the poker tables, where Byrne was scrutinizing the pair of them. When Jo glanced away, she could still feel Byrne watching her.

"Why?"

"You'll have to ask him. He'd kill me if I said anything to you."

"I hope you don't mean that literally."

Caveman sniggered a little. "You're barking up the wrong tree." He scratched the back of his neck.

"Am I? Why don't you redirect me?"

Caveman squinted at Jo, seeming to size her up. "Look, you didn't hear this from me." The smoke began to leak from his lips in a slow whorl. Jo forced herself not to turn her face away; the scent reminded her of her mother, and of her illness. "You can't use this. In your story, I mean." He glanced over his shoulder.

Jo hesitated, but it was clear that she had little choice. "Okay."

"The cops ... I heard them talking about how Marlo got out to the Bluffs. It's quite a trek up there, eh? They got witnesses say that they didn't see her truck in the parking lot at Gertie's."

"So ... she got a lift from someone?"

Caveman nodded gravely. "Looks that way. They said she left Gertie's before closing. Must have met someone in the parking lot. Someone offered her a ride. Most likely someone she knew."

"Huh. So that might rule out suicide, since she may not have been alone."

Something flickered across Caveman's features, some hesitation, before he said, "If I were you, I'd get out of here before freeze-up. Tough to get out once the roads and runway snow over. You could get out via Alaska, but not once the Top of the World Highway closes or the ferry is taken out. Be any day now. You don't want to be trapped here with the rest of us when that happens. Trust me."

"What are you so afraid of? You think the killer is still here?"

"I can't say more than that, okay? It's not safe. I shouldn't even be seen talking to you like this." He cast a look around the room.

"Why? I wouldn't know who to tell. I don't know anything about anything that goes on in this town."

"Now you are dangerous," he said, and he exhaled a thick curl of smoke.

The squeaking of a microphone behind her caused Jo to turn away for a moment, toward the stage, where a young woman with a nose ring and thick sweater began strumming a guitar. Her hands bore an interesting collection of rings with oversized stones and skulls. "This one's for Marlo," the singer said, causing small waves of hushed discussions to ripple through the audience. She began to hum something low and lovely, the eerie strains reaching all the way into the shadows of the bar. When Jo turned back to Caveman, he had already slipped away, and there was a fresh drink that she didn't remember ordering, sweating on the table in front of her.

⥥⥥⥥

The kitchen in Jo's new home smelled like a mixture of mold, chocolate, and something oddly pungent. Sally had been baking again. Various mixing bowls had been added to the pile in the sink, turning the water there an unapologetic shade of brown. The beaters were still in the mixing machine, coated in chocolate, calling to Jo in their syrupy voices. *Eat me … eat me.* She yielded up a finger and scraped off a line of crusty icing, placing it lightly on her tongue. *Mmmmm.* Plenty of rum.

Jo leaned against the doorframe, one ear against a cold telephone receiver, listening to the distant ringing in her father's living room. It was late—almost midnight. She hoped that Frank was still up, watching *House* (he was always a sucker for a bit of misanthropic humour) or reruns of *Law & Order*. She could picture Pepper Spray, Frank's Scottish terrier, barking in disapproval at the telephone, as though it were another yippy dog. Frank and Pepper's heads would turn in unison; their twin expressions (surprise and accusation), closely clipped grey hair, and matching moustaches presenting the appearance of familial relation. They'd be sitting on the plaid blanket that had covered the couch for years.

Jo was eyeing the half-eaten tray of rum-fudge brownies when Frank picked up, compacting the sense of culpability she experienced at the sound of his voice.

"Jo? About bloody time." Pepper was indeed making aggravated little sounds in the background. "Shut it, furball," he said to the terrier.

68

"I'm sorry. I meant to call you to let you know I got in okay, but there's no cellular service here, and things kicked off so quickly." (Jo ignored her father's derisive snort at this.) "The RCMP found a body in the river this morning." This sad fact would at least give them something to talk about, something that wasn't an admission of guilt or a defence.

Jo tried not to blame Frank for persuading her to accept what the VPD had asked her to do: to kill the publication of her story about the tactics of a serial killer operating in the Vancouver area. Her conversations with her father as of late had circled around their mutual feelings of recrimination and self-blame. It was exhausting.

"A body?" Frank sounded alert now.

"Yes. A local politician."

"Foul play suspected?"

"Possibly. She'd been drinking, but the police don't think she was alone before she went into the water."

"Suspects?"

"Frank, they interviewed me. I met the woman last night, in the parking lot outside the local pub."

"Did she say anything relevant?"

"Not to me. To someone I was with." She was loath to say any more. "Who might be a suspect."

"Who?"

"Just someone who was giving me a ride home."

"Name please."

Jo listened to her father breathing into the receiver for a moment as the wind hummed outside. His familiar voice was almost comforting. She wished for a moment that she could tug on the frozen telephone wires to bring him closer. "Christopher Byrne," she said.

"Jesus, Josephine! One week in a new town and you're getting into the vehicle of a strange male in a dark parking lot in a place with no emergency cellular service. Haven't I taught you anything?" His breathing sounded laboured now.

Jo thought of the dire warnings she'd received over family dinners when she was growing up, the stories her parents had told of young women turning up in her mother's emergency ward or disappearing altogether in Frank's district. But she said, "I am an adult, you know."

"Fat lotta good that will do you in an isolated place with the wrong person. You of all people should know that."

Jo had the fleeting image of a woman's body in long grass, a snail leaving a silver trail down one pale arm. The blue necklace of bruising around the throat. One flame-mangled ear. The Surrey Strangler's second victim.

"I mean, Christ," Frank continued. "The police think this Byrne guy had something to do with this?"

"I don't know. Maybe."

"Well, I'm going to find out. Get me his driver's license number or date of birth and I'll run a CRC."

"No," she said, her tone sharp. She cleared her throat, and said more softly, "No. I'll look into it myself."

"But it would only take me …"

"No thanks, Frank." In the ensuing pause, Jo thought of the warm taste of rum-laden chocolate. Comfort food. She crooked the receiver under her chin while reaching for the pan of brownies. "I need to do this myself." She thought she heard Pepper growl at something in the background as she cut herself a thick slab of sweetness.

"If you say so," Frank grumbled, clearly unhappy with the decision. "Let me know if I can do anything. I just … you know, I'm feeling …"

"Oh!" she said, grimacing at the skunky flavour of the laced brownies.

"What? Are you okay?"

"Just bit my lip," she lied, because there was no way she could answer the question without lying anyway, and there was no way she was going to tell Frank that her housemate had cooked up quite a lethal batch of pot brownies. She swallowed down the lie, enjoying the dark, velvet aftertaste.

7

Sharp tongues of flame devoured the vehicle, crackling and popping ravenously as the tires sagged and something—melting rubber around the windows perhaps—dripped ominously. Black smoke billowed from the silver SUV into grey skies as Jo was drawn closer. There was something she needed to know about what was inside, some question she needed answered, but she couldn't quite remember what it was. Then the back window exploded in an angry flash, sending shards of glass raining down everywhere.

The heat of the fire reached her face. She felt her skin melting like snow, running over clean bones, only she couldn't stop because she could see someone in the passenger seat. A dark outline against the blaze. Now the corpse was calling her, but the tone was not what she expected; there was no sense of redress. Something was not quite right. This was not the way the dream usually went, because when the charred skeleton's jaw swung open and it turned its face toward hers in accusation, it merely whispered softly, "Wakey, wakey."

In the muddy hours before dawn, Jo was nudged rudely awake by the long nose of a rifle, her thoughts still milky. The room was dim. The heady scent of Verbena perfume replaced the lingering memory of smoke and decomposition.

"Rise and shine, sweetheart." A woman's voice.

Jo sat up slowly. Her heart was fluttering like a June bug in a glass jar and her mouth was dry. She eyed the gun. She knew this person was going to kill her now. She had made a terrible mistake somewhere …

"Not loaded. Thought we'd be able to skip the coffee this way." A low chuckle. The figure was blurred and shadowy, a soft, surreal extension of the gun.

Jo reached for her dark frames on the nightstand, almost knocking over a glass and spilling the golden dregs of whisky and melted ice. She felt lightheaded. The figure at the foot of her bed snapped into sharper relief as Jo slid her glasses in place.

Sally.

Her housemate was not going to kill her. Jo felt something unexpected then, not quite relief. She felt glad to be alive, here in the middle of nowhere, in Dawson City. The feeling surprised her, a sudden warmth washing over her body. She couldn't remember the last time she'd had that feeling. Not since before things had all gone wrong, since the woman had been found in that car. She knew she should feel outraged, but instead she felt a kind of gratitude toward Sally.

"What the hell were you dreaming about, anyway?" Sally asked.

<hr/>

The sky was just beginning to bruise in violent colours behind a fan of feathery clouds: a showy performance to kick off a mundane Tuesday morning in Dawson City. Sally's thickly gloved hands lifted a white, birchbark horn to her mouth, making a mournful call that echoed in the still air. The two women stood rigidly silent for a moment, as though overwhelmed by the solemn presence of the trees. Then came the distant notes of other hunters playing the same lament, an anguished baying that tugged at the heartstrings. Another lull.

Finally Jo broke the silence. "Can't we just order a pizza?"

Sally whispered, "You wanna make it through a winter in the Klondike, you'd better hope we find us a bigger rack than mine. Here, gimme those binoculars a sec." Sally looked different now. Smaller, mostly, in her sturdy Yukon snow boots. She wore a white quilted parka, trimmed in fur a shade darker than her own hair, which was tightly braided in two sections. Over her coat, she sported a bright orange hunter's vest that gave her an air of pragmatism hitherto undetected and unsuspected by Jo.

Jo handed over the binoculars, watching as Sally scanned the tree line. Fiery slashes of crimson bearberry leaves steeped the foliage in bloody hues. Jo glanced at her watch before clearing her throat. She didn't have much time. She'd need to be at the *Daily* shortly after sunrise.

"So I've been thinking about Marlo …" Jo said.

"Less thinking, more hunting, please." Sally shoved the binoculars back toward Jo, the fur around her throat stirring in an icy gust of wind. She made another call, this time using only her hands around her mouth. A nasal braying sound, softer this time. Imploring.

"Listen, I hate to interrupt you in mid …" Jo waved her hand, searching for the right word "… seduction. And I do appreciate the scenic tour, but I've gotta go. Some of us have to work this morning, you know."

"Tell Doug you were delayed. It's moose season. Everyone will understand. Filling the freezer is the first priority in Dawson." She glanced at Jo. "Yours too. And once you've seen the grocery prices in The General, you'll know why. There are only two choices here: you can be predator, or you can be prey." Sally picked up a pale slab of bone from a leather bag and knocked it twice against a tree trunk, making a hollow sound. "And I need you to survive because I need your rent."

"I'd kill for some good, East-Van Chinese takeaway right now," Jo muttered under her breath, "Soup with dumplings from the Bamboo Garden ... wontons ... hot."

"Shhh." Sally paused as a wolf struck up a melancholy tune. A cold sound that reverberated up Jo's spine.

She shivered and lifted the binoculars. During the night, snow had transformed pine into surreal, Dali-esque shapes. Soft, rounded, alien forms. The world at this hour was shadowy and suggestive, promising both wonder and some kind of unnamed primordial violence. Jo searched the darkest parts of the forest for life, but found no movement. She blew weakly on one gloved hand in a useless attempt to stave off the numbness that was spreading rapidly through her fingers and toes. She heard Sally squeaking lightly through the snow, soldiering ahead, but something held Jo firmly to the stillness of the moment. When she couldn't stand the needling sensation in her fingertips any longer, she wrapped leather binocular straps around her neck, shoved hands deep into pockets, and shuffled through the snow to catch up with Sally.

"You know," Jo said, "it sounds like most of the town was at Gertie's the night of Marlo's death."

Sally whispered back, sharply, "*Will* you shut up? You're like a walking megaphone."

Jo lowered her voice. "But the murder ..."

"If it was a murder …"

"… happened before closing time, right? Or, at least, the murderer likely met Marlo in the parking lot and left with her before closing time. So did you notice anyone leaving early?"

"Aside from you?"

"But obviously I didn't …"

"Not obvious to the rest of us. We don't know you that well."

"Is that why Sergeant Cariboo paid me the visit? Christ." Jo felt something in her chest tighten.

"There's also Peter Wright."

"The mayor?"

Sally nodded. "Yup." Jo thought about his flushed cheeks at the roulette wheel. "And rumour has it that Jack Grikowsky left early."

"Who's he?"

"Manager of Claim 53, out at Sourdough Creek. It's one of Dawson's biggest gold mines."

"Well, at least I'm not the only suspect."

"True. Oh, and May Wong left before closing. I only noticed because she was wearing the most fabulous fur coat I've ever seen." She added, "Wonder if she killed it herself?"

"May … wasn't she at the town meeting?"

"Could have been. She pays pretty close attention to every-thing that goes on in Dawson. Owns her own business in town, a jewellery store called The Gold Digger."

"She was staring at me during the meeting yesterday. Like she wanted to say something."

Sally stopped walking and stooped down to examine fresh tracks, as though they were a secret language written in the snow. "Probably going to advise you to invest in a comb, dear." Sally shot a look at Jo's hair, which was probably sticking out at odd angles under her black toque. "And then there's Byrnie."

Sally looked up at her. The way she was crouched there in the snow, her curious face framed in fur, suggested the appearance of something feral about to pounce.

"What about him?"

"You really don't know?" Sally cackled a little as she stood up again, delighted with the notion of a good scandal, presumably. "Did Marlo see you get into his truck?"

"Yeah, she did. Why?"

Sally brushed snow from her legs. "What happened after that?"

"Well. Actually, I … don't remember much of the ride."

"No!" Sally said it in mock surprise.

"I'm not sure whether or not we went straight back to the apartment. I remember driving through a wooded area …"

"Guess you'll cover that ground on your date." Sally sneered, then began drawing in the snow with the toe of her boot. A heart. A childish gesture that seemed a little spiteful.

"It's not a date." Jo felt defensive. Was the entire town talking about her? Was it a date? The notion of being back in the public eye rankled. "Anyway, I won't have time to go out tonight. I'll be way too busy with my story." Jo glanced at the sky. An egg yolk of a sun was beginning to bleed into a pan of dark cloud like a Northern fry-up. "And I need to get into the office first thing this morning, so if we're about done here …"

"Why do you think about work so much? What happened to you?" Sally shifted the weight of the leather hunting bag on her shoulder, her green eyes bright.

"What do you mean?"

Sally gave her a look that Jo interpreted as, "*Honestly!*" but said, "Everyone knows…"

"What?" Jo felt her breath catch.

"Well. Maybe not *everyone*. A few people, anyway.

"Know what?"

"Know that you were lynched in the press over a big story. A murder case, right? The Surrey Strangler?" She folded her arms across her chest.

"Who told you that?"

"This is a small town. Things just have a way of getting out."

"People know …?"

"Not the *details*," Sally said, her forehead furrowing. "But really, what happened to you?" Jo felt as if a very tight cord that had been keeping her erect had suddenly been released, permitting her body to slouch forward. She tucked a strand of hair back behind her ear, wearied and irritated by all things that wouldn't stay in their proper places.

"I guess I lost something," Jo said. "My perspective."

"But what happened to that woman wasn't your fault …"

"No, it was, actually."

Sally cocked her head, but said nothing.

Jo squeezed the ends of her fingers in a failed effort to bring back the circulation. "I'd been doing a crime blog for the *Sun*. I was following a case the press were calling 'The Surrey Strangler.' "

"Catchy."

"Uh-huh. My father was a police officer and had inside information—he told me that the first body had been found naked, with bruising at the throat. But he was worried that the violence was escalating."

"Escalating how?"

"Well, the second victim had been strangled *and* had her ear scorched off with something. They didn't know what. Maybe a welding torch."

"God!"

"I know. When he told me, we were right in the middle of having crispy spring rolls at Hon's. I may never eat spring rolls again."

"Oh, that's disgusting!" Sally spat the words out.

"Yup. So, not long after that, a woman escaped a third attack and called the *Sun*—and she got put through to me. She tells me that she'd parked her car near the Rowing Club and gone for a run in Stanley Park ..."

"Wait, wasn't he called the *Surrey* Strangler? Stanley Park is in Vancouver."

"True, but only the first victim was attacked in Surrey. The name just stuck. Anyway, when the woman got back to her car, the sun was setting. She notices a flash of silver sticking out of the driver's window. She'd left it rolled down a little to keep the car cool. It looks like a coat hanger. When she steps closer to look, this guy comes out of the bushes in front of the car. He's a young guy, dressed like a police cyclist. You know, black helmet, black vest, black cargo shorts?"

"Let me guess ..."

Jo nodded. "Yeah. He calls out 'Police!' and holds up what looks like a VPD badge. Then he tells her that someone tried to break into her car, but escaped in the woods. He wants her to get into the car and check to see if anything's missing while he waits."

"I hope she didn't do it?"

"Nope. She said ..." Jo strained to remember. It was like going back down a very dark tunnel. "... she said there was something she didn't care for in his eyes. She said he looked too *eager.*"

Sally shuddered. "Like that isn't disturbing."

"Yeah, then she noticed that, although it said 'Police' on the tactical vest, there was no VPD badge on the sleeve of the shirt."

"Good for her."

"Yeah, lucky. It probably saved her life. She ran for it."

"What happened to the guy?"

"He chased her, but gave up once she made it to the seawall. Too many joggers and bikers. She called the police, and they told her that no officer had reported vehicle damage in Stanley Park."

"*Eeeee!*" Sally shook herself. "How does that woman sleep at night?"

"I know. Anyway, this is where my problem starts. Two officers from the VPD pay me a visit. Friends of my father's. They don't want me to report the story."

"Why not?"

"Because it would let the guy know that the police are on to him. If I don't report it, they can stake out the parks. They know who to watch for, how he dresses. They've got a shot at catching him. But if I report it, the guy might just change his tactics. Or do a runner."

"So what did you do?"

"I said I'd let my editor, Kevin Kessler, decide. But they tell me that if I tell him, it's already decided. Because Kessler would print it, and they'd lose the guy. The Strangler."

"So you didn't print it."

"No. And he got another girl. Strangled her in a car and then set the whole vehicle on fire."

"Jesus."

"Yes. The woman who'd gotten away promised she wouldn't talk to anyone. Promised the police. But she changed her mind after that. Can't say I blame her."

"No." Sally cleared her throat and shook her head. It was snowing softly, and she lifted her face to look at the sky. "That's a terrible story."

"I know," Jo said. She felt a tight knot in her throat as she swallowed. "Well anyway, I made the wrong call. My first duty should have been to warn the public." She thought of the smoking wreck. The charred remains.

"But in warning the public, you would have warned the killer, too."

"Yeah."

"Damned if you do …"

"Just plain damned. Like I said, my dad was a cop. When they wanted me to kill the story, they sent over one of the guys my dad used to go drinking with after his shift."

"Sure they did."

"The truth is, a big part of the reason I made it as a crime reporter was because my dad's friends were willing to trust me with an inside scoop. They trusted that I wouldn't use the information carelessly. I would have never gotten another interview with any of them if I'd published that story." A frozen curl of breath escaped her. "But I shoulda done it anyway."

"Well. I'm sorry."

Jo looked away. "So am I."

"What happened to the guy? To the Surrey Strangler?"

"Oh. When the witness came forward, after the last victim, I guess he was tipped off, because the killings stopped. Frank thought he might have left the province, or even the country."

"Frank?"

"Oh, that's my dad. He says they're still looking for the guy, but … maybe we'll never know."

Sally traced a line in the snow with one fur-trimmed boot. "Dawson is a small town. But a good place to find perspective."

"Yes. I had hoped."

Sally nodded and squinted into the distance. The snow was heavier now, silently burying the trail behind them, as though burying the past. Sally made a sudden movement, grabbing Jo's arm, and then cocked her head toward the forest. "*Shhh!* Did you hear that?"

Jo jumped. The back of her neck tingled, that age-old sensation of being watched. She lifted the binoculars and adjusted the focus ring. He was there. There, in the darkness of the undergrowth and thick trees. A majestic bull moose with antlers that must have been as long as her arm. Probably longer. He was perfect.

The beast stared at Jo, frozen for a moment that hung there like a question. Her mouth dropped open, each grey, vaporous exhalation suspended in midair.

"See anything?" Sally was still facing away, toward the trail.

"Not a goddamned thing."

8

Jo placed a few saline drops in each eye to lubricate her contact lenses, which felt gritty in the dry air. Her vision was blurry for a moment as she resumed peering at the *Daily*'s framed collection of archival photographs and stories that decorated the walls of her new office. The articles had titles like "Community Garden Ladies Can Carrots," "Parade to Celebrate Miners," and "City of Dreams Founded on Gold Dust."

"Journalist's Dreams Turn to Gold Dust in Ghost Town," she thought, then chided herself for being selfish. She should feel more fortunate for the second chance, she knew. *People know,* Sally had said. So. There could be no second chance.

Many of the old photographs pictured the haunted faces of long-dead miners, who either struck it rich or died trying. By the time the news reached the newspapers in the South that the Gold Rush had ended, it was too late for most of those faces. The majority of the luckless prospectors who had bought into the story—victims of newspaper headlines that promised "rivers filled with gold"—didn't have the money to leave. Many of them died in Dawson their first winter. The ones who had managed to make any money at all fled then, before freeze-up, leaving everything behind to do so. And so The Rush ended as suddenly as it began. Jo blinked. A pale reflection of herself, trapped in the framed glass, stared back through the hollow eyes of bankrupt miners. She turned away.

Jo knew that what she dreaded was not freeze-up itself, but coming to terms with the choices she'd made to come to Dawson. It was all well and good back in Vancouver to imagine herself curled up next to a cosy fire with a crossword puzzle or a book of poetry, the whiteness of the snow a carte blanche. In the daydream, she'd be listening to her new favourite song, the scratchy guitar string heights making her soul ache and soar. Jo pictured herself with a husky strewn casually across her feet for warmth. Maybe she'd take up the guitar again to fill the long winter nights. She thought of other possibilities, but pushed them away. For a moment, Jo wished that she'd pursued her first love, music, and never started writing about crime. Too late. Too late for so many things.

The harsh reality of life in a small northern town was sure to be less romantic. And Jo had always been an urbanite. She'd aimed to work for one of the nationals in Toronto someday, to immerse herself in the fast-paced, crime-riddled concrete world. The only kind of world she truly understood. Those dreams, and the dreams of others, ended when the body of a young woman was found in a burning vehicle. Now she dreamed of escape, atonement, and, most of all, anonymity.

The light on the *Daily*'s archaic answering machine was flashing. She wondered why everyone in Dawson seemed to have such an aversion to modern technology. She sighed as she pressed the button, pushing aside the yellowing stack of archival newspapers on her desk as she listened to Doug's whispery message asking her to review the old editions for content and style. Then there was a message from Frank, asking Jo to call him. Finally there was a series of staticky clicks and a long beep that somehow made her feel like a telegraph operator listening to naval distress signals.

A woman, enunciating very precisely, said that she urgently needed to speak to Jo Silver. Only Jo Silver. She instructed Jo to call her at home or come by her shop, The Gold Digger, when it opened at eleven. Her voice was high—almost musical—and confident. *May Wong.* May asked Jo to erase the message from the machine as soon as she'd heard it, and to mention the call to no one. Jo listened again and checked the time of the message before deleting it: May had rung just after midnight. Probably about the time that Jo had been holed up in the kitchen scarfing down "special" brownies. She had that slow, creeping feeling that she was on to something as she dialled, but was met with a hollow ring tone. Several more attempts yielded the same outcome. She thought it best not to leave a message.

The morning drained away in a languid succession of duties as Jo waited for The Gold Digger to open. She began by reviewing the most recent copies of the *Daily*. Most of the content was what she had expected—and dreaded. In the *Our Town* column, there was a story about Dawson's boardwalks, "Splinter Faction Debates Wooden Sidewalks." In the *Nuggets* column, there was always a story about a claim striking it rich, speculation concerning the price of gold, or somebody winning a bit of coin at Diamond Tooth Gertie's. In the previous edition, an aging tourist called Myrna Cunningham had been interviewed after she won a whopping $48.50 playing the slots. The headline read: "Tourist Strikes Gold at Gertie's!" There was a regular column called *Sourdough*, comprised mainly of local recipes. The last edition of the *Daily* had provided a collection of tips for freezing moose meat, under the title "The Big Freeze." An *Arts & Culture* column boasted rich content in the summer, when Dawson was rife with visiting artists and summer festivals, but was blatantly thin in off-season. What did surprise Jo a little was *Winning Hands*, a regular column dedicated to card games. The most recent featured a story on Klondike Solitaire, something the article claimed was a wildly popular pastime in the north. This spoke volumes about how much excitement was in store for her in the long, dark days ahead.

She went through Doug's suggestions for story ideas and put them aside. She wrapped her fingers around a negligibly clean mug of bitter instant coffee, warming her hands, thankful that the *Daily* was, at least, home to an electric kettle. In her inbox, someone (probably Doug) had thoughtfully forwarded a photograph of Marlo McAdam for the *Daily's* retrospective. Correction: for what everyone expected would be a retrospective, but what would, no doubt, become something much more complex.

Jo studied the photograph of Marlo, a close-up taken outdoors. She wore a frank expression, with faint lines appearing at the corners of closely set eyes. Jo guessed she must have been in her early thirties. The toothy grin made her look approachable. The fur trim of a parka framed a face that fell just short of pretty, but was beautiful in its openness.

Jo closed her eyes. She pictured Marlo's body, battered and lifeless in the icy waters of the Yukon River. Jo breathed deeply as the memories flooded back. She rested her eyes on the cool palm of her hands and inhaled the calm, dry scent of newspaper and dust. Tried to think of nothing. Tried not to feel the wave of shame and panic that sometimes washed over her. A bell chimed. A door opened. Boots shuffled a little on worn carpeting.

"I did receive your story notes," she said without looking up, steeling herself for battle. Forgetting momentarily that Doug would be at the school.

"Ms. Silver." The voice was tense. "I wonder if I might have a few moments of your time." Sergeant Cariboo filled most of the doorframe, a lanky figure that blocked the only escape route. He swept a sprinkling of light snow from the shoulders of his RCMP parka and stamped his feet. His dark eyes looked serious.

"Certainly," Jo said agreeably, but her shoulders betrayed her by lifting involuntarily. She motioned him to come in. "Would you care for a cup of the *Daily*'s famous coffee? Fresh out of the can."

He waved the offer away. "No, but thank you."

"Guess I didn't sell it very well."

Cariboo took a few steps into the room, but continued standing. Jo stood too, the grey metal desk between them like a shield. "This won't take long," he said. "We're continuing our investigation into Marlo McAdam's death, as I'm sure you know." Cariboo took off his gloves and then the muskrat-fur hat, running a hand through shiny black hair. He didn't look much like a cop. His hair was too long on top. A dark shadow of stubble lined his jaw and framed a generous mouth. He looked more like … what …? Jo thought about what Doug had said, about Cariboo's disappointed dreams. He'd wanted to be a singer.

"Yes," she said. His eyes searched her face, and Jo felt suddenly exposed, a guilty teenager in the presence of her father. The uniform put her on edge. It always had. "I thought you said the RCMP believed Marlo's death was an accident?"

"I'd appreciate it if you would let me ask the questions. It seems you weren't entirely truthful about your whereabouts Sunday night."

Jo's father had always been quick-tempered, something she'd made a conscious effort not to inherit. She had failed miserably. As a child, she had been sent home on more than one occasion for scrapping in the schoolyard, though she insisted she'd been demonstrating a technique that she had learned in one of the plethora of self-defence classes Frank had enrolled her in. Jo clenched her jaw and envisioned pouring gasoline all over Sergeant Cariboo. The pleasant sound it would make as she tossed the match. *Wooosh!* "I was entirely truthful about the fact that my memory of events is hazy at best, Sergeant."

"Convenient for you."

"There was nothing convenient about the way I felt yesterday morning."

"Convenient for you to forget that you were at the scene of the crime Sunday night."

"What …? Where …?"

"Crocus Bluffs."

"That is absolutely …"

"Before you say anything else, you should know that Christopher Byrne admits that the two of you were on Crocus Bluffs Sunday night, during the period when Marlo McAdam died."

Jo felt as though she were on a ship that had suddenly keeled sharply to one side. She leaned over and clenched the desk. "I … you said *crime* …"

"Perhaps you'd be more comfortable coming down to the station to continue this conversation?"

"Certainly, however you'd have to wait for my lawyer to accompany me, and I'm not sure how long it would take for her to get a flight this far north. Off-season, you know." She offered him a weak smile.

He gave her an appraising look, as though considering how much force to exert. His brow furrowed a moment, and the beginnings of lines showed around his eyes when he returned the insincere smile. He looked exhausted. "Was there any particular reason the two of you drove out to Crocus Bluffs the night Marlo McAdam died?" He studied her closely.

"I … believe you are mistaken." Jo sat down hard. "Mr. Byrne simply gave me a ride home. I was … feeling unwell."

"Are you sure you want to stick with that story?" His expression showed disbelief.

"Are you sure that you're still investigating an accident? You seem to be asking a lot of questions for something you've told the public was an accidental death."

Cariboo considered her for a moment. There was a long silence, then he said, "Did you know that Christopher Byrne was sleeping with Marlo McAdam?"

She felt something inside her constrict. "I did not. But it's none of my business. I barely know him." Her face flushed and she experienced a rush of self-loathing. If there was one thing she hated, it was being easy to read. Cariboo looked away, as if finding an answer that he didn't like.

"That's not what I hear. He told me you drove up to his cabin yesterday."

"I was investigating the story for the *Daily*."

"And you have a date with him tonight?"

She didn't answer him. Jo remembered Byrne's eyes on her at the bar. She hadn't been certain whether he'd been serious or not, but now she'd have to make sure that he kept the invitation.

There was a long silence between them, ended by Cariboo. "You know, I can't quite decide whether I'm worried about you, or for you." He gave Jo a penetrating look.

Jo broke eye contact with Cariboo to glance at her watch and then out the window.

A smattering of shops on Front Street that hadn't closed for the season yet, or had decided to tough it out through a Klondike winter, were beginning to show signs of life. The light in the Dawson Trading Post winked on. ("Yes, we sell mammoth ivory!") A well-bundled form disappeared inside The General

Store. The sign in the window of Jimmy's, the DVD rental and bookstore, flipped to "Open." The white metal gates at the mouth of Maximilian's Gold Rush Emporium were sliding back. Jo reached for her parka. She needed time to think.

"Where are you going?" Cariboo asked, the irritation in his voice clear.

"I've broken no law," she said, already pulling on cold rubber boots.

"That you remember." There was a meaningful silence before he added, "Do you think it's wise to be alone with him?"

Jo felt something inside her flare again. "Why? Are you jealous?" Her face was hot with annoyance.

"Yes," he answered.

His boldness shocked her. Was he winding her up? She stared at him, but his dark eyes returned the gaze without any trace of humour or malice. She felt something else pass between them, which she chose to ignore. "Is that all?" She wrapped a thick scarf around her throat, as though to protect herself from further attack.

"For now."

The sergeant's cruiser was parked right outside the *Daily*, causing curtains along Front Street to draw back.

"But don't leave town." Cariboo added, his tone firm.

Jo could have laughed out loud, but thought better of it.

9

The display cases in the window glittered with ostentatious jewellery and lusty nuggets of raw gold. Jo caught sight of her image in the glass. Reflected through the words "Gold Digger," her double's hair appeared to be a tarnished shade of yellow instead of her usual dark brown, and she watched herself brush away a strand that was blowing in her eyes. Her doppelganger frowned. She was tired of waiting, too.

The "Closed" sign had not been flipped to "Open," though it was now well past eleven, the appointed hour for the boutique to open and Jo to meet May. The shop floor was unlit, and the seductive exhibits of tourist gold were unattended. May Wong was nowhere to be seen. Jo backed away, surveying the street, checking for anyone who might be en route to the shop. The air smelled of snow and woodsmoke. A figure in a bright turquoise coat was disappearing down Front with a toboggan full of supplies. Otherwise, the street was empty.

May Wong's house was tucked into the hillside on Eighth, where turn-of-the-century mansions and large homesteads looked down on the town. *Business at The Gold Digger must be prospering.* May's home was of the Victorian variety, with the obligatory Dawson antlers hung over the entry. The front door had been painted blood red. Jo had read somewhere that a red door protected the occupant of a home from evil. She wondered if May had read the same article.

The path to the door had snowed in and bore no trace of footprints in the new snow. The flag on the mailbox was still up and the driveway was empty. Jo trudged through the snow to rap on the front door, making a hollow, empty sound while the wind hummed. Her second knock was met with obstinate silence.

Jo retraced her footsteps in the snow toward the street. She glanced over her shoulder at the stern, black windows of May Wong's home to see if anyone was watching, then around at the neighbouring homes. When she lifted the rusty flap on the mailbox, it made a shrill squeaking sound like an alarm. The mailbox was laden with flyers and bills, the latter stamped with that day's date. She returned the envelopes, took one more glance behind her, and then slipped down the side of the house toward the backyard.

In the back garden, a lone, bony willow stood like a tombstone, while a sagging picket fence told the story of the home's slow surrender to permafrost. At the north end of the property just beyond, the trees leaned in, like a group of conspirators.

It was snowing again, but not enough to conceal fresh footprints—large ones—leading from the forest up to the back door.

This discovery gave her pause as she considered knocking. The sound of a distant wood saw startled her, making her heart race as though she were planning something ill-advised. She rapped on the door and waited. May had told Jo to come to her shop at eleven. Had she been delayed by the arrival of someone unexpected? The tips of Jo's fingers were beginning to go numb, and the wind gnawed at her ears below her toque, urging her to try the handle. It turned easily enough.

Jo swung the door open, placing one rubber boot over the threshold. The lights were off inside, and although she'd already tried knocking, she called out "Hello?" just in case. Silence.

The back door opened into a boot room, where a women's fur coat and parka hung, along with a pair of cross-country skis and a set of modern snowshoes. The room also housed a collection of winter hats and footwear. Just beyond the doormat, a little puddle of muddy water had pooled on the wood floorboards. Jo slipped off her boots and took a few quiet steps around the puddle, through the entry, and into the kitchen. From there she leaned in to a view of an opulent living room with luxurious oriental carpets and rich furs. An impressive set of moose antlers hung over the hearth, yet the walls were also draped with sumptuous kimonos: a strange dichotomy of East meets West. An antique gun display rack boasted two rifles; there was an empty space where a third should have been.

"Hello? Anyone home?" She didn't want to disturb May if she happened to be with someone. Still, she couldn't shake the feeling that something was not quite right.

Somewhere upstairs, a floorboard squeaked. Jo froze. Her heart drummed a frantic rhythm and the inside of her woollen sweater felt damp. She tried to listen above the melody that the wind was whistling. A soft dirge. She was just beginning to think that she'd imagined the noise when she heard a clear scraping sound, like wood on wood, in one of the rooms above her.

She lost a moment or two as she wrestled between dual emotions: terror and curiosity. Then, she moved stealthily through the lounge to find a dim staircase at the front of the house. As she climbed the steps, the wood floors tattled on her approach. She paused at the landing. The second door down the hall was slightly ajar. A chilling draft emanated from the room, as though it were softly exhaling while she held her breath. She moved forward, giving the door a little shove and then stepping back.

Lace curtains billowed like a broken cobweb, waving farewell in the breeze. Next to the open window: an antique desk, one drawer slightly ajar. Jo padded over and drew back the curtain.

The blanched limbs of a skeletal tree clawed the window, making a handy escape ladder from May's office. Jo leaned forward for a better look, searching at the base of the trunk for new footprints in the snow. She had a good view of the ailing wooden fence and the fringe of wild growth beyond that disappeared into the woods. It would be the perfect escape route.

Jo realized her mistake just a moment too late. The only footprints were those leading toward the house: hers and a set of larger ones, both disappearing at the back door. She heard some kind of movement behind her and was just turning her head and raising one hand when the world went black.

10

It was the icy air that brought Jo to her senses. She felt stiff, her body twisted awkwardly as she came to, shivering on the floor. She opened her eyes slowly, blinking against the soft light of a Yukon afternoon after a snowfall. Her head throbbed and her neck ached. Her first instinct was to touch the side of her head, near the back, where she'd been hit. With that realization came a wave of panic that she might not be alone. Painfully, she moved her eyes and sat up, causing a brief ripple of nausea and a distant tinkling sound, like falling glass. The room appeared to be empty, the window still open.

Jo removed her glove and touched a bare finger to her scalp, resulting in a cool, damp sensation. For one horrible moment, she thought that the contents of her skull had been spilled, but when she brought her hand away, it was covered in gold glitter. Jo released a slow breath and moved her head painfully to look around. The floor was covered in shards of glass and a sparkling dust, as though she'd just been hit over the head by a combative fairy. A circle of wood lay at the epicentre of the destruction. She picked it up. A gold plaque along the edge read, "Dawson City, City of Gold." Nearby on the floor, the shiny figure of a miner kneeled thoughtfully over a pan of gold, lost in time and space.

Shakily, Jo got to her feet and crunched across fragments of glass to the window. This time when she leaned out, there were a second set of large footprints below, beginning at the back door and disappearing into the woods. Jo donned her gloves and closed the window.

She picked up the receiver from a rotary phone on the desk and dialled Dawson's emergency number, already dreading another interview with Cariboo. The receptionist spoke maddeningly slowly. Once she'd made the call, Jo took another look at her surroundings.

The soft, new snow seemed to deaden all sound, muffling the distant hum of a chainsaw and the rough laughter of ravens. Jo wondered how much time she had. The only thing that appeared to be amiss was a desk drawer, which wasn't quite closed. It slid open easily, revealing a set of letter-sized files. She flipped quickly through the labels on the file folders. All but one were related to May's shop, The Gold Digger. The last was labelled "Claim 53." Jo withdrew the file, rifling through the documents. Gold production … Staffing … Various articles about the increasing strength of gold on the market. Then a legal document naming May Wong as the owner of Claim 53 at Sourdough Creek, and someone named Jack Grikowsky as the manager. The name rang a bell. Tires crunched on snow in the driveway. A car door slammed.

Jo shoved the folder back into the desk drawer, which she returned to its original position. She tugged on the handles of the other two drawers. One contained innocuous office supplies. The other was locked. Jo knelt down, removed one glove, and felt the underbelly of the desk.

The sharp sound of boots rang out on wooden stairs. A voice called out, "Ms. Silver?" Cariboo.

Her fingertips brushed against cold metal under the desk. She dipped her head to look.

The footsteps reached the top of the stairs. "Josephine!" He sounded both alarmed and irritated.

"Yes!" she called out. "I'm here!" She straightened, left hand still clutching her right glove.

When Cariboo arrived at the door, competing emotions showed on his face. "Why didn't you answer me?" His dark eyes strayed from hers and his gaze travelled to her hands. Jo could feel his suspicion.

"Sorry," she said. "Still a bit dizzy from the whack on the head. Not thinking straight."

The tip of the little gold key in her pocket nudged the top of her leg in accusation.

11

Snow had piled up along the edges of the street in high banks. The SUV skidded a little, and Cariboo steered into the slide to correct. The town flashed by in pastel pops of false-fronted Victorian buildings.

"What if she hasn't gone hunting?" Jo asked, squeezing her gloved hands both to comfort herself and to generate some kind of warmth. Her head throbbed dully with the strobing of the storefronts. Jo winced as she turned to look out the window. She rubbed at the back of her neck, but avoided touching the bruised area on her head, where she now had a sizeable lump.

"You should see a doctor about that. You might have a concussion." He looked concerned.

"It's fine," she lied. "Anyway, isn't the nearest hospital in Whitehorse? I can just imagine what people would say if I had to be airlifted out of Dawson in my second week. Not very sourdough."

"There is a part-time nursing station." He glanced at his watch. "Though it's closed now."

"I'm fine. Really."

Cariboo didn't look like he believed her. After a weighty

pause, he said, "Her gun is missing from the rack. Her vehicle is gone. It's moose season."

"What kind of a gun is it? The missing one?"

"A Springfield. Thirty-aught-six."

"Is that a moose gun?"

"Definitely. It's quite powerful. You'd only use it for big game."

Or self-defence. "But doesn't it seem a bit odd to you that she would leave now?" Jo felt the pain pulsating from the back of her head and radiating to her temples and down her spine.

"It's moose season now. May often goes hunting. Sometimes she's gone for days at a time." Their eyes met, and Jo felt the dark intensity of his stare. She experienced the sensation again that he was looking through her. "Anyway, come by the station as soon as you're up to it so I can take your statement."

"But you already did an audio recording of my statement."

"I'd like you to write it down, as well. I'll buy you a coffee." He smiled at her, but the smile concealed a question.

"You mean you want to interview me as a possible suspect."

Cariboo focused on the road. "I'm just doing my job, Josephine."

"Jo." She felt her face heat up. "And I told you, the door was open. I stepped inside, called out, and heard something upstairs. I thought May might be in trouble."

"Yes. So you've said. But what you were doing there in the first place?" He frowned, as though he didn't like to have to ask the question.

Jo experimented with tilting her head to the right, and was rewarded with a quick jab of pain. "I wanted to talk to her about what happened Sunday night. She left Gertie's early, right? She might have seen something in the parking lot, or given Marlo a lift."

Cariboo shifted in his seat. "I'm not at liberty to discuss that information. And it's not your job to play detective."

Jo wondered what he might be holding back. "But if May did see something and now she's missing, that seems pretty ominous, doesn't it?"

Cariboo glanced at her. He looked like he wanted to say more, but didn't.

She felt shaky, and the jostling and lurching of the SUV seemed to be creating waves in the ocean inside her stomach. Should she tell Cariboo that she'd been invited to meet May at The Gold Digger, and that May had never shown? It concerned her that May had asked her to keep the phone call a secret. She had no idea who to trust with the information. She bounced both knees, squeezing them tightly together. The heater in the front seat roared in a promising way, but the warm air didn't seem to circulate. Jo pictured herself in the airlift helicopter, circling up over the town like a raven, flying away. She shivered, shaking off the thought.

"Anyway, as you know, my memory of that evening is a little fuzzy. I had hoped that seeing May might … I don't know, help me jog it a little." When she swallowed, her throat felt constricted. "I went by The Gold Digger first. It was after 11 a.m., but her shop was still closed. I thought she might be at home." Jo decided she'd talk to Frank later about how much to tell the police in Dawson about the phone call from May.

Cariboo threw her a quick, suspicious look before returning his attention to the road. "Well, I guess you can see about that when she's back," he said.

"You're not even going to look for her?"

"I'll ask around town today, check out the hotel lounges where she might go for a coffee break, let her know about the break-in if I find her … but like I said, she hasn't been missing twenty-four hours and her car is gone, so it looks like she's left of her own accord." He was scowling now, either at the weather or at her questions. When he glanced at Jo again, their eyes locked. Jo knew that Cariboo didn't believe May Wong had gone hunting. "I *will* look for her," he added more softly, though whether to reassure her or himself, Jo couldn't say. He had a curious expression on his face.

"But what about the break-in?" Jo could see the *Daily* now. She straightened up in the seat and rested a glove on the door handle in anticipation.

"The guys will do a routine investigation. Look for finger-prints and photograph footprints. But it was probably just some transient looking for cash. Sometimes it happens when the sum-mer kids leave town at the end of the season."

Jo listened to the squeaking sound of the tires on dry snow, and the soft static of the RCMP radio for a moment while she thought about that. "What if you're wrong?"

Cariboo made a sound that was supposed to be a laugh. "Be quite a story." He gave her a sharp look.

Something inside her flared. "Yes, it would: the RCMP's only witness in a murder investigation goes missing. You'd better hope you're right, because I will certainly make sure people read all about it if you're wrong." Jo began unbuckling her seat belt, anxious to be free of him.

"Please don't leave yet, I'm not finished," he said, shoving the gear shift into park with more force than was really required. He left the car idling and turned to face her. Jo could feel her cheeks flushing. "It has not escaped my attention that Marlo McAdam died shortly after you arrived in Dawson ..."

"An enormous coincidence ..."

" ... and that you were in the vicinity at the time of her death."

"... that would never stand up in a court of law." The tips of her ears felt like they were on fire.

"You have formed some kind of relationship with a person who had a motive to kill her ..."

"This is what you do in small towns, don't you? Blame the outsider?"

"... and you have just been found present at the scene of another ..."

"If you accuse me of anything you'd better do it with my lawyer present."

"This is not a formal accusation."

"Then we're done here. My father is a police officer in Vancouver, Sergeant, so if you think you can bully me, you are sadly mistaken."

"I just think you might want to be careful." Cariboo had a strange expression on his face, but she was too angry now to care. "Also, I consider myself to be a good judge of character, and I know when someone isn't telling the whole truth."

"Thank you for the ride, Sergeant." Jo leapt down from the front seat of the SUV, her rubber boots making an emphatic sound as they hit the snow. She closed the cruiser door as gently as she could when she exited, but she knew it would make little difference. By the end of day, everyone in town would know about Jo's ride in Cariboo's SUV.

12

There are only so many places to look for a person in a decaying frontier town of thirteen-hundred-some-odd people. The Riverside, the only coffee shop in town, had just closed for the season, so that made the list even shorter. The windows of May's Victorian beauty on Eighth remained dark, and the mail untouched. The bars and restaurants in Dawson were almost exclusively located on the premises of a handful of hotels: the Eldorado, the Westminster, the Downtown, and a former brothel, called Bombay Peggy's. Jo checked them all.

No one seemed particularly alarmed that May hadn't opened her shop. During the winter months, store hours became erratic. If the hunting was good in the morning, a waitress at the Jack London Grill informed Jo, a person might just stay "out there." It was moose season, she said, refilling Jo's warm mug of drip coffee.

Jo had not only landed squarely in the middle of "nowhere," she now occupied a shifting terrain where a person could disappear without consequence. If someone couldn't be found "on the map," it was merely assumed that they'd been swallowed up by the ever-encroaching outer terrain called "the bush." She was uncomfortable with grey areas, with life's little uncertainties. She wanted to occupy a space defined by a clear set of fundamental truths. A black-and-white world where gourmet coffee was available.

Jo knew that the RCMP would normally wait twenty-four hours before they began a thorough search for a missing person, though she hoped she'd prodded Cariboo to begin sooner. Still, she didn't trust the RCMP with finding May. May was one of only a few people known to have left Gertie's early the night Marlo McAdam had been killed, and May had urgently wanted to speak with Jo. If she had been the person who drove Marlo to the Bluffs, she might have seen something important. Jo chewed on her lip, feeling the rough, chapped skin. May might be hiding, in trouble, or even implicated in Marlo's death. Whatever the case, doing nothing wasn't an option for Jo. She had no intention of adding to the nightmares she already lived with.

⌘

The lengthening shadows of trees stretched across the Kondike Highway in the path of the old Chevy. Jo felt the contents of her head jostling along with Sally's truck and the Hawaiian hula dancer on the dashboard. Her neck was still angry about her run-in with the snow globe, but her vision was clear and the nausea had passed. What she was aching to do was to go straight to Christopher Byrne and rattle him for the truth about what had happened Sunday night—the night Marlo died. Unfortunately, as Byrne had no phone, she had no idea how to contact him when he wasn't at his cabin or at the pub. She cursed as she hit another pothole that sent a shooting pain up from the base of her skull.

Jo continued east, turning off onto an old mining road toward Sourdough Creek to find Claim 53. May Wong's mine. The truck passed giant, Frankenstein-esque machines, rusted-out water cannons, snow-capped piles of gravel, rotting log cabins sinking into the snow, abandoned dredges and sluices, and "pan your own gold" tourist traps. The landscape was a strange, desolate moonscape of human destruction. She drove slowly. It had stopped snowing, but the wind was teasing drifts across the road. She hoped she wouldn't be long. She had no trouble finding Gold Gulch, which was marked clearly on her map, but she drove by the excavation site the first time. The boulder marked "#53" was set back from the road a bit, next to a sign that read "Beware of Dog." The lane was blocked by a metal gate, which stopped vehicles but not pedestrian traffic.

Jo left the Chevy on the side of the highway, facing in the direction of Dawson. She crunched along a narrow path that finally widened into a battlefield of excavation trenches. Despite two layers of wool socks, her toes were going numb. She thought a little wistfully about that pair of North Face boots in the closed shop window of Wild & Woolly. Fur lined, full leather uppers, waterproof shell, and gusseted tongue. Jo never thought she'd covet a lousy pair of snow boots, but here she was, in a place she'd never thought she'd be. She thought about how quickly priorities shifted in the North, and wondered what Marlo's priorities had been.

The air smelled of winter and earth and diesel. Two men wearing dirty jeans and gumboots stood by the side of a big pit, where gravel was piled up and capped in snow, so fresh it sparkled cheerfully under a powder-blue sky. They were in the middle of a heated discussion. A driverless beast of a machine— all metal tooth and claw—idled dully in the excavation. The men stopped their conversation as they registered Jo's presence on the other side of the pit.

Within minutes, one of the men—the one with the handlebar moustache—stomped over to where she stood.

"Hey! Sweetheart! If you're looking for tourist panning, you're in the wrong place." He wore a disingenuous grin that matched the tone of his voice. His moustache and sideburns were beginning to silver, but he emitted a sense of strength that made him seem younger than his forty-some-odd years. His heavy brows were raised in fine points and his eyes were sharp, the pupils small, giving him an eagle-like expression.

Jo shook her head. "No, no, I'm with the *Dawson Daily*. I'm looking for Jack Grikowsky." She felt the muscles in her shoulders tensing.

"Well, you found him. And he doesn't recall having an interview scheduled."

"Jo Silver." She offered Grikowsky her hand, which he pointedly ignored, reaching for a packet of cigarettes in his pocket instead.

"Look, I'm very busy, *Ms.* Silver is it?" His brow creased as he lit the cigarette and casually exhaled. "I'm trying to hit pay dirt here before freeze-up." That smile again. A crocodile smile.

Jo shivered, and suspected that it had nothing to do with the cold this time. "I won't take much of your time, Mr. Grikowsky. I'm wondering if you've heard from May Wong recently?"

"May? May owns the mine, but she doesn't participate in its daily operations." The cigarette dangled and bounced as he spoke. He had a certain style, Jo thought. He was … *smooth*.

"So you haven't seen her this week?"

"Nope." The smile. "Of course, it's only Tuesday."

"Any idea where I might find her?"

"Not a clue."

"Well, I wonder if you could tell me how well May knew Marlo McAdam?"

"McAdam?"

"MLA North. Body was found in the Yukon River yesterday."

"Oh, yeah. Heard about that. What's that got to do with May?"

Sunday seemed like weeks ago already, but the events of the night played out in Jo's mind like a loop of film that had been spliced at each end: blurry stars, Byrne's hand on her elbow, then Marlo hissing at Byrne, "I'll tell! I'll tell *her*!" Jo pictured the body in the puffy red parka floating in the Yukon River, then Caveman's wide eyes as he said, "Are you here about the mine?" Caveman had said it wasn't safe to talk about that at Gertie's, "especially after Marlo." It seemed to fit.

"Did Ms. McAdam ever come out to the mine?" Jo asked.

"Why would she?"

"She'd been asking questions about the mine recently, hadn't she?" Grikowsky stopped smiling for an instant. "Did you happen to see her at Gertie's Sunday night?"

"Does Doug know you're here?"

"What?"

Jack Grikowsky gave Jo an oily grin, his composure regained like elevator doors sliding smoothly shut. "I thought so. I'll have one of the guys show you to your vehicle." Jo must have looked like she needed convincing, as he added, "Unless of course you'd prefer me to call Sergeant Cariboo and let him know you're trespassing on private property?" Grikowsky threw down his cigarette like a glove.

"Don't trouble yourself. I'll show myself out."

———∞———

A surge of excitement hit Jo like a gust of Yukon wind. Her thoughts wheeled ahead of her as she tromped back to ol' Bettie. It was the insinuation that Doug Browning was somehow in Grikowsky's pocket that really got to her. She was certain that something was wrong at the mine. Jo kept her head down against the wind, and her chin tucked into her scarf, which is probably why she saw it: a thin leather strap poking out of the snow.

Jo bent down with a squeak of snow and cold fabric. She inhaled sharply as she gave a little tug, half hoping the excavated object might be a handbag belonging to May Wong. It wasn't. She wasn't sure what it was.

13

The radio at the *Daily* was set to CFYT 106.9FM ("The Spirit of Dawson!"). On bad weather days, CFYT broadcast a lot of static, but this day sparkled and the sound was clear, if a little tinny. Patsy Cline bayed the words to "Strange" as Jo lifted a steaming cup to her lips. She closed her eyes and tipped back in the chair. The hot liquid was rich, but not nearly strong enough. Already she yearned for the coffee from The Pit pub. Jo placed the bright orange teacup lightly on her desk, next to the leather bag that she'd tripped over in the snow.

There was something very odd going on at Claim 53. She knew it. It was written all over Jack Grikowsky's face, and she bet that Marlo had known it too. Jo eyed the leather bag, then picked it up. Still damp with snow, it looked a bit like a camera case with a broken strap, but she already knew that the device inside was not a camera.

She opened the bag and turned the metal contraption over in her hands again, studying it. The design was sombre in tone: black and tan, and the little needle on the front somehow made Jo think of hospitals. It looked like a medical device. She turned the power switch on, activating a red light, then searched for instructions, or more switches, but found only a power input and something that might be a volume switch. She pushed a little triangular button, and a number appeared on the screen. Jo let out a soft sigh and returned the gadget to her desk, next to the tangerine teacup. The thing that was not a camera made a faint clicking sound.

Perplexed, she picked the little metal box back up and waved it around, listening to its scratchy "t-t-t-tsk tsk tsk" as it neared the cup. A robotic tone of disapproval. Jo swung the apparatus gently away from the desk. It stuttered once or twice, and then was silent.

Jo straightened in the chair as Patsy's lilting, melancholy voice haunted the room. A portable heater in the corner kicked in, glowing orange and clicking in time to the music. She reached for her laptop.

The computer made a grating noise in complaint. The archaic dial-up sound was like cold steel scraping and crumpling. Jo steered her thoughts away from car crashes. Leaning forward, she typed "Geiger counter" into the search engine, waited again, and then scrolled through a long series of images. The search result displayed not only an array of machines with angry needles, but also a morbid collection of links: how to build your own survival bunker, reports on nuclear radiation disasters, environmental reports about the hazards of mining, conspiracy theories about terrorism and uranium smuggling, and the like. France had recently been accused of exporting uranium to rogue terrorist states. There were also several reports of smugglers transporting raw uranium to France via Skagway, Alaska, which was not that far from Dawson. Jo thought she'd heard someone in town say that you could take the ferry to West Dawson and drive straight on to Skagway, weather permitting. At least, you could until the Top of the World Highway closed for the season, which would be any day now.

Jo leaned back in the chair and rubbed her dry, irritated eyes, then gently touched the bump at the back of her head. She was relieved to find that it didn't hurt quite as much as it had earlier. A husky wailed in the distance. Or possibly a wolf. Even then, Jo felt strangely comforted by the close proximity of another being.

Note to self: not to use the orange teacup.

⸎

It took Jo almost an hour to write a few paragraphs about Marlo, as she spun the story again and again, searching for the subtleties, the connection between May Wong and Marlo McAdam, and just the right level of suggestion to trigger a reaction from ... someone. Whoever knew more than they were letting on about May's disappearance or Marlo's death. Jo stopped short of pointing to a police cover-up, noting only that the police had been questioning anyone who left Gertie's early and were looking for the person—or persons—who might have given Marlo a ride to the Bluffs. By the time Jo was finished, she felt confident that anyone in Dawson could line up the dots and see that Marlo's death may not have been accidental, that the police were aware of the fact and had not informed the public, and that May Wong—who "could not be located for comment" on what she may have seen in the parking lot—was obviously missing.

In the waning afternoon light, head down and hands in pockets, Doug arrived at the *Daily*, made late and irritable by parent meetings. It took only a few fleeting minutes for him to kill Jo's story. He looked up from the article, titled, "Police Probe Suspicious Death of MLA."

"Man, we can't say this ..."

"Can't say what?"

"We can't, you know, talk about the 'controversy' sparked by her death." Doug pantomimed quotation marks in midair.

"Why not?"

"We have to remain unbiased. We simply report what the coroner said. 'Death caused by the fall or by drowning after falling into the river.' We won't know more until the pathology report, probably not until tomorrow."

"But the question isn't whether she died during the fall or after hitting the water. The question is whether she 'fell,' " Jo pantomimed quotation marks back at Doug, "or whether she was pushed from a very high cliff. I'm betting on the latter."

"Look, we report only what we know absolutely to be true. Let people draw their own conclusions, eh? What we want is a simple retrospective that's respectful to her memory. That's what we agreed to. Not a lot of wild speculation."

"Why can't we just pose the question? What was Marlo McAdam doing up on the Bluffs in the middle of night? And was she alone? Because she certainly didn't drive herself there." Doug stared at Jo, the kind of calculated study that an opponent gives to a threat. His eyes were shifting and watery behind his glasses. Jo added, "What are you so afraid of?"

There was an uncomfortable silence. Jo had the feeling of looking at something underwater, flitting just below the surface, and not being able to make out exactly what it was. The shape of the thing distorted in the currents of their conversation.

"Were you out at the mine today?" Doug asked.

"I was. I was following a story lead."

"I specifically, like, directed you not to do anything without clearing it with me first."

"I didn't include that particular angle in this piece, so it shouldn't be an issue for you."

"You are not to bother Mr. Grikowsky again. Are we clear?"

"Yes."

Doug looked relieved for a moment, until she added, "We don't ask questions. We don't investigate the sudden death or disappearance of our citizens. And we don't bother Mr. Grikowsky."

The moment hung awkwardly. Doug appeared to stare at nothing for a moment, his pale eyes unfocused as though looking inwardly. Then his attention gravitated to something, or someone, behind her.

"Are you dating Christopher Byrne?" he asked. His voice sounded distant.

Jo turned to follow his look. Byrne's truck had just pulled up on Front Street in front of the *Daily*. He was two hours early.

14

The glassy-eyed stare of the caribou head over the bar made Jo feel unsettled, but not as much as the company she was keeping. She avoided Byrne's eyes as much as possible on her date that wasn't—she reminded herself—a real date. There was something unnerving about the way he looked at her, as though they shared a secret. Jo studied the room instead, meticulously assessing the peeling, Victorian-style wallpaper and the gilded mirrors. The Sourtoe Saloon was located in the Downtown Hotel, popular with the tourists in high season, according to Byrne, but mainly a hangout for the locals in off season. Jo found herself squinting and rubbing her eyes; the room was woven with thick ropes of tobacco smoke, like a giant web. A collection of men in heavy jackets and Klondike boots sat under a string of sad Christmas lights at the bar, several staring openly at Jo. Self-conscious, she missed her shot.

"You have to account for the slope in the floorboards. Sorta like golf," Byrne said.

"Good to know," Jo muttered.

"The buildings here are built on permafrost. When the buildings heat up, the frost melts and the whole structure shifts."

He bent over to line up a shot and artfully dropped a ball in the corner pocket. She tried not to notice his very fine backside.

"Nice," Jo said, and pretended she was referring to his shot.

Byrne smiled at her. It was a very charming smile. "You look great, by the way," he said.

"Thanks. A lot of thought went into this outfit." She was still wearing the same clothes she had worn to work: jeans, a black sweater, rubber boots, and a toque. She felt she was on uneven terrain on more than one level. Byrne had knowledge about the night that Marlo McAdam died that Jo did not possess. He had made Jo an alibi for something she had no recollection of, and the knowledge burned. She was angry with him for using her, for not being forthcoming about what had happened, and she was a little unsettled by him. Still, she felt she couldn't let him know it, or she'd risk losing access to any information that he did have. During the brief drive from the *Daily,* Jo had attempted to question Byrne about the events of that night. He'd quickly hushed her to turn up the road report on the radio, leaning in close to the dashboard to listen, as though they were announcing the winning lottery numbers. Before she knew it, they were at the Sourtoe Saloon.

"So, I had an interesting talk with Sergeant Cariboo today ..."

"So I heard. I suggest we talk about that later. Somewhere more private." The faint suggestion of a smile on his lips made "private" sound lewd, but his eyes scanned the bar, looking for signs that anyone might have been listening.

"Oh." *Where did he hear?* "Well, I have nothing to hide."

"Are you sure?" He looked amused as he watched her reaction.

Jo doubted herself for a moment. A couple of heads turned from their Yukon Golds to listen in profile, feigning indifference.

"Then what do you recommend we talk about?"

He held his cue still, studying her in silence for a moment. "You could ask me my sign. This is a date, after all," he said.

"Is it?" Jo asked, hoping to refute the assertion.

He allowed the question to hang there, ringed in smoke, enabling it to drift through the room. Now thick with meaning. He grinned, fanning the laugh lines around his eyes. "Isn't it?"

Flustered, she began again. "You promised me a reenactment, remember? And today Cariboo said that we were on the Bluffs that night, which you didn't tell me. And he said that you'd been sleeping with Marlo." More heads at the bar turned.

"Jesus." He said it like a fact, putting down his cue and crossing his arms. He glanced around the room, then his gaze came back to rest on her. He looked concerned, but a smile still played at his lips. "You do not want to do this now. Trust me."

"I make a point of never trusting a person who says, 'trust me.'" She leaned over and smacked her ball, which rolled down the tilted table and just missed knocking the green into a corner pocket. She'd grown up hearing all sorts of stories over dinner about the horrid things that happened to trusting women, so her lack of judgement on Sunday evening was something that surprised even her. She'd been drinking too much lately. Since Vancouver. Such a basic form of escapism, but usually she had more control. It couldn't happen again. Jo straightened up. "But I guess we can talk about certain details later, if you insist."

"Good," he said, examining the table, a strained expression on his face.

It pained her to wait. She had to have something now. "But I was wondering ..." She hoped her tone would sound casual. "The night Marlo died, you were working the poker tables, right?"

Byrne held her look. His face gave nothing away. Either he had no response, or Jo didn't have the forbearance to wait for one. She charged ahead. "Did you talk to her at all?" *They were sleeping together.* The thought was unbidden, unwelcome, but surfaced anyway. "Before the parking lot, I mean?"

"We weren't together anymore." Another ball rolled into a side pocket.

"You didn't answer the question."

"I answered one of them. The one you implied, which I thought was more important." He smiled.

Jo missed her next shot. "So, you've never had to work in any of the mines in Dawson?"

He sighed. "You are determined. No, I've been fortunate enough not to have to."

"Fortunate? Why fortunate?"

Byrne lined up another shot and sank it effortlessly. *Bastard.*

"I've done well enough with my art, and when I've needed to, with working the tables here. Others haven't been so lucky."

"Which others?" Jo asked.

"Friend of mine, Mike Cariboo."

"Cariboo? As in Sergeant Cariboo?"

"Yeah, Johnny's cousin. They were quite close until Johnny's father died. I think that changed Johnny. He had responsibilities. You know, not so much time for fishing with his little cousin anymore. And then there was what happened to Johnny's fiancée."

"What?"

"Yeah, a girl called Alice Wolfe. Couple of years later."

"What happened to her?"

"Nobody knows. She was hitchhiking home from a party one night and was never seen again. Mike says Johnny never got over it."

"They never found out what happened?"

"No. That happens sometimes in the North. Especially to First Nations girls, but nobody talks about that." He looked serious then. "Mike says that's when he and Johnny stopped hanging out. Then Mike went to work in the mine."

"Poor Johnny."

"Yes, that's the general consensus. But you didn't come here to talk about Johnny, did you?" Jo felt their connection again. There was an emotional intelligence about Byrne that was undeniable. "At least, I hope you didn't."

"You said Mike was unlucky to work in the mine."

"Yes."

"Why?"

Byrne shrugged. "He said a lot of the guys got sick working there."

Jo set her pool cue down with a slight rattle and stared at him. "Sick with what?"

"Dunno. Mike doesn't work there now. He works for Han Construction. A lot of his family does. In framing. He helped Johnny build his cabin. And mine."

"I'd like to meet him." Seeing the look of surprise on Byrne's face, she added, "I'm serious."

"I know. It's unfortunate. But I'm willing to forgive you on a first date." He grinned, then ran his cue through his fingers, back and forth, and sunk his shot. She wondered if he was trying to be provocative, or whether she just had a dirty mind.

The room was suffocating; the back of her throat burned with smoke. She rubbed her irritated eyes, as though she would not only see better, but she might also gain some greater insight. It felt as though the smoke were clouding the real issue. "Listen, it's not that I don't like … well, it's just that, Sergeant Cariboo said some things today that I need to …"

"C'mon," Byrne said. "Let's get out of here."

Byrne's husky was in the back of his weathered pickup, sniffing the air as Jo approached the truck. The one ice-blue eye, one brown, made the big dog look like two beasts in one.

As though sensing her apprehension, Byrne said, "Don't worry about Nugget. He's part wolf and part husky, but he's all pussycat." Nugget's tongue lolled out in a hungry grin. He looked part hyena. Byrne opened the door for her, then continued round the truck and got in.

Jo caught herself wondering whether Nugget slept on Byrne's bed, and whether Byrne's blankets would be hairy. She put one foot on the running board, then hesitated.

Byrne noticed. He leaned over from the driver's seat. "Look, if I wanted to get you alone in a truck and kill you, I would have already done it, right? You've already survived my company once, though you may choose to forget the experience." He grinned. Jo exhaled icy breath and climbed in.

The seats of his truck were cracked and had absorbed the sub-zero temperatures. As he turned the key in the ignition, a strain of moody guitar filled the cold air. Jo felt strangely enchanted by the music.

Byrne said, "The local station here is quite good. Have you found it yet? CFYT."

"Yeah," she said. "Doug listens to it at the *Daily*." She couldn't believe he was still trying to make small talk, now that they were out of earshot. She cleared her throat. "So what exactly did you say to Sergeant Cariboo? He told me you said that we were at Crocus Bluffs Sunday night. Is that true?"

Byrne gave her an enigmatic look. The windows were steaming up as they huddled in the cab, waiting for the engine to warm up. The vehicle was filled with his scent. Something warm and spicy. *His soap?*

"Yes," he said, as though he'd just read her mind.

"What did you say?"

"What did you say?" His blue-green eyes were searching hers.

"I told him the truth," she said.

"Ah." Byrne threw the truck into drive. Snowflakes caught in his headlights, dancing brilliantly before disappearing into darkness. The gritty voice on the radio sang,

Hangnails and coattails,
The snow sounds like crushed rails
And I have failed at leaving on time
In a frozen town. In a frozen town.

"That I don't remember where we went that night."

Byrne squinted into the snow. "And did he believe you?"

Not really, Jo thought. "Yes," she said.

"Sometimes we don't truly forget; we just refuse to remember." Byrne glanced at her.

"Why would I want to do that?" Jo asked.

"You tell me. Are you ashamed about what happened?"

"I have no idea. What *did* happen?" She felt a hot flash of anger. "I want to hear it from you."

He glanced at her, but she couldn't read the expression on his face. "It would be easier to show you than to tell you … I could take you there now, if you're sure you want to know."

"I think you'd better drive me home, and tell me *exactly* what you said to Sergeant Cariboo when he asked if you were on the Bluffs the night Marlo died."

"I denied it."

"So we weren't there?" Jo still hoped he'd refute the accusation. Hoped it was all a terrible mistake.

"No, we were there. I lied." Jo felt her breath catch in her chest. "Until Johnny told me what had happened. To Marlo, I mean."

He pulled the truck over, letting it idle next to a snow bank, behind Sally's turn-of-the-century house. The parking lot was deserted.

"Why did you lie?" Jo said.

"You really don't know?"

"No! What were we doing up there? I need you to tell me."

Byrne's haunting eyes bored into her, but he declined to answer. Jo began to perspire, a cold feeling. Stupid of her to accept a ride home with him again. She had no idea who he was or what he was capable of.

"What if I told you we were doing a little old-fashioned necking?" Byrne said, his eyes smiling, but also searching hers.

Jo felt a sudden rush of emotions. Elation. Mistrust. "Were we?" She fought to keep her voice calm.

Byrne looked mischievous. "Would it please you if we were?"

"So let me get this straight: you were sleeping with Marlo and you've been placed at the scene of her death. The night she died."

He raised his eyebrows. "Yes," he said, watching her carefully. "Yes, I slept with her. But it wasn't serious. And ..."

"And you may have been the last person to see her before she died." *I should leave.* Frank was forever telling Jo in college that 90 percent of victims know their attackers. She pulled her oversized parka tighter around her body. The air in the cab suddenly felt heavy, and she began calculating how many steps it would take to get from the truck to the front door. The space between them felt electric now, and Jo was overwhelmed by a deep, primal fear. She lunged for the door handle, but his arm shot out, barring her escape. Jo gasped, ready to scream, but felt the weight of his arm as his reach retreated, brushing against her leg as he withdrew. He had only been unlocking the door. She felt heat escaping in her breath, twisting in the air around her, and betraying her emotions. Byrne's hand lingered a moment on her forearm.

Rattled, Jo seized the door handle, thankful for its cool, solid weight. "Well. Thanks for the ... I'd better go," she mumbled.

"I gather I'm not coming in for a coffee then?" His tone was lighthearted, but Jo felt shaken just the same. "What about the reenactment?"

"Maybe another time."

"Jo!"

She glanced at him, without committing her whole body to turn toward him.

"Do you know where Sally was?"

"What?" Jo searched the back of at the house, looking for any sign of her housemate. The bedroom windows upstairs were black, but there was a light on in the kitchen. "Why?"

"Maybe you should ask her. That's all I'm saying." Byrne's face was solemn now.

"Good night," Jo said. She refrained from glancing back or waving as she walked away.

15

As Jo hastened to close the front door, she was met by a fiery blast of air, the squeal of a kettle, and the disturbing vision of Sally dressed in head to toe black PVC leather.

The faux leather glinted at every deadly curve as though Sally had just polished her entire body. She glanced up, snipping a little piece of thread on her sleeve. She picked up a riding crop and examined her reflection in a gilded, full-length mirror in the front entry, looking pleased. "Giddy-up," she said, tapping the crop against her shiny backside. *Thwack, thwack.*

"What the hell?" It was all Jo could think of to say as she rushed through to the kitchen to take the blackened kettle off the wood stove.

Sally glanced at Jo in the mirror from the entry room. "We're hemorrhaging tourists—in a few days freeze-up will be here. Have to have an alternate business plan, so I'm gonna make myself a sweet website." As though that explained everything.

"And here I am without a Halloween costume." Jo headed back to the boot room to remove her jacket, now damp with melted snow.

"You're in early. How was your date?"

"Strange. And it wasn't a date." She leaned in the doorframe.

"Hmm. You be careful with that one." Sally gave Jo a look that was difficult to decipher. It might have been concern, or it could have been something else.

"Why? He seems ... I can't quite figure him out."

Sally pointed the crop at Jo. "Which is ex-*actly* what makes him so dangerous," she said.

"Dangerous?"

"Oh, he's fabulous. Those *eyes*, right? He's just not everything he seems." Sally contemplated her reflection. "Then again ... who is? Speaking of which ..." She grabbed some tissue and stuffed it into her bra. The result seemed to satisfy her, as she put her shoulders back and smiled at herself. Her breasts were robotic and pointy, like some kind of deadly femmebot that might at any moment gun you down with her mammary glands.

"Hmm. Better," Sally remarked.

"That's funny, he seems to be saying the same thing about you."

"Ha!" Sally looked surprised, but not displeased. "Touché!"

"Did you have something against Marlo?" Jo said, shrugging off her wet parka and tossing it onto an already cluttered bench.

"I had very little interest in Marlo at all. She was quite dull." Something hardened in her expression.

"Did Marlo McAdam think Christopher Byrne was dangerous?"

Sally stared at herself in the mirror for a moment without saying anything. Without meeting Jo's eyes. "That I don't know." She turned to look at herself from another angle, turning her back on Jo a little more.

"Do you think Byrne had any reason to kill her?" The heat of the wood stove in the kitchen made Jo's wool sweater feel even itchier. She longed to tug it off over her head, but she didn't want to take her eyes off Sally's reaction for even an instant. She felt snow melting in her hair and trickling down her neck.

"Just because someone has a *reason* to do something doesn't prove that they actually *did* it." Sally raised an eyebrow at Jo.

"Meaning?" Jo tried to sound casual as she reached down to yank her Wellies off. Her cheeks and ears were burning now as they warmed up.

Sally sighed and clattered on high heels back into the kitchen, opening a peeling cupboard and pulling out a tin of Ghirardelli's dark chocolate drink mix and two mugs. "*Meaning* that it's common knowledge that Marlo and Chris had an argument a few weeks back, at Gertie's." Sally rummaged around in a drawer for clean cutlery and then began spooning decadent heaps of chocolate powder into the cups.

"What about?" Jo followed her into the kitchen. She leaned on the counter.

"Dunno exactly, but I do know that Marlo had been following him. They were finished after that. Not that they were ever, you know, *together* together. At least, not in his mind, I don't think." Sally stirred both drinks energetically, then reached into another cupboard to pull out a bottle of Bailey's. She poured liberally.

"Was it about another lover?"

Sally shrugged, but her nonchalance didn't seem quite honest. "That you'll have to ask him yourself." She smiled thinly at Jo.

"What time did you leave Gertie's the night Marlo died?"

"Pardon?" Sally looked surprised, but not particularly upset by the question.

"Byrne suggested that I ask you. Why would he do that?"

Sally laughed again. "Oh, my goddess. He really did throw me under the bus, didn't he? See what I mean? Dangerous!"

"Why would he do that?"

125

Sally blew softly on the hot cocoa, the heat swirling away from her. "Because he knows that there's an exit at Gertie's via my changeroom, so I could have left at any time without anyone noticing."

"And did you?"

"No. But if I had, I certainly wouldn't tell you about it." Sally smiled and shook her head. She took a sip of the cocoa and burned her lip. "Ouch. Needs cream."

Jo watched her housemate. "Why do you keep a photo of Byrne in Ol' Bettie?"

Sally's brow lifted a little, before she snapped, "Because shiny things amuse me. I also like sparkly, pretty objects. And glitter paint." She turned away and began fishing in a drawer for something.

Jo nodded, aware of the subterfuge taking place.

"He likes you," Sally said, pulling a pair of stainless steel beaters from the drawer and popping them into a pink electric mixer on the counter.

Jo avoided Sally's eyes now. "Or he wants something."

"Isn't that the same thing?" Sally teetered over to the fridge and opened the door, leaving Jo with a view of her shiny back-side as she bent to look inside.

"Hey, I was wondering ..." Jo hoped she wasn't pushing her luck. She'd borrowed Sally's truck twice already and had eaten several of her bagels. "... if I could borrow your truck again?"

"Absolutely not." Sally emerged from the fridge with a carton of cream.

"What?"

"I've seen the way you drive in snow." Sally drained cream into a bowl.

"But ..." Jo was interrupted by the sound of cream being beaten into submission.

"Besides, I've got some time to kill." Sally raised her voice over the appliance and grinned. "I'll give you a lift." The machine made a whining noise as the whipped cream was a fait accompli.

"I don't think that's a good idea," Jo said. Sally spooned the cream on top of the Baileys and chocolate and passed the steaming drink to Jo. The cream was already melting in a swirling pattern. "Thanks," Jo said, and took a sip. A dreamy burn of alcohol and chocolate set a course for her muscles while the mug warmed her fingertips.

"Why not?"

Jo eyed Sally's pleather and stiletto outfit and tried not to laugh. "I don't think you'll want to go where I'm going. It may not be totally ... Well, above board. To be perfectly honest."

"Ooh, now I'm definitely coming," Sally said. She pulled out one of the beaters and licked off a thick dollop of cream.

<hr />

Finding Claim 53 a second time proved to be much more difficult than Jo had hoped. The Chevy's headlights strained against the primordial blackness of the bush and the blowing snow. Jo caught herself speculating whether this new storm could be the beginning of freeze-up. Was it cold enough to freeze the Yukon River? It sure felt raw. Jo wondered which roads would close, and whether she would be caught out in the middle of nowhere when it hit. If Sally had concerns, she kept them to herself, humming a little as she peered into the inky nothingness beyond the headlights.

Jo used the speedometer to gauge their progress, rolling the windows down to keep the cab of the old pickup from steaming up while Sally drove. The air was crisp with the scent of pine and snow, keeping her alert. On edge, even. The radio was off, but they were serenaded by the desolate music of wolves in the distance. Jo hoped they didn't run out of gas.

The big boulder marking Claim 53 was almost entirely buried in snow, but the size of the rock marked the entrance like a flag. The "Beware of Dog" sign was already submerged. Sally pulled over and killed the headlights.

"Thanks for the ride. I won't be long," Jo said in a low voice.

Sally was quick to reply. "Oh, no. If you're doing something you shouldn't be …"

Jo interrupted her, "You don't have to …"

"Then so am I."

Jo pointed to Sally's high-heeled boots. "You're not exactly dressed for field work."

"Nonsense. I can play soccer in these." Sally opened the door, hopped down and kicked one sky-high heel toward Jo, as if to demonstrate. Jo frowned. She objected. In the end, though, she had no choice in the matter.

⎯⎯∝⎯⎯

The shaky beam of Jo's flashlight lit the snowy path to the excavation, as Sally stumbled and slid, clutching onto Jo's arm for greater stability. Jo felt like one half of an elderly couple shuffling along, and she silently cursed Sally.

As they approached the lip of the open pit, Jo turned off the light and squatted down. Sally joined her, PVC squeaking as her knees bent. Circles of light bounced in the pit below, where a small night crew laboured near an overhang of cliff wall. Jo leaned against her companion for warmth and whispered, "Does it seem odd to you that they're drilling at this time of night?"

"Hmm," was the only insight Sally offered.

"Damn, I wish I could get inside Grikowsky's office," Jo whispered.

Sally nodded toward a stark, rectangular shape behind the excavation. "Well, I'd bet it's that trailer right there. The cabins back there will be for crew."

Jo saw what Sally meant. Behind the trailer were the dark silhouettes of dwellings, where pinpricks of light indicated signs of life. The main trailer, though, was in darkness.

Sally added, "It's not like he'll be there now ..."

"Well, aside from the fact that I've just come dangerously close to a breaking and entering conviction that would have cost me my career, there's also every likelihood that it will be locked."

Sally rolled her eyes. "This is the Yukon, hon. No one locks their door. So it's not breaking; it's just entering."

Jo hesitated just long enough to allow Sally to go in for the kill.

"Besides, I hate to be blunt, but isn't your career already ruined?"

"Thanks."

"Hey, you wanna know the truth about what's going on down there, or not?"

Sally's breath escaped in a long, broken line, like punctuation.

———∞———

Navigating their way around the pit in the darkness was painstaking work. By the time they reached the trailer, Jo's fingers had gone numb in her leather gloves, and Sally could no longer feel her toes.

"I love this weather," Sally said. "My boots are actually comfortable."

Jo clenched and unclenched her fingers and listened to the crunch of snow as they approached the main trailer: a dull, utilitarian rectangle iced in white like a boxed cake from the supermarket.

"Maybe I should go back by the pit and keep watch in case anyone comes this way? I could moose call if I see anyone," Sally said.

"Yeah, yeah. Good idea." She watched Sally's black figure recede into the night, then climbed the humble plank steps and paused at the door. Jo listened for a moment, but heard only the hollow hum of machinery in the distance and the peculiar cry of wolves and wind. She knew she was about to cross a line.

When Jo was eight, not long after her mother died of lung cancer, she began keeping a flashlight under her bed so that she could do extra homework under the covers after "lights out." Once Frank had caught her, and she was thereafter taken for regular visits with Dr. Rivera, a vivacious woman with a passion for boldly coloured skirt suits and a talent for provoking patients into an emotional response. Dr. Rivera had plagued Jo with questions about her feelings, something she was loath to talk about. Most of the time, Jo was secretly feeling like she was wasting valuable time when she could be doing something more useful. On one particular visit, Dr. Rivera informed Jo that children who lose a parent, either through death or abandonment, often become people pleasers, which can tip over into perfectionism and workaholism if left unchecked. Jo had nodded and pretended that she was listening. Dr. Rivera had reached out and touched Jo's knee softly, heavily pencilled eyes uncomfortably sympathetic. Then she told Jo that lots of famous people were overachievers with lousy personal lives.

It irked Jo now, as she stood at the threshold of Grikowsky's trailer, that Dr. Rivera may have been right about her after all. Jo might have a sharp tongue, but at the end of the day, she was still a people pleaser, not a rule breaker. She had done what the police had asked her to do by killing the Surrey Strangler story. She had also done what Frank had thought was the right thing to do, which was something she might never forgive either of them for.

She thought about Marlo's body floating in the river, hair waving like seaweed. This time, things would be different. Jo placed one gloved hand on the chilly metal handle of the trailer and squeezed tightly. It wouldn't turn.

———

"I thought you said that no one in the Yukon locks their doors," Jo said to Sally when they rejoined on the path.

"They don't," Sally said. "Unless they have something to hide."

"In that case, most of Dawson probably locks their doors. Anyway, I have to get in there."

"We could chuck a log through the window …" Sally offered.

"Too noisy."

"Then … we seduce the miners into giving us a key."

"What, you're just going to sashay down into the pit in the middle of the night? You don't think they'll find that a little suspicious?"

"Shame. I rather like Plan B."

Jo shook her head. "Have you no pride, woman?"

Sally put her shoulders back, forcing her chest into a prominent position. "Actually, I have quite a lot of it."

Jo was about to retort something cutting about the source of her pride, but at that moment they heard low voices coming along the path. They exchanged a panicked look, and Jo pulled Sally forward into a run.

A male voice called out in the darkness. "Hello?"

"Plan B! Plan B!" Sally whispered.

"No!" Jo attempted to propel Sally through the shadows at a more reasonable speed.

"Who is that?" A man's voice, full of doubt and suspicion.

Jo sprinted through the night, Sally a few paces behind now, her heart thrumming at a nightclub beat.

"Stop!" The deep voice rang out; someone was chasing them along the path.

"Faster!" Jo hissed, the thought of Sally's useless boots flashing in her mind. She pictured Sally falling … sprawling out in the snow in slow motion while their assailant closed in on them.

They plunged along the crooked path, arms pumping, the snow-shrouded trees and glassy underbrush leaning in to stop them. The man was gaining on them. Sally, though surprisingly agile given the height of her heels, was falling behind. Jo reached for her companion's hand and dragged her forward again, with a hot rush of adrenaline. Then, Sally stumbled. The moment hung there, frozen in time, like a thrilling circus act that you know will, eventually, succumb to gravity. A delicate china teacup, spinning on top of a white porcelain plate, on top of a long pole. Perfection, however temporary—like Sally's black, PVC-clad curves glinting in the moonlight.

Then they fell. Sally pulled them both down, into the snow and ice. A gunshot split the icy night and reverberated in the darkness. Sally was first back on her feet, tugging on Jo's arm and urging her forward. "Not a good time to take a nap, sister!"

"Me?" Jo stumbled to her feet, staggering loosely forward.

They heard footsteps in the snow behind them, and more voices calling out. "Dave! We've got uninvited guests!"

Jo didn't think things could get much worse, but she was wrong. The excited cry of dogs echoed across the shadowy landscape.

"We've got to split up!"

"Meet you at the truck!" Sally said, and then she was gone, a shapely silhouette in the night, slipping into the undergrowth alongside the path to the right.

Jo veered to the left and crashed into the forest, tree boughs swiping at her like maces as she darted relentlessly deeper into the snowy underworld. The dogs sounded louder now, their clamour more insistent. Jo felt the white heat of alarm spreading through her body, eclipsing all other sensation. She couldn't feel the cold anymore—or the porcupine bristles of frozen pine. Only the sense of panic and the baying of dogs filled her mind.

Jo slipped. Her foot hit a patch of ice and she went down hard on her tailbone. Flakes of snow worried at her as she got clumsily to her feet. Jo was on water. About to pitch through the black skin of ice. There was a loud crack—a rifle firing or ice breaking. Jo didn't know which. She was disoriented. She thought of Johnny Cariboo's father for a fleeting moment, about the way he had died, lost in a storm.

Her mind was beginning to snow in with terror. Jo spun in a circle, looking for the way back to the road. She couldn't find it. Jo had always had a terrible sense of direction. The ice creaked ominously as she moved to what looked like the nearest bank.

Jo couldn't be sure, but this didn't look like one of the big rivers. Not the Yukon or Klondike. It might have been a smaller river, or a very wide stream. Her breath came in clouds that caught wetly in her eyelashes and made her blink as they froze. Jo wondered how long before frostbite would set in, and what it would feel like. Somewhere in the distance a dog howled, and now she considered whether she should run toward the sound and surrender. She might have a better chance of surviving the people than the weather. They might take her inside to question her. *Inside.*

Jo clambered over the bank, back onto solid ground. She moved toward the receding sound of the dogs, now, lurching forward through her own breath like a steam train. A thin sheet of ice had formed across the top of her raw cheeks.

A quick, will-of-the-wisp light flashed in the distance. A flashlight? Car headlights? Jo stumbled through the trees toward the light, but there was nothing further. She floundered in the dark trying to retrace her steps. Trees. Snow. Trees. Snow. Nothing. Then, a clearing.

Jo emerged where she thought the truck should be. She could barely make out the Dempster Highway under the drifting snow, but one thing was clear: there was no vehicle anywhere in sight. Jo beamed her flashlight up and down the highway, the spiralling snow catching in the light. Had she come out at the wrong spot on the road, or had Sally taken the Chevy and left? There was little for it but to pick a direction, start walking, and hope for a ride—an unlikely prospect.

Jo pulled back her hood for a moment to hear better. The lilting cadence of the wind obscured all else. She zipped up the hood tightly under her chin, turned to her left, and began walking into the sting of the wind. She tried not to think about the emptiness of the road. The cold gnawed at her face and fingers. She was just giving over to panic when she saw the bright spray of headlights.

Jo peered into the night. Was it the men from the mine? Was it Marlo's killer? She glanced around for the closest cover, torn between flagging the driver for help or dashing for the treeline. She held up a hand to shield her eyes.

"I said meet me at the truck! This is not at the truck." The window of the old Chevy was rolled down and Sally was leaning out the driver's window.

"You moved!" Jo shouted, but she felt dizzy with relief.

"Only after you didn't show! I've been driving up and down the Dempster looking for you!"

"They fired at us! We've gotta get Cariboo."

"Get in," Sally said.

16

"They let us go," Jo said. In the half-light somewhere between dusk and dawn on a Wednesday morning, she clenched a thermos with gloved hands and breathed deeply, the buoyant scent of coffee driving away persistent swells of anxiety. She and Sally were huddled together on a turquoise bench overlooking the Yukon River, listening to the thunder of the current rushing enormous chunks of ice to nowhere.

"Nonsense. We outran them."

Jo shot a look at Sally's heels, but said nothing.

Sally, noting the silent skepticism, added, "I could play ..."

"... soccer in these boots," Jo finished for her.

Sally straightened on the bench. "Well, I could."

"They shot at us, but missed. They called the dogs off."

"But why would they do that?" The heat from Sally's flask billowed around her as she took a sip.

"Exactly. And why not report trespassers to Sergeant Cariboo?"

"Hmm," said Sally. "How do you know they haven't?"

"Don't you think he would have come calling? Believe me, I've been up half the night waiting."

"Hoping?" Sally's green eyes twinkled dangerously.

"Don't be ridiculous." Jo looked away and took a swill from the container. The coffee had a freshly brewed, hazelnut flavour, with warm, welcome undertones of whisky. Sally hadn't mentioned that the coffee was spiked, or asked permission to spike it. She'd just made the assumption. Jo frowned into the thermos, but refrained from asking why.

When they'd returned home in the middle of the night, they'd convinced one another not to go to Cariboo, fearing prosecution. They'd agreed to sleep on it. Jo found herself questioning whether they'd made the right decision. She'd only had a couple of hours sleep before her alarm had sounded. She'd woken Sally up, clattering amidst the debris in the kitchen, looking for a clean coffee cup. This time, instead of arguing about who was responsible for the disaster in that room, they'd agreed to go out for coffee.

"It's not too late to tell Cariboo," Jo said.

Sally swallowed hard, as though choking on her coffee. "Are you quite mad? You want to give Cariboo a reason to arrest us? You want Grikowsky to know that it was us? I mean, he might not know who it was."

"You have a point."

"Right on the top of my head. Helps keep my hat in place." Sally tapped her Cossack-style headwear. The combination of the sleek fur hat and coat gave Sally the appearance of a Soviet spy, making Jo feel uneasy. *Trust issues*, Jo reminded herself. Sally was probably fine.

Besides, Jo wasn't about to push her luck. They'd been lucky that Grikowsky had let them go: a telling fact that Jo turned over in her mind again and again, polishing it like a stone until it shone brightly. She could not put it down. "What do you think they were doing out there, though?"

Sally considered for a moment. Somewhere a raven chortled over the roar of the river. The sound was throaty and guttural, like a bargoyle after last call. "Trying to sluice up before freeze-up?"

"Sluice up?"

"It's a kind of dredging."

"Oh."

Jo looked toward the water, where jagged shards of ice rushed ceaselessly forward, but her gaze was unfocused. The air was bracing and carried with it the scent of pine. She jiggled both legs to keep the blood flowing.

Sally nodded toward the river. "That's it, then," she said. "You can forget about canoeing out. It'll be frozen solid in a day or two." Sally sounded slightly amused by her own demise.

"Well. There goes *my* escape plan," Jo said. "Good thing there's still an ice pick under your bar." A smile flickered briefly on Sally's face, like fluorescent lights before they dim.

The spreading slabs of ice filled Jo with dread. It was actually happening now. The tourists had fled. The river was freezing solid. The roads were snowing in. Soon the airport would close too, if it hadn't closed already. Jo was either about to miss her last opportunity until spring to escape, or she'd missed it already. Dawson would be cut off from the rest of the world. Jo thought about the shots ringing out in the darkness, and wondered who would be shut in with her.

The ice swirled and eddied in the river: a great, seething cauldron of fate. Jo felt like a passenger on the *Titanic*: as though she were sitting back, putting her feet up and listening to the violins play as the ship sank. She quickly recapped her expenses in the last month, and calculated—again—how much room might be left on her credit card. Could she leave once the story was published on Friday, and Dawson had been warned? If she could scrape together enough credit for a plane ticket out … if the airport hadn't already closed … but what then? How would she earn a living in the South? It was a moot point.

Then there was the issue of what to do about the *Dawson Daily*. The *Daily* couldn't—or wouldn't—go to print until Friday. Two days. Jo had to find a way to warn the town that the RCMP were now investigating Marlo's death as a possible murder.

Jo considered leaking the story to Kevin Kessler, but Dawson-ites didn't read the *Vancouver Sun*. She had to be certain that her voice was heard where it mattered the most. And she had to be absolutely sure that she was right. But at this point, what did she really know?

Jo glanced at Sally and cleared her throat. "The morning after Marlo died … "

Sally turned her cat-like eyes on Jo. Her expression seemed interested. Not wary. "Yesss?"

"Why did you call Byrne?"

"Oh that." Sally's tone was nonchalant.

"Yes. That."

"Because he asked me to." Her expression, too, was unapologetic.

"When?"

"The next day. He called from the pub and said that you'd had too much to drink the night before, and he was worried that you might get the wrong idea. That he'd taken advantage." Some emotion tugged at a corner of Sally's mouth, but she drowned it with coffee and whisky.

"Do you think he would? Take advantage, I mean?"

"I have no idea. I only know that I saw you get into his pickup outside Gertie's, and later his truck was parked out front of my house. And the next day, he was concerned that you know that he hadn't done anything … ungentlemanly." She smiled a strange smile.

"Did he mention that we were up on the Bluffs the night Marlo died?"

"*Were* you?" Sally appeared to be more intrigued than horrified.

Jo nodded. "According to Cariboo."

"The plot thickens."

"Why didn't you tell me that Christopher Byrne had called you and asked about me?"

"Because at the time, I didn't think it was all that important."

Jo placed her numb hands under her arms. "Do you think he did it? Could he have done it?"

Sally considered for a long moment. "I wouldn't have pegged Byrnie as the type, no. But you never know what someone might do when they're really pushed. God help anyone who pushes me hard enough." Sally bounced both knees and leaned forward over her open canteen. A veil of steam screened her face.

The dull rumble of water and ice was ubiquitous, permeating the landscape. Jo watched a lone snowflake land on her glove and cling there for a moment, unique and perfect. Sally's answer had seemed honest enough.

"We need to go back to the mine," Jo said. "Find out what they're mining for at night. Have another look for May."

Sally shook her head and took a slug of her Irish coffee. "If we're caught at the mine again, Grikowsky will prosecute us for trespassing."

"Claim 53 is a gold mine, right?" Jo said.

"Yup."

Jo hesitated only for a second. She had to trust someone in Dawson. "So why would they be looking for uranium in a gold mine?" Jo asked.

"Pardon?" Sally raised her artfully crafted eyebrows. This might have been the first time Jo had caught her off guard, and she could tell that Sally didn't like losing the upper hand in a conversation. Or losing at anything, for that matter. Doubtless it was a rare occurrence.

"I need to get back to the mine, into that trailer ..."

"Shhhh!" Sally grabbed Jo's arm, startling her.

Jo was positive that something terrible was about to happen. "What?" she gasped.

"It's showtime." Sally nodded to the horizon, where a petulant sun had begun a spectacular display. Jo watched, transfixed by the fiery burst of colour that created at least the illusion of heat.

It occurred to Jo later, as she listened to the steady drip of the *Daily's* coffee machine and the dry hum of the heaters, that Sally hadn't asked for an explanation about Jo's uranium theory because she couldn't stand to have to ask. By contrast, Jo couldn't stand not to question. She was only fascinated by what she couldn't understand. She had to know. Then, once she'd figured it out, she lost interest. Probably one of the reasons her boyfriends never lasted. Maybe that was part of the appeal of Christopher Byrne. There was something ineffable, some kind of mutual understanding between them, that prevented Jo from thinking that he had anything to do with what had happened to Marlo. But she had to know for certain. In the back of Jo's mind, she had to consider the possibility that Byrne was using her.

Jo dialled the number May had left her again, thoughtful as she listened to the empty ring tone that she now knew was the phone in May's kitchen.

She glanced at her watch. May had been missing for almost twenty-four hours. Her boutique, The Gold Digger, was supposed to open at eleven. Winter hours. Would Dawsonites believe that

May was missing when she didn't turn up for work again? Jo might have to confess to Cariboo that May had asked to meet her at The Gold Digger and not shown up. It was the only way to show intent. Jo would also have to admit to Cariboo that she had withheld information in her last interview. Not a pleasant scenario, especially since May had asked her not to tell anyone about the phone call. There was something else Jo couldn't help thinking about. *Alice Wolfe.* Johnny Cariboo's fiancé had disappeared. That made made Marlo the second woman, not the first, to come to a tragic end in Dawson City. And Johnny Cariboo had a connection to the first.

Jo chewed on the end of a pen. The cold plastic made her teeth ache. She pulled out a pad of paper and slapped it down on the desk. She wrote the name Marlo, and drew a circle around it. Then, like planets rotating around the sun, she wrote down the names of others in town, forming a circle around Marlo's name. Christopher Byrne. Sally LeBlanc. Sergeant Cariboo. Caveman Cal Sanders. May Wong. Jack Grikowsky. The Mine. Doug Browning. Then she wrote down her own name, in the middle of a circle that overlapped with Christopher Byrne. Next she made lines to connect the circles to one another and to Marlo. What Jo came away with was that one circle in particular had the most connections to Marlo and May Wong: the mine. Marlo had fought against the mine. Grikowsky managed the mine. May owned the mine. Cariboo's family had worked in the mine. Doug seemed to be protecting the mine.

Byrne's offhand remark about workers at the mine had lodged in her brain; he had said that many of the miners became ill. If they were surreptitiously mining for uranium, surely that would have a detrimental impact on the water in the surrounding areas. If she could find any evidence that something illicit was going on at the mine, and might have been factor in Marlo's death or May's disappearance, Jo had until tomorrow evening to support her theory. The *Daily* was printed Thursday nights and distributed on Friday mornings. Jo had to warn the town before someone in Dawson killed again.

If her theory about the mine were correct, Jo knew the story could gain national coverage—and she might find some redemption in the public eye. Perhaps she could even leave Dawson and find work elsewhere. More importantly, if she got it right this time, the nightmares might end. But first, she'd have to find a way to see it printed, despite opposition from those who wanted to keep it quiet: Doug, Grikowsky, and the RCMP.

She rubbed her dry eyes as the *Daily*'s dusty baseboard heaters clicked and whirred. What would happen if she couldn't find enough support for her story to convince Doug to publish it? She could wait until after Doug's retirement party when, presumably, she could publish anything she wanted. *No.* She couldn't sit on a story like this again. She'd have to find a way to warn Dawson's citizens that Marlo's death was not an accident—and that May Wong was missing—even if it put her already lacklustre career on the line. Even if the story was based on unsubstantiated allegations.

Impatiently, Jo pushed around copy for the retrospective on Marlo's life. She'd do the story the way Doug wanted it. But she'd also find a way to expose the truth. She'd start by looking into what kind of public health records Dawson maintained.

⎯⎯ ⠙ ⎯⎯

The morning was bitterly fresh. Sunlight reflected off turbulent water, where great shards of ice still rushed ceaselessly northward, making the riverside walk along Front Street even more breathtaking. Jo glanced at her watch: city hall would open at ten.

She stopped cold just before Queen Street. A new art installation had been erected. Two larger-than-life lovers, clothed only in snow, were engaged in a heated kiss. The male was taller and wore some kind of bird mask possibly a raven. Huge wings were attached at his back, Icarus-style. He had one oversized hand on the woman's cheek, while the other hand gripped the small of her back, just below where her own wings unfurled. The woman also wore a beak and feather mask. Something about the art moved Jo; the scene looked strangely familiar. She brushed the snow away from the gold plaque at the bottom of the statue, which read:

Northern Lights
Gifted to Dawson City by
artist Christopher Byrne, 2004.

Jo stepped closer and lightly brushed the snow from the male's chest and shoulders. The figure was a mahogany colour, showing the polished grain of wood. A long vertical scratch in the wood ran down the man's chest, like a wound. She exhaled slowly, her breath a long, white thread.

As she neared Duke Street, Jo squinted to make out a figure there, just in front of the fire-station-cum-town-hall. Jo heard the man before she saw him.

"Hear ye, hear ye! A gentle reminder that citizens of Dawson are invited to attend a public meeting today! You've got fifteen to get your civic butts to city hall. Special thanks to Mabel for providing refreshments." The town crier fell silent as Jo approached.

"Morning," Jo said, in what she hoped was a neutral tone. More observation than greeting.

"Morning." That was all. No questions about Christopher Byrne this time. The white plumage on the crier's hat swayed in the cool breeze. This paired with a hawkish nose, hunched shoulders, and long, spindly legs brought to mind some kind of birdlike creature, suspicious and wary, that might peck or take flight with any sudden movement.

Jo held herself very still. "You out here every day?"

"Nah," he said. "Just for the odd meeting. The town pays me to publicize 'em." He made a face. "A pittance. I shore it up in tourist season with poetry readings."

"Why not advertise public meetings in the *Daily*?" Jo said.

"Because it isn't daily, eh?" He gave her a look that wasn't difficult to interpret. "They usually forget by the time the meeting rolls around. If it didn't go straight into the wood stove in the first place."

"Oh," Jo said, ignoring the insult. She was already wondering whether he might serve another purpose later. "What's the going rate?" she asked.

The crier looked surprised, but he smiled just the same.

———⚬∞⚬———

Jo climbed the creaking, salt-stained, and snow-puddled stairs of Dawson's town hall. On the second floor landing, a large bulletin board was covered in "end of season" notices for various businesses. The flyers were hand drawn and brightly coloured, lending a festive air to the messaging that did nothing to lift Jo's spirits. She would not be leaving.

At the service counter, an argument had broken out. A belligerent old hunter cursed loudly as he reviewed some kind of application.

"Goddammit, every year there's more goddamned paper-work! Kill a million trees to save one goddamned moose ..."

The long-faced woman behind the desk searched Jo's expression for any outward signs of hostility. Finding none, she rushed to Jo's assistance; a welcome relief from the quarrelsome local she was already assisting.

"Can I help you?" Her eyes had the begging quality of a Basset hound.

"Yeah, I wonder if you could tell me where I might find the city's public records? I'm looking for local health records," Jo said.

The woman looked pleased to have a practical, bureaucratic request. "What kind of health records?"

"Well, statistics I guess. Incidents of different cases of illness, cancer rates, and that sort of thing."

"Oh, that's easy. There aren't any." The woman guffawed.

"Seriously?" Jo had never heard of a city not keeping public health records. But then, Dawson wasn't truly a city, and it wasn't like any other town she knew either.

"Well, not specific to Dawson, anyway," the woman said.

"But ... how do you ensure that something in the environment isn't making people sick?"

"Hmm. That's a good question." She looked thoughtful. "But I can't answer it. Peter might know."

"The mayor?" Jo said. "Where would I find him? Do I need an appointment?"

"Oh, no." The woman looked amused. "Most people just buy him a beer at Gertie's, although he does have an office here. Down the hall. Just follow the signs. But you won't have long. He's got a budget meeting in fifteen."

It was probably time Jo talked to Peter Wright anyway. In a town this size, the mayor would know everyone pretty well. Jo hoped he might know something she didn't. And Sally said he'd left Gertie's early Sunday night.

"Is there anything else I can do for you?"

"Actually, there is one more thing ... I'm looking for any government files on a Dawson mine. I wonder if there might be any information that's available to the public?"

"For which mine?"

"Claim 53."

The woman's face darkened. "You want permitting information? From the EAO?"

"What's the EAO?" Jo sensed that the woman had shifted gears somehow, and wondered why.

"Environmental Assessment Office. That's the agency that reviews proposed projects."

"Yes. That would be a good start. Then which agency monitors the claim once it's been permitted?"

"Probably the DFO. That's Department of Fisheries and Oceans. They send out inspectors who check on the mine."

"Yes. Any DFO reports on 53 too." The woman was still standing still, looking at her with obvious suspicion, so Jo said, "Please." Perhaps a little curtly.

"It just seems a little odd," said the woman, who stood her ground behind the counter, her expression now defiant.

"What does?"

"That's just what Marlo McAdam asked for before she died."

17

The waiting area outside Mayor Wright's office was covered in framed articles and photographs, mostly documenting the town hall's original function as the fire hall. A black-and-white archival print circa 1911 showed three horse-drawn carriages bursting out of the station, answering a fire call. Jo stood for a better look. The figures looked ghostly, blurred by the motion of the carriages.

It seemed Dawson had a long history of tragedy involving fires, documented in great detail on the old station's walls. The original town, dubbed "Boomtown in a Bog," was built with wood and canvas in a time when people depended on fairly primitive wood stoves, candles, and coal oil lamps to procure any heat in the arctic temperatures. It was easy to imagine the problems this caused once weary gold miners and boozy dance-hall girls were added to the mix. Jo's favourite story had to do with Dawson's earliest fires. The first fire, on Thanksgiving Day in 1897, during not-so-toasty temperatures of fifty-eight degrees below zero (*fifty-eight below zero!*) occurred when tempers flared at the M&N Saloon. A fiery dancer threw a blazing oil lamp at another gal and *wooosh!* The whole saloon went up in flame, along with the saloon next to it and the Opera House. A year later, the very same hotheaded young lady left a candle burning on a block of wood. Twenty-six buildings burned to the ground. Jo imagined the dancer wouldn't have been very popular after that.

Along with the archival shots and stories, there were also a few recent photos taken by Doug for the *Daily*. Images of Peter Wright smiling, shaking hands and wielding a broad shovel as he approved new snow removal bylaws. Then there was a photo of a woman who had just been elected MLA North for the Liberal Party. Marlo McAdam. The accompanying article in the *Daily* posited that McAdam promised to push for greater ecological protection, despite fears by some about what that might mean for Dawson's mine-based economy.

Chairs scraped somewhere behind the closed door. Jo hoped that the mayor was wrapping up his last meeting; they had only a few moments before the town's budget review. Restless, she wandered down the hall, where there were more photographs. She stopped at another door with a plaque that read, "Marlo McAdam." A notice had been pinned there, informing the public of a wake for Marlo at Diamond Tooth Gertie's. Jo tried the handle, but it was locked.

Just then the mayor emerged from his office, followed by Sergeant Cariboo, still in mid conversation. "… asking a lot of questions about the pathology report." Cariboo had his back to Jo and was pulling on his blue cap.

"What sort of questions?" the mayor asked.

"The level of diatoms in her lungs indicated that she was alive when she hit the water."

"I see." Peter looked pale. "But that doesn't eliminate suicide."

"True, but she had some bruising around the throat that the pathologist did not think was consistent with a fall. Now, it's important that we keep everyone calm …"

Something inside Jo felt as though it were sliding. She made a mental note to get a copy of the pathology report.

"And May?"

Cariboo was about to answer when he turned and noticed Jo. Both men swung around to look at her, assessing how much she had overheard. Cariboo's eyes locked on hers.

"Mayor Wright!" Jo called out, but it was too late. She was intercepted by a pair of giant, walking salmon with placards that read, "Run for Salmon" and "Long Live the King (Salmon)." Cariboo looked as though he were going to say something, then turned on his heel and strode off toward the meeting room.

Further along the hall, the receptionist was vying for the mayor's attention. "It's time, Peter! But you'll want to speak with this lady later." Peter glanced back at Jo, before the woman leaned in and whispered something in his ear. Jo was pretty sure she heard the name "Marlo."

———⚬⚬⚬———

Homemade cookies on a Victorian-style, three-tiered china plate disappeared rapidly, marking the time as Jo tried to pin the mayor down for a conversation after the town budget was passed. Once the meeting had adjourned, the mayor had been swarmed by townspeople hoping for an audience with him. Many had questions about Marlo McAdam or May Wong. Dark whispers about May's absence had begun to circulate.

At last, Jo caught a glimpse of the mayor alone in a corner, pondering a lumpy chocolate biscuit.

"Mayor Wright, I wonder if I could ask you a couple of questions."

He grinned, his greying beard full of crumbs. "Only if you agree to try one of Mabel's macaroons. I shouldn't eat these. I'm watching my girlish figure." He winked and patted his expansive waistline.

Jo accepted a cookie and chewed politely while she decided how best to question him. She wished she had the province's file on Claim 53 already, but the receptionist had delayed in handing it over, saying that she'd have to retrieve it from Marlo's office, and would require police permission to do so.

"Mmm, not bad," Jo said. An understatement. The warm blend of tropical coconut and creamy chocolate seemed to dissolve Jo's sense of urgency as it melted on her tongue. Heaven. This Mabel would put the pastry chefs of Vancouver's largest coffee chains to shame, given half a chance. Jo had always wondered how coffee bars in the city could get away with selling stale pastry at such an outrageous price. They must make a killing.

The mayor beamed. "I told you. They're to die for. So, what's on your mind?"

"Well, Marlo McAdam and May Wong, to be frank."

"Ah," he said. "Yes," and bowed his head a little.

"Any news on May Wong?" Jo didn't mention that she'd overheard his conversation with Cariboo about the pathology report on Marlo.

"Sadly, no."

"But the RCMP are looking for her?"

Peter nodded. "They think she may have gone hunting. If only they could find her."

Jo wasn't sure what to make of his insincere tone.

"You were at Gertie's the night Marlo died, weren't you?"

"You bet." He added, "So was most of the town." His eyes crinkled good-naturedly as he blew softly on a steaming cup, fanning the spicy scent of bergamot orange.

"Right. I noticed you were at the roulette wheel."

The mayor chuckled. "Yeah, I was down on my luck a little, if I recall."

"You know everyone in this town," Jo said. "Did you notice anything unusual that night? Anyone acting strangely?"

Peter frowned and shook his head. "Not that I remember, no. Well, there was a bit of a kerfuffle at the bar ..."

"Really?" Jo wished she'd spoken to the mayor sooner. "About what?"

"I'm not sure. Something between Rusty—that's Gertie's barkeep, she's a good gal—and one of the miners. I heard her say something about water ... that it wasn't clean."

"Did anyone else see the argument?"

"Oh, I expect so. You'd have to ask Rusty."

"I'll do that, thanks. Did you happen to notice anyone leaving early?"

"I must admit I was having too much fun to notice," he said.

"How late did you stay that night?"

The mayor laughed. "Unfortunately for my pocketbook, I stayed until closing."

Jo smiled. Peter Wright was an easy person to like. He was down to earth and made a person feel comfortable. But he was a liar. Sally had already told her that he'd been seen leaving before closing. "There's one more thing I wanted to talk to you about."

"Oh?" Peter lowered the cookie he had been about to polish off. Jo caught a flicker of something in his eyes.

"It concerns public accountability in Dawson. I understand Marlo McAdam had been asking questions before her death."

The smile faded from Peter's wide face, but before he could respond, they were interrupted by the belligerent hunter Jo had seen at reception earlier. The old man's whiskery chin was thrust forward in challenge as he addressed the mayor in a voice like an unoiled hinge. "Peter, I need to know where you stand on these new goddamned hunting regulations. And by the way, what's this I hear about May Wong and a hunting trip? If I catch her poaching on my land again ..."

Peter looked at Jo and rolled his eyes. "Sorry—it's moose and caribou season ..." He threw up his hands as if to say, *what can I do?* But he looked relieved by the distraction. "Look, why don't you book some of my time with my secretary when I'm back in town."

"You're leaving?" Jo asked. She had the sudden suspicion that he might not be back.

"Business in Whitehorse tomorrow. Just for the day, but I've gotta squeeze in one more meeting before the airport closes. I'm catching a flight right after we finish up here so I'll have to dash."

"Oh," Jo said, wondering what she could do to stop him.

"Have Judith—uh, that's my assistant—have her pencil you in when I'm back. I'd be happy to help you in any way I can." The wide smile was back.

Jo looked up to see Sergeant Cariboo heading through the crowd, in her direction, his dark eyes fixed on hers. He was using his hands to clear a path, shovelling bodies to one side with gentle pressure to the small of a back here or a shoulder there. Jo nodded her head to the mayor as he left, but her attention was on Cariboo now. The sergeant's path was blocked abruptly by the two bearded men in salmon costumes, who had become embroiled in a heated discussion with a very large, red-faced miner and were waving their placards about in a threatening manner. She thought Cariboo would stop, but the altercation barely slowed him down.

"Ms. Silver," he said when he reached her. His face looked a little flushed. "Could I have a word?"

"Yes," she said, more like a question than an answer.

There was usually more of a quietness about Cariboo. This was the first time she'd seen him flustered. "Well, it's about what you may have overheard today." She waited. He had a habit of taking a long time to speak, weighing his words carefully before he laid them down. "About the pathology report."

"Okay," she said, noncommittal. She liked his stillness, she realized. Something about him made her feel calm. But at this moment, she was reluctant to hear what he was going to say.

"That information was not for public sharing."

Jo had a quick little flashback to a Vancouver restaurant on Main, and the police officer who told her she couldn't write the story. "Was she murdered?"

"Inconclusive."

"There was bruising around the throat?" Jo felt her face growing warmer.

"Yes."

"I have a duty to warn the public if there has been a murder."

"But not if there has been a suicide or an accident. We don't know for certain."

"And May Wong?"

"No sign of her. We just don't know."

"Funny time to disappear."

"Yes," Cariboo said, holding her look. Jo had the uncomfortable feeling that he knew that she knew something about May Wong.

"About that … I didn't tell you everything about the day I went to visit May Wong." Johnny Cariboo didn't say anything, but to his credit, he didn't look surprised either. "May left a voicemail for me at the *Daily* the night before …"

"Monday night?"

"Yes. She asked me to meet her at The Gold Digger at 11 a.m. on Tuesday."

"Let me guess," he said. "She didn't turn up."

Jo nodded. "I'm sorry. I should have told you sooner."

"Why didn't you? Don't you trust me?" He had a strange expression on his face.

"I don't trust anyone," Jo said. "So you shouldn't take it personally. And in the message, May made it clear that I shouldn't tell anyone about the call. I took her meaning literally."

"Then why tell me now?" He looked curious.

"Because I think she's dead, so it doesn't matter if I keep her confidence."

"I see." Cariboo looked away. "And yet you trust Byrne." He glanced back at Jo to see her reaction. "Don't you?"

"I haven't decided yet," Jo answered truthfully. "Maybe."

"Well, you'll have to come downtown with me to amend your statement," Cariboo said, already zipping up his parka. Jo nodded. "By the way," he added. "I saw the new art installation."

"Oh," Jo said, feeling foolish.

"At least he doesn't kiss and tell." Cariboo turned on his heel and Jo had no choice but to follow.

18

In his cage at the *Daily*, Marshall-the-guinea-pig nibbled thoughtfully on another headline ("Price of Gold Soars!") while Jo chewed on the end of her pen, her takeaway sandwich from the gas station sitting largely untouched on her desk. She was running out of time to present the story of Marlo McAdam to the public, and she was still unsure how best to set it up. She had the information that Caveman had given her, that someone had driven Marlo to Crocus Bluffs and had not come forward. The only people known to be in the vicinity at the time were herself and Byrne, but Jo knew that they hadn't given Marlo a lift. And it followed that if someone else had driven Marlo to the Bluffs and not come forward, that person was either the killer or knew something about who was.

Jo thought about Sally and the disdain she seemed to have for Marlo. Sally had been watching Byrne and Jo in the parking lot that night. She could have seen Marlo and gone out via the exit in her changing room. Or what about the mayor? He had lied to Jo about the time he'd left Gertie's. He had an office across the hall from Marlo and they were both politicians, but Marlo was opposed to the mine. Was Peter? Now there was the pathology report, which said that Marlo was alive when she hit the water and had bruising at the throat that was inconsistent with a fall.

Everything seemed to connect to the mine at Sourdough Creek. Marlo had been asking questions about Claim 53 before her death. The owner of the mine had contacted Jo and then gone missing, and her home had been broken into. Someone had been testing for radiation out at Sourdough Creek. Grikowsky, the manager, was operating the mine in the middle of the night. Jo couldn't, however, prove that these events were related, or even that May had been a victim of foul play.

Jo had to go to print the next day. If both women had been attacked, then she had to warn Dawsonites before the roads closed, before the killer struck again. But how could she definitively tie either Marlo's death or May's disappearance to the mine? She couldn't. Everything she had was speculative. She withdrew the Geiger counter from her desk drawer and waved it in the air. It made a single, sullen *click*. She placed it on her desk, next to a smudged glass of water, and lifted the glass.

Water. The mayor had said that there'd been an argument between the bartender and a miner the night of Marlo's death, and that the conflict had somehow related to unclean water. *Who else had overheard?* Marlo McAdam, prominent politician? May Wong, the mine's owner?

Cariboo's cousin, Mike, had told Byrne that those who worked in the mine became ill. If the manager of the mine were surreptitiously mining for uranium, surely the water surrounding the mine at Sourdough Creek would be polluted. Jo needed to see the bartender at Gertie's about the dispute. She returned the Geiger counter to a desk drawer and grabbed her parka.

The urgent ring of the *Daily's* landline startled Jo as she was leaving. She cleared her throat, then changed her mind and let it go to voicemail.

"Jo?" Doug's voice, whispery and anxious. "I'll need to see the article on Marlo before we print it tomorrow. But since I'll be at the school then, it would be good to get it tonight. I usually print everything after school on Thursday, you see. I hope you understand. It's my last week at the helm and I'm responsible for anything that appears in the *Daily*."

Jo bit her lip, attached a file in an email, and hit "send." She had no intention of printing this story. Or at least, not this story alone. But there was no point in worrying Doug until she had to. She didn't have time for an argument if she wanted to find out what had happened to Marlo McAdam and May Wong before freeze-up.

Diamond Tooth Gertie's was an entirely different place without its patrons. Jo's footsteps echoed on the sticky, hardwood floors that smelled of stale beer. Without the boisterous clientele, she could imagine the quiet rustle of long skirts: the ghost of Gertie Lovejoy, an enterprising cancan dancer who mined the deep pockets of prospectors.

"We're not open yet," the bartender said.

"Yeah, I know. I'm sorry to disturb you," Jo said. "I'm Jo Silver with the *Daily*." She offered her hand to the bartender, who eyed her warily before shaking it.

"I know who you are. You can call me Rusty," the woman said, folding her arms across her chest. The name suited the timbre of her voice, which sounded like the long, low scrape of a barstool on wooden floorboards. Jo made herself comfortable at the bar, wanted or not.

"I just have a couple of quick questions for you. About the night Marlo McAdam died."

"I don't know what I can tell you that I haven't already told the police, but fire away. Hope you don't mind if I work while we talk, though, 'cause I've gotta get the bar stocked before opening."

"Sure. No problem," Jo said. "What did the police ask you?"

"Oh, you know. Whether I saw anything suspicious. Whether I saw anyone leave early." Her laugh was a low growl.

"And did you?"

"I'll tell ya the same thing I told them. I'm a bartender, not a babysitter. I'm much too busy slinging Gold to keep tabs on who's coming and going." As if to demonstrate, she bent over a case of Yukon Gold and hoisted it onto the counter. Jo hesitated, wondering how best to phrase the most important question.

"I heard you had a bit of a disagreement with a miner that night."

Rusty looked at her sharply. She straightened up. "Did you now." It wasn't phrased as a question.

Jo didn't answer. She had created a tension between them, and she knew she had to be careful not to accuse. Rusty picked up a dirty bar rag and began polishing glasses.

"What was all that about?" Jo said.

"What's your stake in it?" Rusty glanced at her and looked away, her mouth tight. "Is it for the newspaper?"

"For Marlo McAdam. I'd just like to … put things right."

Rusty put the glass down and sighed. All the energy seemed to have gone out of her body. "Bit late for that, isn't it?"

"Maybe," said Jo. Both were silent for a moment. Outside, the dull roar of a snowplough could be heard as it trudged wearily along Queen Street, in an ongoing battle to carve out civilized paths amidst the wilderness defined as Dawson.

"Jack Grikowsky," Rusty said simply, without looking up. "He ordered a whisky. Got quite upset when I served it. At first I thought he'd caught me giving 'im a blend, but it wasn't about that. I'd made a mistake and served it with water." She shrugged. "He didn't even notice that it wasn't single malt."

"Does Sergeant Cariboo know about the argument?" Jo asked.

Rusty scoffed. "Hardly."

"What did he say when you served it?"

"He said, 'Didn't order a goddamned water.' Had his knickers in a right twist, that one. Took this *tone*, so I thought he deserved a bit of winding up."

"So you said?"

Rusty shrugged. "Just took a bit of a cheap shot. I said, 'What's the matter, Jack? 'Fraid it's not clean?' The water, I meant. Because everyone knows that placer mining is a dirty business."

"Do they?"

Rusty nodded. "Oh yeah. That's why they're not allowed to do it in certain areas, because of the wildlife. They can't do it in rivers or streams with certain types of fish. A lot of people here hate placer mining." She turned away and began fumbling through an old shoebox full of audio CD cases.

"What about Marlo McAdam? Did she hate placer mining?"

Rusty paused for a moment and gave Jo a strange look. "With a passion." She selected a CD and hit an eject key on a monstrous black piece of technology mounted over the bar. The metal disc player swung open like robotic jaws. "Marlo supported a strike a couple of years back that caused a *huge* ruckus in town. 'Black Friday.' Half the people picketed, and the other half—the miners and their families—were ... well. There were more than a few fisticuffs in the bar, I can tell you. Then people started putting up the stickers you see in the windows around town, the ones that say, 'We Support Placer Mining.' " Rusty fed the CD into the drawer and nudged it closed. It made an angry grinding sound.

Jo thought for a moment. "What happened to establishments that didn't put the stickers in their windows?"

"Well …" Rusty said, "let's just say they weren't too popular, eh? Some didn't last the winter."

"I see," said Jo, though in fact, the more questions she asked about Dawson, the less she felt that she truly did *see*. It was like diving down into a cold, muddy river to see beneath the surface, and finding that all visibility was obscured by silt and debris. Then the currents took you in directions that you did not intend to go. "Did you happen to notice whether Mr. Grikowsky left early that night?"

"I just know he left the bar area after our … tête-à-tête." Rusty chuckled, and the sound turned into a rolling, hacking cough. She paused to pull out a cigarette and light it. "I couldn't tell you where he went, or whether he left the building," she said as she exhaled. "I can only tell you that I was glad to see the backside of him."

Jo stood and made to leave, saying, "Thanks." Then added, "Oh, I almost forgot. I don't suppose … I don't suppose you were working the night Christopher Byrne and Marlo McAdam had that argument?"

Rusty straightened up and looked at Jo appraisingly. "Don't suppose you're the first one to ask after Byrnie. Don't suppose you'll be the last, neither." She smiled at Jo, in a way that Jo didn't like.

"So you did hear it?"

Rusty took a long drag on the cigarette, squinting through the smoke. Her face looked like a store receipt left in the bottom of a handbag for too long. "I hear a lot of things, eh? You sure you're still asking for Marlo? Or some other reason?"

"It's all part of the same thing," Jo said quickly. Her face felt warm. "What did they argue about?"

Rusty looked thoughtful as she tapped ashes from the cigarette into an empty beer bottle. "Marlo had been following him."

"Why?"

"Dunno. Thought the woman had more sense than that, but there you have it. People do stupid things when they're in love." Rusty punched the "play" button and, after a prelude of vinyl static, a low, bluesy growl of instruments plucked a slow tempo, accented with a pop of Klondike-style piano. Jo recognized the tune. "Frankie and Johnny."

"Was it love?" Jo asked.

"For her. Or maybe just obsession. At any rate, Marlo followed Byrnie and found out something she didn't like much, I guess. I heard her say, 'I know what you did!' with this terrible look on her face. Byrnie hushed her up right away, and they went outside. That was it. I think it ended badly." Rusty took one last pull on the cigarette and added, "Like most things," then thrust the butt of the cigarette into a bottle where it fizzled out in the dregs of someone's Yukon Gold.

Outside, the streets had been half cleared, but the snow-plough was idling in neutral, grumbling like a malcontented old man. Curious, Jo peered through the frosty windows, then abruptly wished she hadn't. Sally was sitting on the driver's lap, lips locked, his hand reaching inside her fur coat. Jo looked away, at the dirty ditch snow, thinking about the song that Rusty had chosen to play.

19

A hostile sun was just dipping over the rolling hills along the highway as Jo approached the mine. The cold seemed to permeate everything now, the truck, every layer of clothing, her very bones. She had to keep moving, jiggling along with the truck and the box of dog biscuits on the passenger seat. Jo alternated hands while driving to keep one hand shoved coolly between her thighs while the other went numb on the wheel. It was her toes that worried her the most. Jo couldn't feel them anymore.

She turned her attention back to the mine, thinking of something her father used to say all the time: "Things in law tend to be black and white. But we all know that some people are a little bit guilty, while other people are guilty as hell." Frank's world view had eventually become her own: everyone was guilty—it was only a question of degree. She had run out of time for asking polite questions, questions that seemed to centre on the mine. Jo wasn't sure what to make of Christopher Byrne yet, but she was betting that Jack Grikowsky was guilty of something. This time, she couldn't let it go. She couldn't trust it to the police. Jo stirred the embers of her emotions, prodding and poking until she had a bright, steady heat. That low flame drove her forward, to the mine.

Sally's dashboard hula dancer bounced and quivered in anticipation. Jo didn't dare park in front of the gate, so she turned off her lights and pulled over on the shoulder of the highway, far enough away that the truck would not be visible. In the half-light, she waded into the woods behind the mine. Back to where Jo thought she'd stumbled onto the ice.

A frozen creek snaked its way through hard banks of snow. Jo followed the path of the water to where it widened, listening to the crunch and squeak of her rubber boots as she approached the edge. One thing was clear; she couldn't do without proper Yukon boots any longer. She'd layered on two pairs of wool socks but couldn't feel a thing. She silently cursed Kessler, who had told her that she could pick up a pair when she got to Dawson.

Jo crouched down in the looming darkness, withdrawing from her pocket a plastic film canister that she'd liberated from the *Daily*'s ancient stash. Jo planned to experiment with the film stock over the course of the winter, documenting the slow demise of all the decaying houses collapsing into the ice.

She chiselled down into the stream until she'd captured a chunk of ice in the container. The closing lid had just made a satisfying, self-congratulatory "pop," when she heard them coming for her. The dogs. A howl like a canine call to arms rang out across the whiteness and lengthening shadows, and was answered in kind. Dogs, or wolves. Jo sucked in her breath so deeply that the air felt like it might cut right through her lungs. She shoved the canister in a pocket and ran.

The scenery flashed by in jumpy bursts of pine and creek and fleeing sun. She could hear them gaining on her, barking their excitement. Quite close now. She fumbled clumsily for the biscuits in her pocket and threw them down. Still the dogs came. She felt her heart sink with the pale orb in the distance.

Jo could see Sally's truck now. She knew that she should not look back, but curiosity overcame her. She glanced over her shoulder. She caught a quick glimpse of two massive, wolf-like dogs with lolling tongues and eyes the colour of a Yukon sky. Then, her right foot hit a patch of ice and she began sliding forward. She overcompensated by leaning back, and went down hard on her tailbone. Jo found herself blinking at the heavens for half a second, observing where the sun bled into cloud. She heard it coming and leapt to her feet, but it was too late. The first dog was on her, lunging and snarling.

She kicked at the crazed animal so that its bite glanced off a rubber boot, but now the second dog sank its teeth into her thigh, causing her to cry out. She pounded on the beast with a gloved fist until it released. The husky sank into an aggressive stance, tail held low and teeth bared, preparing to spring again. Jo threw down more brightly coloured bones, which sank pointlessly into the snow.

Jo managed to open the door of the Chevy and place her body most of the way into the cab before the dog attacked again in a frenzy of fang. She kicked it hard in the nose with her boot and slammed the door on its head, so that it fell away from the truck with a howl. The moment she slammed the door shut she could hear claws on the metal as the huskies threw themselves at the truck. Their heads appeared at the window, jaws wide and eyes wild. Jo started the truck with trembling hands and prayed that the engine would turn over. It didn't.

A gunshot sounded, echoing across the white landscape. Jo forced herself to wait a moment before trying again. The engine spluttered and coughed. She was going to die in this godforsaken wilderness and be eaten by mad dogs. She wrenched the key again.

The next bullet shattered the left mirror. The next whizzed through ice and snow somewhere near the tire. He was going to take her tires out, she realized. But the engine was rumbling. Jo knew she needed to wait for the truck to warm up, but another shot reverberated in the cold air. She hit the accelerator and threw the truck into gear with a violent spray of snow.

20

Smoke twisted and wreathed in the flickering beam of a projector. Larger-than-life images of Marlo McAdam flashed on a screen mounted over the stage at Diamond Tooth Gertie's. Below the screen, Johnny Cariboo was seated on a wooden stool, playing a worn guitar. He was wearing street clothes: jeans and a charcoal grey Thaw-Di-Gras T-shirt. His arms, usually covered when he was working, were—Jo realized with surprise — adorned with tattoos. First Nations art, like you'd see on a totem pole, in striking reds and blacks. Eagle. Salmon. Wolf. He was painted right down to his hands. His strumming hand was tattooed with a word across the knuckles, but the motion prevented Jo from reading what it said.

He began singing the song Jo had heard on the radio in Byrne's truck.

> *Light up that cigarette, fingers exposed.*
> *It's the first one in months, and I blame the cold.*
> *In a frozen town. In a frozen town.*

Through the undulating smoke, Marlo smiled down at the bar from the two-dimensional safety of the screen, her expression knowing. Cariboo bowed his head as he worked the strings of his instrument, also playing the heartstrings of those left behind.

Now that I'm back in town,
I don't want me around.
Hangnails and coattails,
The snow sounds like crushed rails
And I have failed at leaving on time
In a frozen town. In a frozen town.
Wind to me, wind to me, you're steaming away
In a century old way
I call out the names of the ghosts of this place
That have loved us, and locked us up tight
In a frozen town. In a frozen town.
And it's tooooo cold,
It's too cold for car thieves tonight.
And it's tooooo cold,
It's too cold for car thieves
And everyone's hanging on tight
In a frozen town. Everyone is hanging on.

He cast a spell that swirled around them in the cigarette smoke and hushed conversations. Doug was right. Cariboo was good. He could have been someone, something, big—if he'd left Dawson.

Too cold for car thieves, but not too cold for murder. The patrons of Diamond Tooth Gertie's, bundled in warm sweaters and toques, leaned in to one another to speak, glancing furtively at one another. A few waved their lighters against the darkness as Cariboo sang. Jo caught low snippets of conversation about Marlo and May; there seemed to be an uneasy sense of disbelief among Dawsonites. They huddled together and murmured softly about the coming storms. A collective sense of isolation and grief and anxiety permeated the room.

As Cariboo finished the song and the room filled with quiet applause, Jo moved up to the stage to get a better look at the block letters on Cariboo's playing hand. *A L I …* She couldn't make out the rest, but it was enough. Now she understood the reason he wore the bandages at work. With a sick feeling, Jo remembered her dig about him cutting his knuckles shaving.

When she looked up, he was watching her. Ashamed, Jo turned away, Cariboo still haunting her as she limped to the bar.

Jo had treated her thigh with rubbing alcohol and wrapped it in stretch bandages with enough gauze to stop the bleeding. She didn't think she needed the airlift to the hospital in Whitehorse. In a way, she was relieved that there was no choice in the matter. If she couldn't seek treatment, then she wouldn't have to explain how she'd been bitten.

Her favourite jeans had been torn clear through and she'd had to dispose of them. Her backup pair were uncomfortably snug, particularly over the Tensor bandage and long johns, making her gait strangely stiff.

She found Sally behind the bar, dressed in a black pencil skirt, a 1940s-style peplum jacket, killer heels, and a pillbox hat with netting. Rusty was there too, wearing faded jeans and a navy sweater that was beginning to pill.

"Hey Sal, nice hat," Jo said.

"I think Marlo would have liked it." She smiled and tugged gently on the veil to make an adjustment. "Is that what you're wearing?"

Jo looked down at her jeans. "What? They're black."

"Black … *denim.*" The word "denim" seemed to stick in her throat.

Jo caught Rusty's eye, who smirked and looked away. "Anyway," Jo said, "seen Caveman around?"

Sally nodded her head toward a back corner of the room, where Caveman stood, hands shoved deep into pockets, black felt hat low over his eyes. Next to him swayed the two giant salmon, attempting to swing their lighters in time to the music without setting their fins alight.

"Thanks." Jo began to walk away, but Sally stopped her.

"Hey, are you all right? You're walking kinda funny."

"Yeah, it's nothing. Just an old track injury acting up."

"Is that a fact." Her tone conveyed disbelief. Still, she leaned forward and whispered, "Well, I have news for you."

"I'm on the edge of my bar stool."

"Remember how I told you that Jack Grikowsky left early the night Marlo was killed? After he had the fight with Rusty and stormed off?"

Sally and Rusty exchanged a knowing look.

Jo turned to Rusty. "I thought you didn't see him leave?"

"I didn't." Rusty said. "Mavis did. The piano player."

Sally nodded. "Yes. Grikowsky told Cariboo that he went home, but the thing is …" She leaned in even closer. "No alibi!" She folded her arms over her partially exposed bosom, looking smug.

Jo thought for a moment. "Why would Cariboo tell you that?"

"That I can't say," Sally said, but she smirked as she ran both of her hands lightly over her skirt to smooth the material, then brushed away imaginary lint from her suit jacket, thrusting her shoulders back so that her bust was featured prominently, goosebumps and all. There was no need to ask again. Sally glanced back toward the stage, where Cariboo was talking to someone Jo didn't know. "He shines up nicely, doesn't he, our Johnny?" Sally wore a wicked smile.

"By the way," said Jo. "How difficult is it to get parts for Bettie?"

Sally folded her arms tightly across her chest, her smile now a thin line.

Caveman refused to talk with Jo inside, because "They"—with an uppercase "T"—might be listening. The problem was, Jo couldn't get a clear sense of who "They" were, why "They" were so interested in the comings and goings of Caveman Cal, or whether "They" existed at all. Much of Caveman's paranoia seemed to concern city hall, where he'd been an employee for a time. Jo hoped that Caveman might still have some connections there, and enough practical knowledge about the machinations of the town—under the layers of paranoia—to prove useful.

Jo also had to wonder, as she and Caveman stepped into the back alley, whether Christopher Byrne was a part of upper case "They," or whether he just liked the way her jeans fit. She could feel his eyes boring into her as she exited the bar, though he remained firmly entrenched at the dealer's table. Jo definitely got the impression that Byrne didn't like her stepping outside with Caveman, whatever the reason.

Caveman squinted against the yowling cold and blowing snow as he sucked on his hand-rolled cigarette. "Smoke?" He offered the cigarette as though it might provide some protective warmth. A gust of wind nearly took his hat.

"No, thanks. I wanted to show you something." Caveman raised an eyebrow, and for a moment Jo felt ridiculous—a child playing an adult game with sexual innuendos. She opened her leather satchel and flashed a little peek of the handheld, electronic gizmo. It looked embarrassingly ordinary, and even Caveman seemed to be underwhelmed.

"What?" he asked.

"Take a look."

He took the device and began examining it, waving it around a little. It clicked once. A sedate sound. He looked surprised.

"Where'd you get it?"

"What if I told you it was found out at Claim 53?"

"At Sourdough Creek? But these are used in uranium mining. Not gold. Fifty-three is a gold mine."

Jo smiled, making her papery skin feel as though it might crack. Dawson had a way of draining all moisture from a person. "Exactly. Or another way of saying it is that Claim 53 is *licensed* to mine gold, not uranium."

Caveman studied Jo carefully. "Now you have my attention." His eyes flared with the cigarette, then he peered more closely at the device.

"Is it possible? I mean, that they're mining one thing by day and another by night?" Jo asked.

Caveman tugged at his thick black beard. "Well, it's possible … Depends how much money is at stake, like anything in Dawson." He laughed. "You'd need a rock out-cliff where you had a bit of gold next to pure pitchblende uranium ore. But without a permit …"

Jo felt a shivery thrill that, this time, had nothing to do with the weather. She whispered a little louder than the wind. "They have a permit. A permit for gold."

Caveman glanced quickly over his shoulder. "They'd have to bribe a lot of people to keep it quiet. Possibly even someone from the DFO … someone who would test the water might see residue."

"The DFO?"

"Department of Fisheries and Oceans."

"Oh, right." The woman at Dawson city hall had mentioned the DFO, too. "So … if it's true, it goes pretty high up." She caught herself wishing, just for a fraction of a second, that she were still in Vancouver, so she could go to the Press Club with Kessler and the others to celebrate a big lead. It would be raining, her black Converse sneakers would be soaked through, and she would buy the first pitcher. Then she remembered that Kevin Kessler had been the first to sell her out when the story broke. He'd fired her without even breaking up with her. She supposed that to Kessler it was the same thing.

Caveman gave Jo a look that she couldn't quite interpret. "If it's true, you're getting in way over your head at a bad time. Top of the World Highway just closed. Ferry's lifted—had a helluva time getting over here in my canoe today. Alaska Highway's snowin' in. By the end of the week it'll be purrrrdy tough to git out, eh? And we'll be left with just a couple of small town cops."

"Still …" Jo persisted.

"But what would they do with it?" Caveman argued, though Jo could see that he was as excited about the possibility of a conspiracy as she was.

"Smuggle it out, I guess, and sell it somewhere. Maybe to rogue terrorists. Who knows?"

"Huh. You can git to Skagway from West Dawson, depending on weather, of course. A lot of smugglers take stuff out via Alaska. But, now the highway's closed, you'd have to do it by snowmobile." He shook his head, as though in awe of the scope of the crime.

"Know any smugglers that fit the bill?" Jo prodded.

Caveman snorted. "Only half of Dawson."

"Which half? Anyone in particular?"

Caveman suddenly looked uncomfortable. He shoved the device toward her, his ardour cooled. "I couldn't say. Anyway, I should git going. Fuckin' freezin' my nuts off out here, eh?" He waved to someone behind Jo, then skulked away in the opposite direction, down the alley, shoulders hunched. Jo turned to look.

The back door to Gertie's swung shut. Christopher Byrne had his head down, bracing against the wind with a determined expression. Jo noticed with both envy and admiration the thick parka, and the way the fur trim framed and complimented his strong features.

Byrne looked up and smiled at Jo, as though guessing what she'd been thinking. "Something I said?" Byrne nodded towards the departing figure of Caveman.

"Something *I* said." Jo stamped her feet a little in the snow, even though she could no longer feel them, hoping that he'd focus on her boots while she zipped up the shoulder bag to conceal the Geiger counter. Jo couldn't be sure whether he had noticed the thing or not.

He was still on the stairs, looking down at her with a peculiar expression. "C'mon. I want to show you something," Byrne said.

"What?" Jo said, feeling blood rush to her cheeks. She hated herself for enjoying the warmth.

Then Byrne did something surprising: he took off his glove. He reached out and took Jo's hand, removed her glove too, and held her hand firmly while he shoved it into his own fur-lined pocket, his fingers entwined tightly with hers. Jo's fingers tingled with feeling that she thought she'd lost.

"C'mon," he said. Jo knew she was an idiot, but she went just the same.

21

The husky in the back of the pickup truck narrowed its eyes at Jo. Or possibly Nugget was just reacting to the cutting wind—it was impossible to know for sure. Either way, watching the wolfish form made Jo's thigh throb: she thought of the raw puncture marks there and winced. Still, she worried about how cold the creature must be.

"Is he okay back there?" she asked.

Byrne glanced at the husky in his rearview mirror. "Nugget?" he said, eyes smiling. "Nugget's fine. He loves it back there." Byrne glanced at Jo again, and she found herself wishing that he would keep his eyes on the road. They were in the middle of nowhere, the roads were unpaved, and the trees loomed overhead like Edward Gorey ink drawings. Byrne turned up the radio a little. Something mellow was playing, folksy vocals with guitar and fiddle accompaniment. It was cosy in the cab. Byrne reached out his hand over the heater to check the temperature. "Warm enough?"

"Yeah," Jo said. She swallowed. She wasn't sure why, but she felt unsettled. She wondered whether Byrne felt it too, or whether she was projecting. She glanced at him, the strong outline of his profile, the sensual mouth, and felt suddenly, inexplicably giddy. *Dangerous*, Sally had said. Jo sincerely hoped that she wasn't the type of person who was attracted to dangerous men. Byrne must have felt the weight of her gaze and turned to look at her. Jo returned her attention to the road, embarrassed.

"So, what did Caveman say about me?" Byrne said.

"What makes you think we were talking about you?"

Byrne's tone was playful. "Maybe I just hoped you were. But we can talk about you instead. Did you finish your book?"

"We talked about books?"

"Yes. You like historical crime fiction. You're reading *Name of the Rose*. You wish you'd written it. When you were a teenager you wanted to be a reporter for *The Rolling Stone*. Your mother died when you were eight. She spent most of her time nursing others, even after she found out she was terminally ill. You were angry with her for a long time about dying on you. You wish she'd focused more on living. Your father sent you to therapy ..."

"Christ, did I ever shut up?"

Byrne laughed. "Not really. But this is meant to be a reenactment. So you're meant to be doing most of the talking."

"But I don't remember what we talked about."

"I told you I understood how you felt—you know, that feeling of abandonment—because my mother left when I was nine. I don't blame her anymore—I couldn't have lived with my father either. But I was angry, too, for a long time."

"Oh, I'm sorry. What about your father?"

"His liver finally gave out. I still see my mother. She's an artist. Very talented. Lives in Whitehorse."

"Not that far away."

"Not in summer. But in winter? Dawson might as well be on another planet."

"True," said Jo, thinking of the the wall of mountains surrounding the town, and the closed highways. The truck's headlights illuminated the snow drifting across the dark road. "So, you think you inherited your talent from your mother?"

"Possibly. My father had his moments, though. On his good days, he was full of wonder and imagination. He had the most fantastic telescope. Used to spend a lot of time watching the night skies. Some nights when I was a kid, he'd wake me at midnight, bundle me up in furs, and take the huskies out for a sled ride under the stars."

"Wow. I'd love to do that."

Byrne looked pleased. "Then I must take you."

Jo felt herself falling for him and tried to pull back from the abyss. *Too late*, she thought.

"I have a theory about you." Byrne glanced at her.

"Oh, what's that?" Jo felt apprehensive. She never liked other people's theories about her.

"When you drink, you let your guard down. You talk more about yourself. Usually you ask all the questions so you give nothing away." He glanced at her. "What is that, some kind of defence mechanism?" He had a mischievious expression.

"Yes, and you've just triggered it. My turn to ask the questions."

"Fire away."

"What are you reading right now?"

"Poetry mostly. Wallace Stevens. But I've already told you that and you've forgotten." His voice was low and had some gravel to it. It was the kind of voice she could listen to for a long time, late at night, like rain on a tin roof. Not a hard rain, but a soft, steady kind of rain. Comforting. Something you could listen to while curled up under a thick quilt.

"Favourite poem?"

"'Thirteen Ways of Looking at a Blackbird.' Remember?"

"No. Favourite food?"

"A good moose steak. Medium rare. I'll make you one some-time. You?"

"Chinese dim sum."

"You used to go every Sunday with Frank. In East Vancouver. You thought he was avoiding Sunday dinners without your mother."

"I talked about Frank? Wow." She thought for a moment. "You're a good listener." She meant it, and the realization came as a shock. "And you have an excellent memory."

"Only when it's important. Have you called him yet?"

"Yes." She stared out the window for a moment, watching the endless loop of trees. He was intuitive enough not to ask for more information. She added, "So, where are we going?"

"Somewhere to help jog your memory. That's what you wanted, isn't it? A reconstruction? I promised you." Said with a smile.

"The Bluffs?" The skin around his eyes crinkled, but he didn't respond. "Well, there's something I wanted to ask you about."

"Yes?" he said.

"About the argument you had with Marlo a few days before she died." Byrne stared straight ahead. Jo said, "What was the disagreement about?"

The folksy ballad harmonized with the whispered secrets of the wind. Byrne cleared his throat and shifted in his seat. "Marlo was jealous. Actually, possessive might be a better word."

"She followed you?"

He nodded. "Marlo was ... how can I say this? I don't want to speak ill of her now." His eyes met hers. There was an undeniable spark between them. "Let's just say there's a fine line between passion and obsession. She was like that in her work as well."

"So Marlo found out something she wasn't happy about."

"Yes," he said, returning his attention to the narrow tunnels of light the low-beams were casting into the darkness, twin spotlights for dancing snowflakes.

"What was it?"

He gave no answer, but slowed the truck and pulled over into a parking lot, next to a wooded trail. A snow-burdened sign read "Crocus Bluffs." Byrne opened his door, allowing a rush of wintry air to encircle her throat, but Jo didn't move. She inhaled the scent of pine and fir.

"You wanted to know what we were doing up here the night Marlo died," he said. "It was awkward to explain ... easier to show you."

"Show me?"

Byrne circled the truck and opened the door for Jo, which might have seemed chivalrous at another time. "Hop out!" he said. Jo wasn't sure whether he'd intended it as an invitation or a command, but suddenly the grinding cold seemed like the least of her problems. *I could refuse,* she thought. But if she refused, she might never know the truth. Reluctantly, she left the relative comfort of the cab. As she slid down from the torn leather seats and landed stiffly on the icy snow, Jo noticed a large warning sign in the parking lot. "Caution: bears and wolves in area." *Perfect.*

"Come with me." Byrne took her by the hand again. This time without removing gloves.

"This is where they think Marlo might have ... fallen?" Jo already knew the answer to the question, but felt overwhelmed by the need to fill any silence between them. Her voice sounded artificially cheerful. Byrne nodded but said nothing. Jo found herself doing something that Frank had taught her: to always search an area for escape routes. She wondered whether she'd be able to find her way to the road if she darted off into the forest, or whether she'd wind up running over a cliff and washing up at Caveman's doorstep. "Why can't you just tell me why we were all the way up here that night? Why didn't you just drive me home?"

Byrne's profile looked determined. He didn't turn to look at her when he responded. "It's not the kind of thing you can tell someone. Particularly not you."

Jo thought about this for a moment. If the reason were something innocent, why wouldn't she accept it? Why couldn't he just tell her? *Because the reason is not something innocent.* Despite the jagged breeze, she began to perspire, creating cold patches under her arms.

"You know, I have to be up early in the morning. I probably shouldn't hang around …"

Byrne ignored the comment. "Here. This way." His grip tightened on her hand as he led her firmly down a narrow forest trail into the darkness.

Jo heard the river long before she saw it. It sounded angry. They emerged from the woods into an icy clearing marked "Crocus Bluffs," with an arrow clearly directing the way.

Jo focused on her feet as Byrne pulled her forward, struggling to gain her footing as her rubber boots slid here and there. At the edge of the Bluffs, a tiny, waist-high wooden fence was all that stopped a body from pitching into oblivion, into the darkness and the river below. It would be easy to fall. Easy to throw someone over, too.

"This is as good a spot as any," Byrne said gruffly.

Jo stared down, transfixed by the black emptiness below and the sound of a rushing, watery death.

"Look up." Byrne said.

Was this some small kindness on his part? Like blindfolding a man before you shoot him? Jo didn't want to die, and she sure as hell wasn't going to make it easy for him. Frank had always told her, in a worst-case scenario, leave as much forensic evidence as possible. *Get his skin under your nails.* Jo dug her nails into Byrne's wrist. A pointless effort since she was wearing gloves.

"No. I don't want to." She squeezed her fingers as hard as she could, but her fingers were so numb she wondered if he could even feel her grip. Jo had to make a decision. She wondered if she could pull off a judo throw, but he might go over the railing. She had to be certain.

"Just look up."

"No."

Byrne moved behind her and wrapped her in a tight bear hug. Jo tried to wriggle free, but his arms crushed hers and held her still. If only she were turned to face him, she could knee him in the crotch. She felt a rush of panic. Smelled the scent of winter in the air. Tasted snow on her tongue.

"Look."

Jo looked. The sky was an alien shade of green, a swirling curtain that housed the strangest theatrical production she had ever seen. Playful meteors of light bounced across their celestial stage as though they were line dancing. *The northern lights.*

"Omigod ..." Jo said.

"Yes."

"It's so beautiful." She thought for a moment. "I saw this before? This is what we were doing up here?" An intense wave of relief flooded her muscles and she felt his hold on her release. Her knees were shaking. She hoped Byrne wouldn't notice and mistake the feeling for something else. Jo turned to look at Byrne and saw that he was smiling, but still he didn't answer her. Jo said, "It's so strange the way they move. Almost spooky."

He nodded. "According to legend, it's very dangerous to whistle at the northern lights. If you do, the lights will come and cut your head off. When we were kids, we used to stand up here and dare one another to whistle."

"That's ridiculous," she said. Byrne shrugged. "Didn't you ever do it?"

"No way."

"Well, I'm going to do it." Jo said.

Byrne looked worried. "Why?"

"To prove it isn't true. Don't you want to know the truth?"

"There are some things I don't need to know that badly," he said.

Jo took a deep breath, pursed her lips to whistle and watched as the lights went crazy, playing racquetball across the universe. Byrne leaned in quickly and kissed her.

It was a kiss full of promise and possibility, and when it came to a reluctant conclusion, Byrne said, "That's what we were doing up here."

22

She could still taste the warm kiss that Christopher Byrne had given her, still feel his mouth against hers, although the office at the *Daily* was cold and dark. Her muscles ached for bed, but Jo hadn't trusted herself enough to let Byrne drop her at the house. She knew she'd want Byrne to come in with her, and she also knew that it wasn't a good idea. She didn't trust him. Not yet. She didn't know whether or not to believe that they'd been innocently kissing under the northern lights the night Marlo died. It seemed like an awfully big coincidence that they were in the vicinity when his ex-lover was murdered. For all she knew, Byrne could have killed Marlo while Jo was sleeping it off in the truck. Jo shivered and opened her eyes.

She had used the excuse that she needed to work on her story. This was partly true. She had already finished the story for Friday publication in the *Daily*, but she'd decided to publish her own version before then. She needed to tell the truth, as she knew it, or as much of it as she knew. And now, she needed to know for herself what the truth was. It was getting uncomfortably personal.

Jo unzipped her satchel and extracted the Geiger counter, turning it thoughtfully in her hands, considering its robotic whispers. It clicked meaningfully, like a puzzle piece falling into place. If only it were that simple. She sighed and slid open the bottom drawer of her desk, dropping the thing inside. As the drawer slid to a solemn close, she thought she heard something outside. The crunch of snow.

Her hand gripped the cool metal handle, suddenly conscious of the lateness of the hour and the gaping black windows that made her feel exposed. The wind whined like a hungry husky. Jo listened for several moments until, satisfied that she was being paranoid, she turned on the radio and settled down to work. A woman's voice rose above the wind as Jo began laying out her story—the real story, not the story she had already submitted to Doug. Not a retrospective of Citizen Marlo, Good Dawsonite. This story featured the same photograph of Marlo, offering a Mona Lisa smile for the camera, but the headline read "Police Probe Mysterious Death: Suspect Foul Play." The article fleshed out the hypothesis that someone met Marlo McAdam in the parking lot and drove her to Crocus Bluffs, and had not come forward. That person likely knew something about what Marlo had been doing on the Bluffs that night. They may have even been involved in Marlo's death. Jo's piece stopped just shy of accusing the police of a cover-up. Next to the spread on Marlo McAdam, Jo laid out a story on placer mining, called "The Yukon's Silent Killer." While the story didn't directly accuse Claim 53 in particular of any wrongdoing, the title, placement, and content would make certain connections in the reader's mind. Finally, a column titled "Where Is May Wong?" linked the disappearance of the owner of Claim 53 to the murder of Marlo McAdam. This article noted that May Wong had been seen leaving Diamond Tooth Gertie's at about the time that Marlo had accepted her fatal ride, making it clear that May was likely to have been either the driver or a witness, and had since disappeared. Jo read through the finished articles, then hit "Save."

This is how Jo would run the story if she were the editor. It was difficult to judge what the fallout of publishing the articles independently might be, but at least this time Jo would have done her duty to warn the public.

When Jo had finished uploading the articles for her new blog, *The Dawson Insider* (which would provide editorial comment on events described—or not described—in the *Dawson Daily*), she turned out the desk light, leaving her laptop open only slightly. The eerie, greenish glow provided enough light to locate her keys in a leather shoulder bag. Jo paused, leaning back in her chair for a moment. She closed her eyes. For the first time in quite a long time, Jo felt she deserved some little reward.

That kiss. Generous. Sensual. But he had avoided answering her questions about the argument with Marlo.

The front door handle turned, startling her. A rush of cold air swirled into the room as a man in a dark parka, black nylon gloves, and a black balaclava opened the door. He held her stare, and the moment hung strangely between them.

The figure in the ski mask hesitated, fingering something in his pocket as if trying to make a decision. His eyes were wide with surprise. Jo stood then, turning her body to the side as she had been trained to do, preparing for a fight. Her muscles were tense. Knees bent. Ready.

The man raised his hands slowly, in supplication. "Only me," he said, and giggled nervously as he removed the black wool cover from his face. Doug Browning.

Jo didn't smile even when the mask was lifted. Her body was still angled away from him. She nodded slightly. "What are you doing here?" She kept her tone cool. There was something about his behaviour that unnerved her. He had taken too long to speak.

"I could ask you the same question." He took a step forward, tentatively. He slipped one hand back into his pocket. "I like to come in here and putter when I can't sleep," Doug continued, withdrawing a glasses case from his pocket. "Didn't mean to scare you. Couldn't see who it was without my glasses. They fog up." He opened the case and gave the spectacles a polish.

"Oh," Jo said, relaxing then. She straightened her knees. *Ridiculous. Soon I'll be as bad as Caveman.* "That's okay."

Doug bent down to see the *Daily's* small mascot. "Hello, Marshall. You keeping warm?" His voice was like two pieces of paper rubbing together. The rodent stood on his hind legs and sniffed the air curiously.

Jo glanced toward her laptop, still open a little on the desk.

Doug followed her look. "Still working on something?"

"Nope. All done," she said. "You got the articles?"

"Yes," he said. "Hours ago. I really appreciated that you kept the tone … neutral." He sounded surprised. And suspicious. "You need a lift?"

⌘

The SUV fishtailed toward a snow bank before correcting its path. When Jo finally exhaled, her breath was a wistful coil.

"Sorry," Doug said, rolling down his window a little. He kept his gloves on as he drove, his posture erect, fingers tightly gripping the wheel. The heater was rattling away but the windows were still frosted, making the world appear patterned with feathery fissures. When Doug glanced at Jo, his expression was difficult to read, cold glasses clouding his eyes.

Was it his driving that was causing Jo to feel uneasy? Or something else? Maybe it was the car Doug was driving—a Volkswagen Touareg. She'd expected a VW, but an old-school campervan, not a modern SUV. It looked fresh off the lot, aside from the chipped windshield. Of course, a VW campervan would never last a Yukon winter.

She couldn't put her finger on what was making her so jumpy, but she had the distinct feeling that something was wrong. *Instinct*, Frank would have said. *Always trust your instinct.* Perhaps she shouldn't have taken Doug up on the offer to drive her home, but the whole misunderstanding at the office had made Jo think that she was just being paranoid. They turned off Front, but now there were no streetlights. Most of the curtains in the windows were drawn against the night, against the coming storm.

"So." Doug's voice, before soft and papery, now sounded snake-like to Jo. "Thank you for the articles."

"No problem. It's my job." Her eyes remained on the road. It was snowing again, and the snow created an eddying effect in the headlights: each individual snowflake a minute whirling dervish assailing the vehicle.

"Yeah, well, you did a good job of keeping it upbeat. The retrospective on Marlo, I mean." He was watching her carefully. "I know it wasn't easy for you. I know you would have done it differently."

"Honestly?" she said.

"Of course ..." He smiled faintly.

"I think we've botched it. I think the *Daily* has just helped the police cover up a murder. Okay, probably 'cover up' is too strong. But certainly helped a murderer remain at large in the community ... And I think he's already killed again."

"What?"

"At a time when the community is most isolated. We'll be trapped with him all winter."

"You know we have different opinions about the evidence, which I believe is wanting." Doug said, his whisper-voice rising for the first time. The car slipped a little again, lurching to the left, then recovered its course.

"Yes. And I respect the title of editor." She added, as an after-thought, "I try to."

"I appreciate that." He didn't sound sincere.

"Which is why I think we should be above board with one another. You should hear what I have to say first before the rest of town hears it. To be fair."

"What? We've already discussed it. You've sent me the story and I'm printing it tomorrow. As is."

"After the last time, there's just no way I can sit and watch this kind of thing happen again. I hope you'll understand my decision."

"Which is?" Doug said.

"I'll be publishing a series of articles independently tomor-row. Call it a blog if you will. *The Dawson Insider*."

"You may be in breach of contract if you do."

"Perhaps. But I don't believe so. And even if I am …"

"Wait a minute—series? You said 'a series of articles.' "

"Yes."

"Something about the mine? About Claim 53?" Doug licked his lips.

"By the way, I've been meaning to ask you. Why is it that when I went out to interview Jack Grikowsky, he asked me whether you knew I was there?"

Doug's mouth fell open, then closed tightly. "I have no idea." He leaned forward, as though searching for a path through the snow. For a way out.

"Interesting." She punctuated this last comment with a silence long enough to be uncomfortable. They listened to the sound of the wipers labouring against the snow. "Anyway, I'll let you read the articles tomorrow. With everyone else, of course.

But as it is an independent publication, I hope you'll appreciate that I'm not obliged to discuss the content in advance."

"You can't do this." Doug jerked the steering wheel to avoid a gaping pothole and overcompensated into another slide.

Jo clutched at the door, now seriously concerned about Doug's erratic driving. The fractures in the windshield—the result of Dawson's stubborn refusal to pave the roads—now seemed to loom over her. "I already have," she said, but she hoped her tone was gentle. She found herself feeling sorry for Doug Browning. Whatever was going on with him, it was clear to Jo that Doug was in over his head, and suffering from the stress of it. She wondered if that could be why he had resigned his position as editor of the *Daily* and was planning to retire and leave Dawson.

"I won't let you." He slowed the vehicle, turning into a small shared parking area behind Sally's house, wheeling around and stopping abruptly next to a fresh bank of snow.

"You won't *let* me?" Jo set her jaw firmly.

He took a deep breath, one gloved hand raised to his mouth. The expression on his face relaxed, but the soothing tone of his voice was unconvincing. "I'm sorry. I didn't mean it to sound like that. Of course I respect your decision. I know you went through a lot in Vancouver." He leaned over and put a hand on her shoulder, the other glove disappearing into his coat pocket.

Jo flung the door open, bumping it hard against a stubborn drift before she could finally squeeze out. She didn't like the look on his face, or the purposefulness of the hand in the pocket. Her breath came in quick jabs of cold air, but her movements felt clumsy as she slammed the door and scraped along the side of the SUV toward the light of a second-floor window at the back of the house. If she needed to make a run for it, she'd have to sprint all the way around to the front because she didn't have a key for the gate yet.

The headlights on the SUV winked out, though the motor was still running, throwing the back entrance to the house in shadow. Jo heard the car door open, and turned to see her editor moving stealthily through the snow toward her. Doug hesitated when he saw Jo watching him, but his face still bore a malicious expression. Maybe it was just the way his glasses fogged up in the cold, obscuring his eyes. He looked strangely faceless. Or at least eyeless. Instinctively, Jo bent at the knees a little, in preparation. "What are you doing?"

"The walk might be icy. Just wanna make sure you get home all right."

If he'd wanted to help Jo navigate the path to the back door, surely he would have left the lights on. Jo wanted to glance up at the bedroom windows to see if she could see Sally, to know if anyone would hear her if she screamed, but she'd had it drilled into her in self-defence classes never to turn your back on anyone you didn't trust. As a result, Jo rarely turned her back on anyone.

"I'd see better with the headlights on," she said.

"Oh," Doug said flatly. "My battery is weak. Need a new one." Yet aside from the damaged windshield, his car looked new. Doug stood his ground in the snow, but his mouth fell open and he nodded his head a little, like some sightless, carnivorous worm listening for its prey.

"It's all right, I've got my keys. I'll be fine."

"Oh," he said again, but not as in, "Oh, I see." More like an, "Oh!" Like he had just remembered something. He rushed back to the car and flipped on the headlights.

Now Jo was blinded. She held up one hand to shield her eyes, attempting to see if Doug had exited the car again. The vehicle began to reverse. Jo knew he was going to run her down. The car surged fiercely, and when he hit the accelerator, Jo was already moving. The truck burst forward, and then, to her surprise, spun away with a spray of snow, shooting back down the alley and disappearing into the night.

Jo listened, heart juddering, to the sound of tires on snow retreating in the distance.

23

Jo slept fitfully, plagued by fiery nightmares, but when her alarm sounded she had almost forgotten the night's dark tapestry and was dreaming of a kiss. The Kiss. The warmth of that remembered contact saw her through to the aromatic promise of the day's first cup of coffee.

Thursday. The world outside steamy windows was black, and the thermometer read minus twenty-five. Jo cupped a hot porcelain mug in her hands and closed her eyes. Her lips met his again.

"Morning!" Sally's voice was too loud and cheerful for the hour, startling Jo. Sally surveyed Jo's appearance. "Whoa. Rough night?"

"Fine. Just not a whole lot of sleep."

"Oho! Up late with your new boyfriend?"

"Boyfriend?"

"Don't play dumb with me. Half the town saw you and Chris playing pool together at the Sourtoe Saloon. Wonder what Johnny Cariboo thinks about that?"

"Why should he care? It's none of his business."

Sally shrugged. "Are you sure about that?" A knowing smile. Jo couldn't be sure whether Sally thought Cariboo's interest would be professional, or private. "And rumour has it you left Gertie's with Byrnie last night." Sally winked. "He show you his ..."

Jo aimed a warning look at Sally ...

"Cabin?" Sally said. "I hear it's quite large."

Jo shrugged and took a cautious sip of coffee. It was bitter. "Perhaps I should dedicate the front page of the *Daily* to our conversation, so I can answer the whole goddamned town's questions in one go?"

Sally shuffled across the kitchen in her leopard-patterned bathrobe, collar turned up against the cold, one hand clutching the throat closed. She wore pink pyjamas with ruffled edges and fluffy slippers. "Might increase readership. But the headline might have to read: Big City Crime Reporter Does Time with Convicted Smuggler."

Jo felt her insides tighten. "What?"

"Oh ... Byrnie didn't mention that? How odd." Sally smiled and flounced away, pleased with herself.

───⊗───

Sometime during the night, the Yukon River had finally frozen solid. The silence of the river was disarming after days of icy furor. *So this is freeze-up.* It felt like the calm before the storm.

Jo stood listening, waiting for something intangible while the steam of her breath moistened her woollen scarf. The sky was still grey, reflected in charcoal shades in the ice beneath blowing snow, like a child's messy chalkboard. The ferry had vanished, as though the river had claimed another victim. Jo wondered how thick the ice would have to be before it could be crossed. She pictured herself skating away on it, doing slow, graceful loops until she disappeared into the horizon line.

Jo did not go directly to the *Daily*—a fact that she was questioned about later by the RCMP. Instead, she continued northeast on Front, along the river. She stopped in front of the fire hall, which she now knew was also city hall, and there she met Glen Idlett, the town crier. *The Village Idlett*, she'd heard him called. He nodded his head to her.

"Morning."

"Good morning."

"So, are you and Christopher Byrne an item?"

Jo ignored the comment. "I brought your fee."

"In cash?"

"Yes. And here are the headlines for today." She handed him a typed list, as well as some bright strips of paper that contained the URL for the newly launched *Dawson Insider*.

He gaped a little. "Is this all true?"

"Read it and see." Jo said.

He looked at the headlines again. "Geez …" He shrugged. "Well, looks like you're asking for some crazy trouble to me, but it's your money, eh?" He cleared his throat and began to ring his bell, splitting the silence of the sleepy town with a violent crack of steel on steel. "Hear ye, hear ye … Get the truth about Marlo McAdam's death at the DawsonInsider.com. Read all about the Yukon's silent killer: the placer mining industry … Find out about the strange disappearance of May Wong …"

As the town crier called out Jo's words, figures began to emerge from the dark doorways and still-closed shops along Front Street. Jo wondered if the person responsible for Marlo's death and May's disappearance was among them. There were some notable absences: *Grikowsky. Doug. Peter. Sally. Caveman. Byrne.* Anyone who was not in range (those who lived across the river like Caveman, or up the Dempster Highway like Byrne) would hear about it soon enough.

Jo turned away from the onlookers. She was still on salary at the *Daily*, for the time being at least, and there was work to be done. But she had one more errand to do first.

At shortly after ten on Thursday morning, Jo's package bound for Vancouver via Whitehorse achieved liftoff. A lonely stretch of snowy pine bore mute witness to the departure of the small turbo-prop aircraft with four passengers and Jo's water sample on board. Jo suffered a feeling of deflation as the plane disappeared over a ridge of firs, the bright orange dorsal fin sinking like a setting sun. She wondered whether she was watching the last flight out of Dawson for the season.

Her boots squeaked in the empty, one-room terminal as she approached a pay phone. She deposited a cold coin, which made a cheerless clinking sound as it fell. Jo breathed in the scent of stale cigarettes as she dialled.

Frank didn't pick up. Jo listened to his voicemail message and then left careful instructions to meet the Air North flight in Vancouver. She hoped he would get the message in time.

Jo felt a little lighter as she shuffled back along the icy wooden boardwalk toward the office. She hung onto the warm feeling inside her despite numb fingers and toes. She had done it. She'd made a choice she could feel good about and her journalistic ethics were intact. Maybe now she could put the past to rest. As she climbed the wooden steps to the *Daily*, the shrill cry of a raven sounded like laughter.

There was a plastic mail pouch hanging on the front door.

Jo unhooked it and fished in her shoulder bag for the key. Jo was looking at an envelope stamped "City of Dawson Y.T." as the door swung open, so the first thing that struck her as unusual was the sound of the space heater running. She must have left it on, which was strange; Jo thought she'd turned it off last night before leaving. *Stupid.*

When Jo looked up she saw the blood. Rust-coloured prints on the floorboards that looked like paw prints. In fact, they were paw prints. Paw prints that led away from the desk and toward the water cooler, where a small rodent cowered, its bloody whiskers twitching. "Marshall, what happened to you?" For a moment, Jo thought the guinea pig had been injured, but it scampered away easily when she spoke. She looked back in the direction of the desk.

The top of the desk was now empty. Her laptop was gone, as was the black rotary phone that had perched there, gargoyle-like, a technological monstrosity from years gone by. On the floor behind the desk, two legs protruded at odd angles.

24

The body of Doug Browning lay in a pool of congealing blood behind the desk, one hand still holding the tangled mess of phone line that was wrapped around his throat. Jo shuddered. She clenched her hands into fists as she leaned in for a better look. He was bleeding from numerous places on his body, about the chest, hands, and throat. The slashes on his hands looked like defensive wounds. His eyes bulged and, magnified by pop-bottle lenses, exaggerated the shocked expression on his face. Then Jo noticed his ear. Jo felt her insides drop like a roller-coaster ride. Three dead, if you counted May Wong. At least two had bruising about the throat. Doug's ear had been mutilated. This was all beginning to feel uncomfortably familiar.

Jo fought to slow her breathing and stay calm. She had to call Cariboo, but she hesitated, reluctant to touch the phone for fear of hampering any investigation by altering a crime scene. *Cell phone* ... Before she could even finish the thought she remembered that Dawson had no cellular service.

She glanced around the room, feeling panicky that someone might still be there, though the blood was evidently not fresh. The filing cabinet drawers at the far side of the room were open and the files had been dumped all over the floor. The main desk drawer was completely extended, and others had not been closed properly. *The Geiger counter.* With one gloved hand, Jo gently slid open the bottom desk drawer: the Geiger counter was still there.

Jo picked up the device and stared at it. What had the intruder been looking for, if not the Geiger counter? She tucked it into her coat pocket and then picked up the phone, doing her best not to disturb the position of anything. This meant that she had to lean forward into the tangle of phone line—which made her think of intestines—in order to reach the receiver. Doug gawked at her from the floor, their faces close, almost in a position of intimacy. No dial tone. It had been yanked from the wall in their struggle, evidently. Jo had to unwind some of the cord and plug it back in. Although the call was short, it felt like a purgatory.

While Jo waited for the RCMP, she couldn't resist inspecting the open desk drawer to see what, if any, files may have been removed. The answer didn't surprise her. A raw gust of air swept through the office, rustling the documents scattered about the floor near the filing cabinets. She hugged herself tightly and walked toward the draft, which seemed to originate from the small bathroom at the back of the *Daily*.

The door to the bathroom was open. Inside, the window had been shattered. Shards of glass lay strewn about the cracked linoleum floor like fractured ice, making Jo think of the river. For a moment, Jo pictured herself falling through the dark crust of the Yukon River, floating under the ice, green bubbles of breath trapped just below the surface while the current carried her far away.

Jo breathed deeply as she navigated the glass and then leaned out the window to look into the alley. There were indents in the snow, along the side of the building, but the tracks had largely been snowed in.

The RCMP office in Dawson was small and had an intimate feel to it. There were no photographs on the wall of the interview room, and the overhead lights had the queasy yellow tinge of fluorescents, but the room was equipped with a surprisingly comfortable tweed couch and matching armchair. Jo could almost imagine that her visit was merely a social call, but for the fact that Cariboo had just videotaped her statement.

A large husky with cloudy blue cataracts wore dog tags that read "Justice." The dog snapped at the powdery bit of doughnut that it was offered. "He can't see a thing anymore, but his nose still works." Cariboo nodded toward the dog. "Had him since I was a kid." He leaned forward, offering Jo the box of dough-nuts, dark eyes studying her. His knuckles were bandaged over again. Cariboo looked weary, and also concerned. "Cruller?" he prompted. "You've had a shock. Sometimes a bit of sugar helps."

Jo slouched down into the worn loveseat and waved the doughnut away. "I'm good, thanks. She felt a wave of fatigue that the blood-hued sofa wasn't helping, and she could feel herself shaking. She hoped Cariboo hadn't noticed.

Cariboo returned the box to the desk. "More water? Or are you ready for coffee now? It's Tim Hortons—only Dawson's fin-est for you." He smiled. Jo couldn't quite tell whether or not he intended the irony. She decided that he did.

"I'm fine, really," she lied. "What about the tracks in the alley?"

Cariboo frowned. "A lot of snow during the night. We've tarped over them to preserve them as best we can and photo-graphed them but ... We're also dusting for prints."

"Oh," she said, thinking, *he'd have been wearing gloves.*

"We're looking for anything we can get in the way of DNA samples."

"Do you have a forensics team up here?"

"No. We'd like to send for one, but … freeze-up is going to make that tough. The body will be preserved in the freezer at the rec centre at Minto Park, under police guard, until weather permits it to go to Vancouver for examination, along with any DNA samples."

"I see."

"It is possible that someone just broke in to look for cash and was surprised," Cariboo said.

"But Doug was murdered."

"True, but it doesn't appear to have been premeditated. Cause of death was probably strangulation, but the body showed wounds inflicted from a fairly small knife, possibly a jackknife. Not something a guy typically uses to plan a murder."

"So, escalated violence like a serial killer—and yet, it seems to have been a crime of necessity, if the killer was startled by Doug's sudden arrival."

"Yes. That it is … curious." Cariboo looked at Jo with an odd expression. "It does seem unlikely that the intruder expected to find Doug at the office, given the hour. Unless, of course, some-one arranged to meet him there … By the way, do you know what Doug was doing there?"

"What? No," Jo said, not liking his tone. What she didn't say was that she suspected Doug's nocturnal visit to the *Daily* had some-thing to do with the story on her laptop. Perhaps he had gone back to read it, to learn who Jo was pointing the finger at … whether it might be him. Jo didn't want to raise the issue of her story with Sergeant Cariboo if she didn't have to. Not yet. She wondered if he'd heard about her blog already. "So. Dawson's had two breaks-ins in one week. And possibly three murders."

"Two deaths, by my count."

"Have you found May Wong yet?"

He looked away. "The break-in bit is not so unusual this time of year. Folks get hungry. A couple of years ago there was a prospector out in the bush; his claim went bust and he was starving. The guy broke into a cabin and was in the middle of stealing some bread and peanut butter when the owner came home. The intruder panicked. Shot him in the head. He killed a man for a peanut butter sandwich."

"Even two murders in a town this size in the space of a week is …"

"Doug was murdered. Marlo's death is still under investigation. And as far as we know, May is only missing."

"With all due respect, someone drove Marlo up to the Bluffs, and that someone is still unaccounted for. Plus, the pathologist pointed to marks at Marlo's throat that could not be explained by the fall. That makes it two murders. At least. More if May's been … Well. You've got a serial killer on your hands. Did you notice Doug's ear?"

Cariboo straightened in his chair. "We are exploring a number of possibilities. But do you know what I notice? And I wish I didn't have to … I notice that you were on the Bluffs the night Marlo McAdam was killed. You were also the last one to see Doug Browning alive."

"You can't seriously think …?"

"And you found Doug's body."

"You're not suggesting …?"

"I'm not suggesting anything. I'm just observing." He considered her for a moment. "However, the facts are certainly suggestive." His tone was cooler now.

"Do I need a lawyer?" Jo folded her arms, hands in armpits, searching for any last vestige of warmth.

"Did you leave Gertie's last night with Christopher Byrne?"

"Yes, and I lived to tell the tale."

"Are you sleeping with him?"

"None of your business."

"How well do you know him?"

"Why do you hate him so much? What have you got on him?"

Cariboo's bandaged fingers tightened on the arm of the sofa. "Why don't you ask him that question?" His expression was dark.

"So. May Wong is still off hunting?"

"Now that you mention it, you were also on site at the break-in at May's."

"Oh please." Jo said it with attitude, but secretly she was making her little circle chart again in her head. This time, she imagined herself in the middle, with Marlo, Doug, and May's names in circles surrounding her, with lines drawn to her name. She felt things spiralling in.

"Look, the only thing to tie these incidents together is you," Cariboo said, as if reading her mind.

"So I suppose I stole my own laptop." The dog, Justice, turned his head with a jangle of tags as Jo raised her voice.

"I'm just saying …"

"And my file on Marlo McAdam."

"He took your file?"

Jo nodded solemnly.

Cariboo's forehead creased. He looked tired suddenly. "Why didn't you say so?"

"You didn't ask about the files."

He rubbed the dark shadow of facial hair around his mouth. "Look, I've got a team here of five guys—good guys—working around the clock on this. But they are all young, junior officers trying to earn their stripes. We don't have a forensics expert. For most of the guys, this is their first homicide. We're doing a good job, by the book." He paused. Jo could see how Cariboo had advanced so quickly in the RCMP. He took his time and thought things through. He was calm under pressure. "We don't want anyone in town to panic."

"Meaning, what—that they have reason to panic? That someone in this town is on a killing spree, and no one in town can get out now that freeze-up has hit?"

"Meaning that I don't need you to create a sense of hysteria with your inflammatory articles about the RCMP handling of the investigation. It isn't helping the situation." Cariboo stood, his dark eyes flashing. *So he has read my blog, or at least knows about it.* "Meaning that I've already given you one warning about getting in the way of the investigation, and that your own involvement is being watched. Closely."

"I see," Jo said, just as Justice-the-dog lifted his heavy, grey-ing head and gave her a curious look with unseeing eyes. Justice sniffed the air a little, licked his lips, and rested his chin on thick paws again. "So, the story is, a guy breaks into the *Daily* to steal some cash … or possibly some peanut butter …" Cariboo shot her a warning look, which Jo ignored. "Doug arrives on the scene. The thief attacks Doug with a Swiss army knife, then proceeds to stran-gle him to death. Why would he do that?" She waited for Cariboo to say, "Do what?" but he refused to take the bait, allowing the silence to linger instead. "Why would he bother strangling a guy with a telephone cord when he's got a perfectly good knife, even if it is a bit small? Why not just drive the knife in one more time?"

"Exactly," Cariboo said. He had a curious expression on his face. "It's as if it were somehow important to the killer that Doug was strangled, too." He sat back down on the arm of the sofa across from her, leaning forward.

He means me. Jo swallowed.

Cariboo raised an eyebrow, his expression conflicted. A rip-ple in still waters. "It's almost as if we're supposed to think that it's the Surrey Strangler."

Jo felt something inside her icing over. "You don't really think …" Jo realized with a cold shock that she might be the RCMP's prime suspect.

"The victims of the Surrey Strangler—they had their ears mutilated, didn't they?"

Jo nodded. She didn't trust herself to speak for a moment, but Cariboo waited. "They were burned. Their ears. Then later …" Jo thought of the burning vehicle. The charred corpse. Cariboo allowed the silence settle back over the room, until she was ready. "You can't think that he's here? In Dawson?" she asked. She jostled her legs again, unable to find any heat in her body. *Was it possible?*

Cariboo frowned. "Frankly, it's difficult to know what to think. I'm focusing right now on what we're *meant* to think." He was watching Jo in that particular way of his that made Jo feel as though she were transparent.

Jo thought about the bruising at Marlo's throat.

"One more thing," Cariboo said, his brow furrowed. "If I were you, I wouldn't get involved with Christopher Byrne."

"Why not?" Jo crossed her legs and jiggled her foot, wondering if the lack of heat in the room had been strategical.

"Do you know where he was when Doug Browning was killed?" Cariboo's eyes narrowed a little.

Jo crossed her legs the other way. She was about to say that Byrne had been at home. That's where he had been headed when he dropped her at the *Daily*, before she left with Doug. Then it occurred to her that she had no proof that Byrne had actually gone back to his cabin and, as he lived alone, he wasn't likely to have an alibi. She wondered why Cariboo disliked Christopher Byrne so much. Jo thought about what Sally had said—that Byrne was a known smuggler. Jo tried to stay calm, but she had that feeling she got whenever she found a hair in her mouth. First revulsion. Then panic. "No," was all she said.

25

An antique radiator in the bathroom had been painted gold, the gilded strokes spilling over onto the wall behind. On top of the radiator perched a cherry-red radio, filling the cold room with warm strains of jazz that mingled with the beguiling scent of vanilla.

As hot water filled the peeling, claw-foot bathtub, Jo reread the letter. It was a copy of a classification statement for Claim 53 at Sourdough Creek, on Department of Fisheries and Oceans letterhead: the information that Marlo McAdam had requested before her death. Jo couldn't see any particular importance to the correspondence. After a brief salutation to Mr. Jack Grikowsky from the inspector who had visited the mine, it confirmed the mine's classification for the mining of gold. The document stated, "Claim 53 at Sourdough Creek—Classification: 4B (Defined as a tributary creek, no salmon or other species of fish present)."

Jo returned the letter to its envelope and placed it on the counter. She lifted a coffee cup full of warm whisky. Yukon Jack. Normally she wouldn't drink whisky on its own, but today it was required with only a little boiling water and a slice of lemon. She swallowed a mouthful of liquid fire. The stuff tasted like rancid honey, and she felt it burn a path clear through her digestive tract. *That's the stuff.* She turned off the tap, disrobed, and slid into the bath with a soothing squeak of skin against porcelain.

A cake of soap labelled "Wash your sins away!" rested in a wall mounted dish. *If only.* Jo picked up her dog-eared, paperback copy of *The Name of the Rose* from the edge of the tub and began to read, letting the scalding water soothe taut muscles. She spent a few peaceful moments chanting with monks, until she stumbled on a line about seeing through a glass darkly. Distracted, she put the book down, only vaguely aware that the pages were damp. She'd lit a single tea light, housed in a Mason jar on the counter. The flickering candle was somehow comforting in its persistence, if not its strength.

Jo sank deeper into the tub, sending soft curls of fog up into the chilly air. At some point, the bath had been painted a bright pink, but the paint had bubbled and was chipping away in spots. Jo took a deep breath and submerged herself in the water, willing away the images of the day: Doug lying in a pool of blood, the tangled mess of phone cord, the bloody paw prints across the floor. She opened her eyes under the water, watching her dark hair flow out around her, like a siren. Jo released her breath slowly, following the path that the bubbles made to the surface. Then the lights went out.

She sat up abruptly, sending water sloshing over the edge of the tub. Now the candle cast eerie shadows in the room as the music on the radio died. She stood up, allowing the warm water to run off her body as she reached for a towel. Her wet skin rose in bumps at the shock of cool air.

Somewhere below, on the first floor, hushed voices were arguing. A male voice said, "Did you say anything?"

"No, don't be dense." Sally.

"Do you think she suspects?" The man's voice sounded familiar.

"Of course not. Why would she? Okay, where did I just put those goddamned matches?"

"I dunno ..." It wasn't clear whether the male voice was speaking to the issue of suspicion, or whether it was referring to the location of the matches.

"She's completely clueless about most of the stuff that goes on in this town. Ah, here ..."

Jo rushed to towel off, hoping to catch the rest of the conversation. She was shivering now, but only partly from the cold.

⊸∞⊷

Sally and Christopher Byrne were sitting inches apart on the sofa when Jo arrived in the living room. "That's a good look for you," Sally said, making Jo feel suddenly self-conscious about the ratty bathrobe, towel on her head, and gooseflesh on her pale, skinny legs.

Byrne stood, as though to increase the distance between himself and Sally. "Oh hey, Jo ... didn't see you there."

"Evidently," Jo said, clutching the Mason-jar candle. "Thought you might need a light."

Sally and Byrne exchanged a look, and she felt something unsaid pass between them.

"I was just in the neighbourhood," Byrne said. "Saw the power go out and thought I'd check in on you guys." Jo studied his face, the fiery mask of new beard that framed his frown.

"Your cabin is forty-five minutes away on the Dempster Highway," Jo said.

Sally chimed in, a little too brightly, "Well. I'll just ... go ... do something fun, like read the obituary column." She took a deep breath. "Again." She sashayed off.

"You okay? I heard about Doug," Byrne said.

"Yes. I'm fine," she lied. "So, what are you really doing here?"

"Okay, I lied. Actually, I wanted to bring you something. I didn't want to say in front of Sally."

"Why not?" Jo could hear the cynicism in her voice, and thought she sounded like her father, who always made you feel like you were lying. Even when you weren't. Frank always assumed the worst in everyone. Sometimes there was just no escaping the past.

Byrne reached inside a khaki backpack. "Here," he said, holding out a burgundy leather book with gold embossing. "I thought you might enjoy these," he said.

Jo turned the book over to see the spine, which read, *The Collected Poems of Wallace Stevens.* "Oh." she said. "That's … well, thank you." Jo stared stupidly at the book, both flattered and apprehensive. She shoved one hand into the pocket of her bathrobe. "That's very kind of you." She didn't want to accept the gift, but she couldn't think of an appropriate reason not to.

Byrne nodded. "Looks like the power is out all over town. If it doesn't come back on shortly, you might want to make alternative plans. It's minus thirty or so out there already."

"Oh! No!" A surge of dread washed over her. "It's electric heating in here, isn't it?" Jo could already feel a stealthy front of cold advancing, curling around her legs like a cat.

"The town does have a backup genny, but it can take a while and it's not always a sure bet. You're welcome to come by my place. I have a wood-burning fireplace in my cabin. Well, you know that." He smiled.

"Thanks. I'll call you if I run into trouble." Jo hugged the book to her body like a shield, but refrained from inviting him to stay.

Byrne cleared his throat a little, expectantly. "It's just that I don't have a phone."

"Yes, of course. I forgot."

"Thought you might like to come back with me now." He scuffled his feet. His expression was difficult to interpret, but looked evasive somehow. Their eyes met and Jo felt a rush of panic, and something else. She glanced away.

"I'm gonna hold out for the backup genny, but thanks for coming by." Her mouth felt dry.

Byrne looked like he was about to say something, then changed his mind. He nodded and turned to leave, when there was a knock at the door. "Excuse me," Jo said, but before she had a chance to escape, Sally was there, still chewing a bit of bagel with salmon, leading Johnny Cariboo into the lounge. Cariboo was carrying a Wild & Woolly bag in one hand. "Well!" Sally said, her tone bright, "This is entertaining! I didn't know that I was going to get dinner and a show!" She took another bite of the bagel, looking expectant and amused as she glanced back and forth between Bryne and Cariboo like she was at a tennis match.

An awkward second or two passed while Cariboo registered the presence of Christopher Byrne, and vice versa. Jo could sense the tension between them. "Mr. Byrne was just leaving," Jo said to Cariboo.

Byrne smiled at Cariboo without showing any teeth, hands shoved in pockets. "Good evening," he said to Cariboo. His smile twisted a bit when he noticed the Wild & Woolly bag. Cariboo nodded without smiling. Byrne kissed Jo on the cheek as he passed. "Later," he said. Sally walked him to the door.

Jo was still holding the book, which felt like stolen goods as Cariboo eyed it suspiciously. She was reminded momentarily of Frank.

"Good book?" he asked.

"Haven't read it yet," she said, dropping it lightly onto a sideboard. "Was there something you wanted to see me about?"

Now Cariboo looked embarrassed. "I'm sorry. I didn't know you had company."

"I wasn't expecting him. Seat?" Jo motioned to a wingback, but he waved her away.

"No, this won't take long," he said. "I just wanted to say sorry, if I was hard on you today. I was just doing my job."

Jo felt her shoulders relax a little. "That's fine," she said, but knew she didn't sound convincing.

"Also, I wanted to bring you something," he said, handing her the carrier bag.

"What's this?" she said, surprised, but she was already lifting the lid off the shoe box inside. She realized with a thrill that they were a brand new pair of white, fur-lined North Face boots.

"I thought … you know. They might keep you warm," he said. When Jo didn't say anything, he added, "I noticed the boots you've been wearing aren't all that …"

She thought about her cold rubber boots with the skull-and-crossbone pattern. "What, you're not partial to pirates?"

He smirked a little. "Well, I might be."

Jo realized with a shock that Johnny Cariboo was flirting with her. She wondered whether this was some kind of good-cop-bad-cop routine, all rolled into one person. Jo found herself looking down at her grey woollen socks, embarrassed.

"I can't accept them. They must have cost you a fortune." She put the boots back in the box and attempted to hand them back to Cariboo, but he resisted. He pushed them toward her.

"Go on. It was nothing. My buddy owns Wild & Woolly. I keep an eye on the shop for him during off-season, so I was able to barter with him."

Jo's fingers closed around the boots reluctantly. "You shouldn't have. That's very kind."

"Don't worry about it." Cariboo looked relieved to have the conversation finished.

"Wait, how did you know my size?"

"Ah. My constable photographed and measured all of the footprints in the snow at May Wong's after the break-in. Yours too."

"Oh, right."

"If you need anything … if you have any problems. Well, here's my card." He handed it to her. "And I'm working late at the station if you need somewhere to stay warm this evening." There was a long, meaningful pause. "Because of the power outage, I mean."

Jo took the card. "Thanks." He looked hopeful, until she added, "But I'm fine." Jo hoped that Sally hadn't overheard their conversation. She was sure that Sally wouldn't let her live it down if she had.

26

Not long after the power blinked out in Dawson with a knowing wink and a nudge in the ribs, Jo laced up the new North Face boots Cariboo had given her and, with Sally, trudged directly to the nearest pub with a crackling good fireplace: Bombay Peggy's.

Sally might not have been Jo's first choice of drinking partner, given what she'd just overheard, but there was little choice now—unless Jo wanted to go back to the interview room. Both women needed to go somewhere to stay warm and survive, at least until Gertie's opened, or until the power came back on. *Any port in a storm.* They were headed in the same direction, and Jo wanted to ask about the conversation she'd overheard between Sally and Byrne. It was a job best done over drinks.

They leaned into the wind as they approached the building: a white, Victorian queen among inns, aptly placed on the corner of Princess and Second. According to Sally, the former brothel and bootlegging headquarters was rescued from its swampy fate when the current owner, a woman named Terra, spotted it sinking into the marsh a few years back and recognized a diamond in the rough. Terra had the sagging house dragged from the bog at the north end of town, where it had been quietly decomposing for half a century, and relocated it to Princess, restoring the structure to its former glory, if not its original purpose. Much of the original décor was maintained, including the framed black-and-white photographs of the lovelies who worked at Peggy's when it was a house of ill repute. Sally said Peg's was to die for.

On this particular Thursday evening, the mood at Peggy's was as dark as the town. Patrons were seated in small, uneasy clusters around the fireplaces, or huddled along the gleaming, walnut bar. The conversation died as Jo and Sally entered the room.

Sally held her chin high and thrust her shoulders back as she crossed to the bar and pulled out a stool for Jo. Sally dropped her white fur muff on the counter with an air of "ain't it wonderful?" and called out, "Two gold diggers." The way she said it made it sound like an introduction instead of a drink order. Jo's shoulders slouched forward a little and her chin dropped down deeper into her parka. She avoided making eye contact with the others at the bar, who gradually resumed speaking, albeit in hushed tones.

"Honestly, must you call out so much attention to yourself?" Jo said to Sally, giving the white muff a look of ridicule. "What is that, some sort of self-esteem issue?"

"What, you have a problem with my muff? You liked it well enough last night." Sally said it loudly, so that it could be overheard by the men in the general vicinity, and stroked the fur muff in a provocative way. Her smile lit her up like a fun fair. More wattage than was really necessary.

"I think you have me confused with someone else. Probably that stray husky you've been …"

"Him too," said Sally, undaunted. The men at the bar wore a dazed expression, like fish in an aquarium, their mouths falling silently open.

A bartender in a shapeless black dress brought the drinks, landing them hard enough on the bar that the liquor sloshed over the edge. "Careful, Terra," Sally said, making a little tsk-ing sound with her tongue, "don't stain my bar."

"*My* bar." Terra said it firmly and crossed her arms. She was a petite woman in her thirties, wore her sandy hair in a closely cropped, spikey style, and sported glasses with dark frames.

"For now," Sally said, lifting the martini glass for a demure sip, enjoying herself.

The woman looked crestfallen, and she left suddenly without making change for the large bill Sally had placed on the countertop.

"What was all that about?"

"Oh, nothing. Seems Terra is in a spot of trouble."

"What, financial trouble?"

"Something like that."

"But … you're not thinking of buying her out, are you?"

"Me? You can't even *begin* to imagine the things I think about."

"You make that kind of coin at Gertie's?" Jo straightened on the barstool. She already knew the answer, but hoped Sally would elaborate on how she planned to obtain the money, or perhaps had already come into it. Not a single family portrait graced the walls of their shared abode, so Jo thought it unlikely that Sally had inherited from a close relation. Jo felt she was on the verge of something, as though Dawson, the town, was finally sharing one of its little secrets.

"Of course not." Sally frowned. She fumbled in her handbag for a lipstick, which was just a shade too dark for her. The colour made her mouth look severe. Or perhaps it was the way the low, flickering candles and scarlet walls cast a strange light on the townspeople, giving them an unnatural pallor.

At that moment, if someone had told Jo that she had just stumbled into a vampire coven, she might have believed it. Dawsonites stared wanly back at her, the smoky figures leaning in to one another, whispering. Jo hoped she was imagining the dark looks aimed in her direction.

"Looks like you're not winning any popularity contests today," Sally said, following Jo's look. "That's what happens in Dawson when you attack miners."

"Do you think that's what happened to Marlo? She was going after the mine." Jo took a sip of her gold digger, which was laced with flakes of gold. Jo wondered if they were real.

"The problem is, everyone has family or friends connected with the mining industry. Peg's isn't even a mining crowd and look at it—you've stirred it up like a hornet's nest." Sally sipped her drink, a delighted expression on her face. Bits of gold sparkled in her lipstick as she lowered the glass.

Jo glanced at the townspeople around her, their fiery, inflamed expressions. Jo thought she could see something else flash in the eyes of the townspeople, too. "I think they're afraid."

"You've just suggested that someone among us, possibly right here, right now, is a monster, and has killed three people thus far. The roads out are closing. Of course they're afraid. You expect them to thank you for it?" Sally tilted her martini glass back and forth, watching the gold sparkle in the half-light. "No one is going to rest easy tonight. Everyone is second-guessing their neighbours right now."

Jo thought about that. If the town needed someone to blame for her revelation, she certainly made an easy target. "How long do you think it will take for the town genny to kick in?" Jo asked, her gaze dropping as faces turned in her direction.

"Well, I think we'd better prepare to hunker down at the bar for a good while. I remember one time it took the city forty-eight hours to get the heat back on. Temperature dropped to minus thirty-nine." She shivered, her mouth a hard, dry line of lipstick.

"What!"

"Yes. They say the outage was responsible for quite a few fall babies." Sally seemed to shudder at the thought. "Survival 101, isn't it? Take your clothes off and crawl into a sleeping bag with a friend." She raised her glass to the idea.

"Doesn't look like there'll be much of that tonight." Jo took another sip of the cool, oily tincture. It had a metallic aftertaste.

"Oh, don't sell Dawson short. The night is still young." A smile tugged at Sally's lips, revealing needle-like eye teeth. "Wait until the liquor kicks in. Anyway, some of us may not be able to go home tonight. And that's a fact. But since you've got everyone in town looking at one another like we've all got two heads, the question is: who to bunk with? Or, more to the point, who not to?"

"Yes," said Jo, thinking of the conversation she'd overheard between Sally and Byrne. *She's completely clueless about most of the stuff that goes on in this town*, Sally had said. "Speaking of which," Jo began, planning to ask Sally about what she'd overheard. A sudden sharp stab of pain in her back stopped her. She saw a flash of someone's elbow as they stumbled away, toward the bathrooms. "Hey!" Jo called out, rubbing her back as the dark parka in question reeled through a door marked "Prospectors," already gone. She turned to Sally. "Do you get the feeling that wasn't an accident?" Jo felt a rush of adrenaline. She considered going into the men's room after the guy. She wanted to. Jo slid off the barstool and stood, hands clutching the bar as a swell of ugly emotion rose in her.

Sally didn't reply. She was looking at something that had been dropped on the well-polished wooden countertop. An ordinary white envelope with Jo's name on the front. In type. Sally raised an eyebrow and put a hand on Jo's arm.

Jo picked the envelope up, considering. "It doesn't appear to be ticking."

"Don't be so sure," Sally said.

Jo hesitated for a moment, then ran her finger under the seal. Inside, there was a one-way ticket from Dawson City to Vancouver via Whitehorse, on Air North. The passenger name was listed as Josephine Silver. "Ah, fan mail," Jo said, secretly wondering if the airport had closed yet, already fantasizing about using the ticket.

Sally leaned over her shoulder, close enough that Jo could feel her breath, warm, on the back of her neck. She wasn't sure whether Sally's breach of personal space was the innocent result of curiosity, or whether the move had some kind of subtext, or what that subtext might be.

Jo had the sense that attempting to attribute meaning to anything in Dawson was like trying to look at something underwater, where the shape and size of a thing changed when you reached toward it. Jo covered what she knew was the strong profile line of her jaw, suddenly self-conscious. "Somebody sure wants to see the backside of me," she said, rushing to fill the silence.

"Yeah." said Sally. "Looks like you've got a blue ticket."

"A what?"

"Dawson has a long history of giving its undesirables free one-way passage on the next steamboat out of town. You've just been blue-ticketed."

"You're kidding me." Jo looked around her and caught the hard stares of several patrons.

"Well, you know what they say. 'The only thing worse than being talked about is not being talked about.' Something I personally couldn't stand." Sally straightened up on her barstool and smoothed out the lines in her dress.

"But … this is so unfair. I went out on a limb to protect these people by telling them the truth …" She hated the self-righteous tone of her voice, but it was true. *Wasn't it?*

"You think they feel protected?"

"They'll be safer knowing they need to watch their backs."

"People are happier being oblivious to the truth until there's something they can do about it. Now they just feel helpless. They're angry, and they want a target for their emotion."

"Now you sound like Sergeant Cariboo," Jo said. "He didn't want me to go public with the possibility that Marlo had been murdered until there was more proof. He thought that people might panic when the roads snowed in and the airport closed. Maybe he was worried they'd take the law into their own hands."

"Maybe he was right, my dear. Dawsonites do have a way of taking care of things themselves, you know. And I'm not just talking about chopping their own firewood." Sally drained the last of her gold digger.

That gave Jo an idea. A terrible idea, she knew, but she could feel it lodged somewhere inside of her, pressing her with the urgency of a small, gold key in her back pocket. She hesitated for a moment, wondering whether she could trust Sally with her secret. She had the sense that what she had heard earlier had been taken out of context, and yet … Still, she had to choose someone to trust. Jo took a quick swill of her drink, watching the flecks of gold swirling around in the funnel of glass like atoms, a little microcosm of chaos theory. She knew she was about to set something in motion, an irrevocable chain of events. But she had to know …

"So," Jo said. "I overheard Byrne asking you earlier if you think I suspect …"

Sally raised an artfully drawn eyebrow. "Oh?" Without missing a beat, she added, "And do you?"

"Yes, I do."

"What exactly *do* you suspect, my dear?" Sally's green eyes glittered. She didn't look alarmed at all. Surely if they were talking about Marlo's death and Byrne's culpability, or Sally's involvement, she would look guilty. *Unless she were truly evil.* Sally smiled, as if on cue.

"That Byrne murdered Marlo?" Jo said.

Sally laughed. "Oh! If I thought that were true for even one second, I would have something more to say to Byrnie about that, don't you think?"

"Then, what were you talking about?"

Sally was still smiling. "It was a private matter, and I've been sworn to secrecy, and if there's one thing I'm good at, it's keeping a good secret. I pride myself on loyalty. I can, however, swear to you on what little honour I have that it had nothing to do with Marlo's sad demise."

"Why can't you tell me?"

Sally shook her head, still looking amused. "You'll have to ask him, I'm afraid. It isn't my place to tell you."

It was Sally's casual, relaxed demeanour that finally convinced Jo to accept her answer. "Okay," Jo said. "I guess I trust you."

"Then you're even more foolish than you look," Sally returned, but she raised her glass to Jo before downing it.

"What bothers me—I mean aside from that fact that another person has just been murdered—is that I feel like I was getting close to something. I got the distinct impression that Doug was protecting the mine, or maybe Grikowsky."

"But why would he?" Sally said. "Editors live for stories."

"Exactly."

"I guess we'll never know."

"Yeah. Except ..."

"Except?"

Jo pulled the antique key out of her back jeans pocket and held it up for Sally to see.

27

"This is a colossally stupid idea."

"Should I point out that it was your colossally stupid idea?" Sally smiled briefly, before burying the lower part of her face into her fur coat and scarf.

"No," Jo said. "Last time the door was open."

They stood in front of the red door at the back of May Wong's house, hands deep in pockets,

"Maybe the police locked it on their way out? They would have searched her house."

"I suppose. Still. It's odd." Jo brushed away a long strand of hair, pinned to her cheek by her toque. She needed to feel like she was doing something useful with her hands. There was nothing worse to her than feeling useless.

"Looks like you stole the wrong key." Sally glanced at Jo, fine lines around her eyes spreading as she smiled, a geisha's fan unfolding.

"I didn't *steal* it." Jo's tone was a little defensive, and she knew it, which made it worse.

"Whatever."

Nothing was said for a moment. A husky, or perhaps a wolf,

cried into the night, and the sound captured some sense of great sorrow or injustice.

"What were you planning to do the last time if it was locked?" Sally smirked.

Jo glanced around the yard, in lieu of a response. She swallowed. Her mouth was somehow too dry, and still tasted like sour flakes of gold. There was a woodpile near the back of the garden.

Sally followed her look. "Ah, I see. Subtle, but effective. I like it."

"Good. Then you do it."

"Get some ovaries, Sherlock. This is your mystery. I'm just along for the ride." Sally turned up the collar of her fur coat a little higher against the gnawing cold.

Jo sucked in an icy breath of air, set her jaw firmly, and began the knee-deep trek to the log pile, silently cursing Sally. *Useless, furry eye-candy.*

The sound of crunching glass under a brand new pair of winter-white North Face boots rang out through the jagged window, across the yard, and into the night. Jo hesitated for a moment, causing a soft collision as Sally bumped into her.

"Bad place to stop!" Sally hissed.

"Sorry," Jo said, almost tripping over something dark at her feet. "Watch your step," she whispered, illuminating the frozen log with her flashlight. She hoped that the neighbours would be out, holed up somewhere with a woodstove or a fireplace, like the rest of Dawson: waiting for the power to come back on. Perhaps the outage would work in her favour. Of course, if the neighbours had a woodstove they might be home. Or they might have just gone for the police.

They padded up the staircase to the landing, where Jo paused a second time. She had the uncomfortable feeling that she was being watched.

"What?" said Sally in a hushed tone.

Jo listened for a moment, but heard only the wind. "Nothing."

Sally held the flashlight as Jo inserted the antique key into the desk drawer lock. The key turned loudly. Jo and Sally exchanged a look. Jo opened the drawer and reached inside, withdrawing a sleek, silver laptop.

"Nice machine," said Jo. "Business must be going well …"

"Yeah," said Sally. "But in the Yukon, the question is always, *which* business?"

Jo opened the notebook computer and waited a moment. A window was already open on the screen: an image of Front Street, dimly lit by streetlights, with the river behind a great, black void. A red pickup truck was crossing through the frame. "What is this?" said Jo.

Sally leaned in closer. "Town webcam. It's over the bookstore."

"Oh. So it's a live feed."

"Yeah."

"Then it looks like the power's back on. Streetlights are on." Jo felt her stomach do a little cartwheel. If the neighbours had been out, they would be on their way home now. "So … May's keeping an eye on Front Street?"

"Apparently so. Though you're not supposed to camp on that site. It overloads if too many users sit there at once."

"Yeah, it seems to have frozen."

"Like everything else in this godforsaken town." Sally said.

"You could leave."

"No way. Better to be a big fish in a small pond. And I like to be a very big fish." Sally grinned. The light from the computer screen spilled onto her from below, giving her a deranged appearance.

Another window on the screen was also open. When Jo clicked on it, an Excel spreadsheet opened, revealing columns of initials and amounts. The last few entries showed the name "Peg" and initials "JG" and "MC." "Whoa! She's doing more than keeping tabs, then."

"Blackmail?" Sally said it with a tone of admiration.

"JG could be Jack Grikowsky. But who is MC?"

Sally shook her head. "Dunno. But Peg might be for Bombay Peggy's. Could be Terra. She has certainly been short of cash recently." Sally smiled to herself.

"I wonder if May saw something on Front Street that she shouldn't have."

"Of course not. She's gone hunting, remember?"

"I wonder why she called me, then. Either she was going to put me on her client list because she knew I was out at the Bluffs, or she was going to warn me about something or someone."

"She called you?"

"The night before she disappeared. She wanted me to meet her at The Gold Digger the next day, but she never turned up."

"You have been keeping secrets." Sally sounded impressed.

"Maybe she chose the wrong person to blackmail." Jo felt inside the drawer with her hand to see if she had missed anything while Sally flashed the light around. Jo's fingers bumped something soft at the very back of the drawer, making them tingle. Jo withdrew her hand, revealing a small, velvet sack. She placed it on the desk and clenched her fist once before shoving bare, numb fingers inside, where they were met with two cold lumps of something startlingly flesh-like. She gasped and released whatever it was, still inside the bag.

"What?" Sally said, peering over Jo's shoulder. "What is it?" Jo didn't look at Sally, but could hear the edge of excitement in her voice.

"It feels like ... " Jo held her breath as she grasped the objects again and removed them. She opened her fingers. "Skin." What looked like two shrivelled brown eggs sat in the nest of her hand. "Whaddya think these are?"

Sally squinted a little as she leaned in with the flashlight. "Bear balls."

"Jesus!" Jo dropped the offending objects, shaking her naked hand as though it had been burned. "Oh!"

Sally calmly leaned over and picked up the first, then knelt down to find the second, which had rolled away on the floor.

"That's disgusting!" Jo was still wiping her hand on her clothing. "What would May be doing with them?"

Sally was on all fours under the desk with the flashlight. "Illegal trade of animal parts is big business here. Very valuable on the Chinese market. Whatever she's doing, I'd bet it's lucrative in off-season." Sally located the missing object and held it up in the beam of her flashlight for closer scrutiny. She looked pleased.

"We should get out of here before the neighbours get back." Jo stuck her hand in the desk drawer one last time and, feeling blindly until her fingers met something cool and flat. She tugged on it.

"Yes, and power or no power I'll be expected to turn up for my bar shift at Gertie's."

"I thought Gertie's had closed?" She withdrew a thick rectangle of paper from the desk, about the size of a tourist flyer.

"Only to the tourists, dear. Stays open to the locals a little longer. Care to join me?"

Jo shook her head. "I need to print out copies of the *Daily* for tomorrow and figure out something to say about Doug. Hang on ..."

"Better hope the power is back on at the house, too. Might not be on everywhere yet."

"How much time do you have before your shift?" Jo asked, holding up the thing that she'd thought was a flyer. The beam of the flashlight illuminated a cheerful pop of blue and orange: a ticket that read, "Air North Gift Certificate" across the front.

"Holy crap—May was blue-ticketed too?"

Jo opened the ticket. "Dawson to Fairbanks. One way."

"Sweet Jesus."

"How much do you want to bet that Marlo received one too?"

"But that means you're ..." Sally said.

"Yes." Jo felt something inside her swan-dive at the thought. "I think we'd better swing by the airport and ask some hard questions about who has been buying these things." Jo returned the other items to the drawer, including the key. Then she folded the air ticket in half and tucked it into the pocket of her parka, where it seemed to hold some kind of secret promise.

28

Snow drifted across an abandoned runway like tumbleweed. Dawson City's airport terminal, a squat, utilitarian building that looked beaten down by sky and weather, had been locked up and abandoned to the elements. A low, slouchy peak over the front doors expressed apathy, like rounded shoulders. The white-domed outbuildings and orange sheds, home to the old Hawker Siddeley air fleet, were silent. Jo pressed her nose against cold glass, peering at the unmanned ticket desk. "Closed," she said, wincing at her own penchant for stating the obvious.

"Mmm," said Sally. "That's probably for the best, since Sergeant Cariboo told you not to leave town."

"I wasn't actually going to leave. I just wanted to see if I could find out who bought the tickets." Her breath fogged up the window, forcing her to step back.

"Are you sure about that?"

Not entirely. "Of course."

"I hope so." Sally's frosted lips were pursed.

They turned away from the one-room terminal and watched the blowing snow in silence for a moment. Jo wasn't sure that she would have actually left, that she could have left without knowing what had happened to Marlo McAdam, Doug Browning, and May Wong, but she was experiencing a strong urge for self-preservation, especially since she had just been blue-ticketed. She was also bothered by the knowledge that everyone in town would be talking about her right now because of her blog. The whole point of coming to the North had been to escape all that. Now, not only had she landed back in the public eye, she was also trapped for the winter in this remote, isolated community with someone who in all probability was seeking to harm her.

Jo reached inside her parka and withdrew the white envelope that had been dropped on the bar at Bombay Peggy's. She removed the ticket. The Air North logo was a compass, a nautical image that made Jo feel somehow adrift at sea in an ocean of snow. The northern point of the compass formed a dagger, which impaled the "N" in "North": ominous, under the circumstances. The certificate provided one-way, open-ended travel, listing Josephine Silver as the passenger, but gave no information as to a credit card number or the purchaser of the ticket. Most likely it had been paid for in cash.

"So if the airport is closed, how was I supposed to use the ticket?" Jo held it up for Sally to see.

"Maybe they didn't know when the airport would close. In fact, they couldn't have known; it's dependent on the weather. Must have been open when they paid for the ticket."

"Or maybe the ticket was never intended for usage. Maybe it was just a message. It may not even be a real ticket."

"A message meaning what?" Sally narrowed her eyes.

"I don't know," Jo said. Initially, she had just assumed that the ticket had been purchased by an irate miner who disliked her exposé on placer mining. Now she wondered whether the ticket might be interpreted in some other way. And might have been sent by someone else. "An invitation?" Jo eyed Sally.

"An invitation? What kind of an invitation? To join the mile-high club?" Sally flashed her teeth in a demonic smile. "One time, when I was on a flight to Las Vegas ..."

"I don't even want to know." Jo waved the story away with her hand, but in the back of her mind she was speculating about how Sally had enough money for wild trips to Las Vegas.

"Back when they still gave out those blue blankets and free drinks ..."

"Stop!" She turned her back on Sally and began to walk around to the other side of the building, where Jo thought she could see smoke. On the way, she had the disturbing feeling that she was getting it all wrong. The lone airline ticket from Dawson City to Whitehorse was just one more clue that she couldn't decipher, or had already misinterpreted.

In detective stories, the detective hero is always one step ahead of the criminals and two steps ahead of the law. Here, the heroes and criminals all blurred together, and no matter how hard Jo worked, she was always one step behind the town.

An invitation. An invitation to come to the airport alone, with only Sally to drive her. Perhaps the recipient of the ticket was never intended to leave. Sally could have slipped the envelope from her fur muff and put it on the bar when Jo was distracted by the elbow to her back. Sally earned more money than a part-time bartender and dancer should ... What did she have on the owner of Bombay Peggy's? May Wong had been into blackmail. Were they in league? Sally hunted, owned a gun, and was quick to recognize illegal animal parts like the bear ... bits ... at May's house. Then there was the conversation she'd overheard between Byrne and Sally. *Do you think she suspects?* Jo turned slowly to look at Sally, while fighting to keep her breathing calm and her face blank. Sally's lips framed a wicked smile.

Jo would never make it back to the truck, she knew, even as the shot rang through the frozen landscape. She sprinted forward, away from Sally, crunching and sliding. As she rounded the corner, Jo could make out the source of the smoke now: an ugly black shape set in sharp relief against the snow. The burned-out skeleton of a vehicle, still smoking. "No," Jo said, stopping in the snow. The world seemed to fall away from her then. Her feet in her new boots looked oddly distant. There was a dark crumpled mound inside the car. Jo knew what the hideous thing was. She put a hand over her mouth, choking back bile and fear. May Wong.

A second shot exploded nearby, causing a flurry of wings and the sharp accusations of ravens on the airport roof. Jo felt a yank on the sleeve of her parka. Sally had caught up to her and was attempting to drag Jo away from the wreckage. "Get back to Bettie!" With that, Sally made an awkward high-heeled dash to the relative safety of the pink Chevy pickup.

Stunned to find that Sally was not the shooter, Jo hesitated a moment before following, her head full of tangled plots, wary that Sally might be in league with the killer. Yet she could see no other way forward. She ran after Sally.

Sally was throwing Bettie in gear before Jo had even shut the door. "What the …?" Jo said, thrusting a hand to the ceiling to stop herself from bumping her head as they hurtled forward, over a drift. Sally cranked the wheel.

"Someone out there is thinking murderous thoughts. Time to leave this party."

Jo was still bouncing wildly. "But then … you're not the killer? You didn't have anything to do with that … in the parking lot?"

"Me?" Sally threw her an incredulous look. "Why would I want to kill Marlo or May?"

"And Doug Browning."

Sally waved her hand in the air, dismissively. "Oh, well, everyone wanted to kill *him*, dear. Some people just make you want to kill them."

Jo glanced over her shoulder to see if anyone was following them, but the parking lot was empty and the woods that encircled them were silent.

"But why you'd think I had it in for May and Marlo, I don't know." Sally shifted in her seat as she glanced at Jo. Bettie lost traction for a moment on a patch of ice, causing Jo to suck in her breath. The truck recovered. "Relax!" Sally snapped.

"Relax? I dunno, you seem to know a lot about illegal trade of animal parts and you do a fair bit of hunting. And, like May Wong, you've been running at least one little business on the side … something quite profitable." Jo was keeping one hand on the ceiling to help keep her balance.

"One? Please. Give me more credit than that."

"Blackmail, or something like that. What have you got on the owner of Bombay Peggy's? Were you moving in on May's territory?"

Sally's gaze shifted briefly back to Jo before returning to the road. She looked less self-assured now. "I won't deny that I've always wanted Peggy's. Terra wasn't born here, and Dawsonites don't like 'The Old Whorehouse' being run by an outsider. Besides, Terra is entirely too frumpy and boring for Peggy's. Peg's is our jewel, and I will make her shine. What's required is someone with a little imagination … a little style."

"So Peg's is to die for. That's what you said."

"Absolutely. But that doesn't mean I'd kill for her."

"Were you and May partners?"

"I didn't kill May Wong," Sally said, stiffly. "May was useful to me. She'd buy anything I happened to shoot or happened to make, no questions asked. But I have no idea what happened to her. And

I'm sorry she's gone. May was all right." Sally looked sombre for a moment. "I think we lost him." She glanced in the rearview mirror. There were no headlights to be seen there.

Jo's cheeks still felt hot. Her heart was accelerating along with the truck, and she wondered whether anyone was following them, and whether Sally was telling the truth. It felt like the truth, mostly. Sally slid forward on the pink leather seat. Thick lines of snow-covered pine flashed by. Sally's thin lips were pinched together and her lip liner had smeared. Jo still suspected that Sally was keeping something back. Something important. "What about Marlo?" Jo asked.

Sally turned to her. "What about her?"

"Did Byrne kill Marlo?"

Sally's features relaxed and she laughed. "Are you still all worked up about that little chat you overheard? You're going to laugh when Byrne tells you. It's nothing."

Jo's temper pulsed brightly and she felt a rush of heat. "Yes, I'm goddamned worked up about it. Someone murdered Marlo, and Doug, and I'd be willing to bet anything that was May Wong back in that sick bit of barbeque." Jo fought to slow her breathing. "Plus, I've got the next victim-ticket—and someone back there was taking potshots at me. Not to mention, Sergeant Cariboo seems to be labouring under the impression that I might somehow be involved. So yeah, I'm upset. It isn't 'nothing' to me."

Sally waved Jo's concerns away. "Don't worry about Cariboo. He's a pussycat."

"Only if you're a cougar," Jo said.

Sally straightened up in her seat, lifting her chin. "Then maybe you should be one. If you ask me, you could use a good ..."

"Did. Byrne. Kill. McAdam? What was he afraid I might suspect?" Jo felt her ears burning.

Sally looked irritated. "You know, you're making me want a good stiff drink. I truly have no idea who killed Marlo McAdam, but I doubt very much that it was Byrnie. If you have something you want to ask him about what happened the night you"—she paused, raising her eyebrows—"conveniently lost your memory, then you can ask him yourself."

"What was he so afraid that I'd find out?"

"He swore me to secrecy. And I always keep my word."

Jo snorted. "Oh, so you're the moral type now, are you?"

Sally looked amused. "Pot? Kettle?"

"Fuck you," said Jo.

"The pleasure would be all mine," said Sally.

29

A bright red light blinked at the top of the camera, like a hot, all-seeing, all-knowing eye. The power had returned to Dawson.

This was not the casual interview room where Jo had been before; there were no worn sofas and easy chairs here. The walls were a stark white, and the only furniture consisted of straight-backed chairs. Jo shifted uneasily in her seat, cradling a steaming cup of black coffee with both hands. The warmth of the porcelain mug was only somewhat comforting. The solemn-faced constable, the one called Scott, adjusted the focus ring and read out the time of the interview.

"So, let's go over it again," Sergeant Cariboo said, scraping a chair across the floor, positioning it uncomfortably close to Jo. He sat facing her, knees spread wide, expression stern. "What were you doing at the airport?"

Jo avoided his eyes. "Like I said, someone slipped me an airline ticket when I was at Bombay Peggy's. I wanted to go to the airport to see if I could find out who had purchased it."

"You didn't get a look at who left it on the bar?"

"No. Someone elbowed me in the back, so I turned to see who had done it. When I turned back, the envelope was on the bar. I didn't see who had left the envelope or who had struck me. Might have been an accident, except for the envelope. I saw someone heading for the bathroom, but it didn't look like anyone I knew and I could only see him from behind."

"But you could see that it was a male?"

"I thought so, and the person disappeared into the men's room."

Cariboo looked skeptical. "What time did you leave Peg's?"

"Time?" she repeated.

"Yes. What time?" He leaned in closer.

Jo dipped her head to take a sip of the coffee while she thought. "Hard to say." *Technically true. It was very hard to say.* "Might have been around ten." *Well it might have been. Though it wasn't.*

Cariboo frowned. "Are you saying you don't remember? And you don't remember the events of Sunday evening, when Marlo McAdam was murdered?"

"So it is murder now, is it? For Marlo, I mean?" Jo took another sip of the coffee. Artificial sweetener.

"Where were you last night after Peg's, before the airport?"

Jo's heart stuttered a little. "Sorry?"

"Did you go directly from Bombay Peggy's to the airport?" He was leaning so close to her now that she could almost feel the warmth of him. There was an intensity about Johnny Cariboo that made it difficult to meet his eyes. She found herself not wanting to lie to him—in the face of that earnest expression he was making—but she could hardly tell him the truth. She hesitated. Jo could tell that he knew something about where she was last night and what she was doing.

"Am I being accused of something?"

"We have a witness who identified you entering May Wong's home last night."

Jo stared at him. She was beginning to feel very warm.

"What were you doing there?" His eyes were such a deep shade of brown, they were almost obsidian.

Jo looked away, glancing at the camera. The operator lifted his head, as though waiting for a response, but none followed.

Cariboo ran a hand through his black, spikey hair. "Look. The first body turned up within days of your arrival. You found the next two bodies. Are you saying that's a coincidence?"

"You're not serious." *Was he?* She had sudden flashbacks to old films she had seen. Westerns mostly, concerning the fate of outsiders in small towns. *You're not from around here, are you, boy?* But some small part of her also felt something else. Doubt, perhaps. The strangulation marks. The escalating violence. Setting the later victims on fire inside their cars. The Surrey Strangler. *Sally knew about that. So did Doug. Who else in Dawson knew?*

"You were on the Bluffs the night Marlo McAdam died." Cariboo was watching her closely.

… *Me?* Jo could feel cold patches developing under her arms, but she held his look. "I'd like my lawyer present for any further questioning."

"How well do you know Christopher Byrne?"

Jo flinched despite herself and felt her shoulders tense. "Maybe you didn't hear me. I said I'd like my lawyer."

"Christopher Byrne and Marlo McAdam were lovers. She broke it off. That gives him a motive," Cariboo said.

Jo crossed her arms in front of her body and lifted her chin a little. "It doesn't give me one." *She* broke it off? Hadn't she heard it the other way around? Had Byrne lied, or had Marlo, and what did that mean?

Cariboo shrugged. "You needed a story. You'd fallen out of grace with the public in Vancouver. Maybe you thought one good story would get you out of Dawson, get you back where you belonged."

Jo waved a hand. "Speculation."

Cariboo's expression was closed. "By all accounts, you'd had too much to drink."

"If having too much to drink were a crime, half of Dawson would be locked up by now." She thought she heard the camera operator snigger a little. Cariboo shot him a stern look.

"How badly did you want a story? Badly enough to create your own? Badly enough to help Byrne?"

There was a long silence, which Jo restrained herself from breaking. Cariboo blinked, but refused to look away. Jo averted her gaze, then stared down at her feet. At the boots he had given her.

"Maybe you wanted to be back in the papers again?" He smiled knowingly. "Maybe you like being in the spotlight?"

Jo felt a rush of blood to her cheeks. "Lawyer," she said, emphatically. It was a Mexican standoff in Dawson. She raised her chin.

Cariboo sighed, turned to his colleague behind the camera, and said, "Book her." He turned back to Jo. "Looks like you'll make the headlines again after all." It was difficult to tell whether he meant it or not. He glanced at her North Face boots, then didn't meet her eyes again.

There was a knock at the door. A sandy-haired officer in a black RCMP parka leaned into the room. Fresh snow dusted his shoulders, catching the light. "Johnny? Got a minute?"

Johnny Cariboo stood up and announced that the interview had ended. The constable behind the camera hit a button on the video recorder and the bright red eye faded away.

Jo shifted on the metal cot, leaning uncomfortably against a cold wall. She fought to stay calm. She'd been sifting through her memory of the night Marlo had died. She vaguely remembered getting into Byrne's truck, and had blurry memories of the drive ... somewhere. She just couldn't remember much in any detail after that. When she thought about it, she remembered sliding out of the truck and the wind hitting her hard in the chest, making her gasp ... Byrne putting his arm around her ... The problem was, she couldn't say for sure whether that was on the Bluffs or in the parking area behind Sally's. She had vague flashes of staggering into furniture at Sally's ... she and Byrne laughing ...

In reality, she could have passed out cold anytime during the ride home and Byrne could have made up the story about looking at the northern lights. The RCMP suspected his involvement in Marlo's death, and, in Jo's experience, the police often knew the truth before it could be proven. Sally had said that Christopher Byrne had been involved in some kind of criminal activity in the past involving smuggling. Still, it didn't feel right. Jo might not be ready to trust Christopher Byrne, but she had to admit that she did like him. She found it hard to believe that he could be responsible for harming anyone.

Who else had motive or opportunity? There was Jack Grikowsky, who managed May Wong's mine. He was hiding something, and Jo felt certain that he had something on Doug Browning. If Grikowsky were double mining for gold and uranium at the same time and Marlo had discovered the secret, she may have threatened to expose him. He left Gertie's early and had no alibi the night Marlo died.

Still, there was the problem of the Geiger counter. Doug's killer hadn't thought it important enough to take with him. Or her. It occurred to Jo that Sally knew about her past, and she'd had the opportunity to drop the envelope containing the blue ticket on the bar. Sally wanted to buy Bombay Peggy's and was willing to do almost anything to get it. Jo had caught her up to something in the kitchen—she wasn't sure what, exactly. It looked like Sally had been making artificial caviar. Frank had once told Jo about the spherification process used to trick caviar consumers in Chinatown into spending their money on expensive junk. She wasn't sure how this might involve Marlo or May, though. Jo thought about the photograph of Sally and Byrne that she'd found in Old Bettie. Was Sally in love with Byrne? Had Marlo gotten in the way?

Then there was Peter Wright, and the way his face had fallen when Jo had said she had questions about public accountability. Jo pictured the mayor's face the first time she had seen him, the beads of sweat on his forehead as the roulette wheel spun. He'd been smiling, but he looked feverish. He'd also looked distraught when May Wong had asked him about the town's budget. Jo sat up stiffly on the cot. *Of course.* Peter Wright was a gambler in charge of public funds. His office was across the hall from Marlo's. MC. The intials in May's blackmail ledger. *Meter Cheater.* He'd told Jo that he'd been at Gertie's until closing on Sunday night. He'd lied.

Jo had to free herself to learn the truth about what was going on in Dawson. She glanced around. The cell was surprisingly clean, to the point of sterility, but the window was just a small glass rectangle near the ceiling. The stainless-steel sink and toilet in the corner shone dully. None of the cells she'd seen at Frank's station in Vancouver had looked like this. *Frank.* She knew that she'd be permitted to make a phone call shortly, and that she'd have to call him. He was the only person who could help her. He'd know what to do, but *damn*, she'd never hear the end of it at family dinners. She'd have to stay in the North forever just to avoid a meal with him. Would he even be able to scratch together enough to bail her out? On a cop's pension? She doubted it. She could just imagine the headlines. "Shamed Journalist Questioned in Murder Investigation." Or, "Cop's Daughter Arrested in Triple Murder Investigation." But surely they wouldn't be able to make the charges stick? She'd had nothing to do with Doug's death. With any of their deaths. Jo felt a swell of panic and self-doubt. The RCMP suspected that Jo was reinventing the Strangler story to resurrect her career. And Cariboo had said that there'd been a witness to Jo breaking into May's home. Jo could be prosecuted successfully for that, and would have a criminal record. And Frank, she now remembered, had sworn that if she ever got into trouble with the law, she'd be on her own.

There was a pitiful sound then, the squeak of wet boots on cold floors. Someone was coming. Jo lifted her head and tried not to feel too hopeful. She operated on a strict policy of optimistic pessimism. Less chance of disappointment if you kept expectations low.

"Ms. Silver?" It was the constable called Scott, who had taped her interview and read out her rights. He was green enough that his face still communicated a willingness to please, a youthful certainty that all disasters could be happily resolved by the end credits. It hurt something inside Jo to look directly at that much naïveté, so she turned away as he said, "You can make your phone call now."

The telephone made a hollow, desolate sound as it rang almost two thousand miles away. Constable Scott looked embarrassed as Jo muttered, "C'mon, pick up …" She wondered what would happen if no one answered her one call, and whether she'd get another. *C'mon old man* … She broke her own rule and felt a rush of hope as the line made a clicking sound.

"This is Frank."

"Frank! It's me. I need some help … And I need that water analysis …"

"… I'm not here right now. Or maybe I am, and I'm just sitting on my couch in my skivvies watching reruns of *Hawaii Five-0*. Either way, leave me a message, maybe I'll get back to you. Hate these damn things." A high-pitched sound added insult to injury. *Beeeep!*

30

Something was not quite right. The woman walking in the snow had her head down, long tendrils of hair waving in the wind, obscuring her face. She wore an ankle-length fur coat and white Timberland boots trimmed with rabbit fur. With each step, the boots made a crunching sound, yet left no impression in the snow.

The wind screamed across the barren landscape, sending a chill through Jo, yet the approaching figure wore no gloves. The fingers were blue. The sharp air carried the scent of smoke and burning flesh, though no fire was visible. Still, this did not feel like that dream. It was all wrong. When the fur-clad woman finally lifted her chin, a gust of wind scattered the hair from her face, the face of another dead woman. May Wong.

There was a strange sound then, like metal bones rattling. Jo started, and was conscious of the fact that she was lying in a horizontal position, somewhere quite hard and cold. Sharp footsteps approached in what sounded like an empty, indoor space. She opened her eyes, feeling shaky and cotton-mouthed.

Constable Scott jangled a key ring, searching for the right thing to say as well as the correct key. Jo thought he must have seen her waking up. She took advantage of his silence to distance herself from the dream. Her usual nightmares were much more passive: the corpse in question had always had the good manners not to move about or physically threaten her. The tone of her recurring dream had always been one of quiet accusation. This was different. It felt urgent. Jo stretched, feeling the knotted muscles in her back, and felt thankful for the pinch of cold that reminded her that she was in the here and now.

Scott chose to ignore anything she might have said in her sleep. Jo was not unappreciative of this small kindness. "Your bail's been posted," was all that he said.

"What?" The cell door slid open with a rattling finality. She wondered if Frank had posted bail, but it seemed unlikely. "By who?" She caught herself wanting to correct the question to make it "By whom?", but decided to cut herself some slack for a change.

"That dancer, I believe."

No name. Just "that dancer." But it was enough information.

Jo stood, taking a moment to massage a muscle at the back of her neck.

"But Sergeant Cariboo said to tell you not to leave town," he added.

Jo laughed. A hearty, earnest sound that resonated in the small, empty room.

Sally was waiting in the reception area, legs crossed, wearing a full-length fur and suspiciously thin leather gloves. She stood as Jo entered. "Enjoy the new digs?"

"Much cleaner than your house, actually."

"But not nearly as stylish, my dear." Sally looked a little worse for the wear, as though she'd been up all night. Jo avoided following through on that particular thought.

"Thanks for the ... um ..."

Sally waved her comment away. "Forget it."

"I'll pay you back."

"Don't bother. You'd be paying back half the town. Anyway, most of them owed me in one way or another." Sally smoothed the wrinkles in her curve-hugging pencil skirt before doing up the buttons on the luxurious coat.

"What?"

"I took up a collection at the bar."

"You what?"

"Have you had your hearing checked recently? You're repeating yourself, dear."

"So everyone knows?"

"Uh-huh. This is Dawson, pretty lady."

"So, no secrets."

"Oh, there are plenty of those. Haven't you learned anything yet?"

"No," said Jo. And she meant it. Sally took Jo by the arm and steered her toward the door.

<hr />

The front cover of the *Dawson Daily* on Friday morning read, "KILLER CLAIMS THIRD VICTIM." The subheading followed up with "Dawson's Season of Darkness." Jo burned through numerous ink cartridges printing the black cover and photos of Marlo, Doug, and May on the front page.

Jo's first edition at the helm of the *Dawson Daily* may have been thin, but it was packed with controversial content. Now, no one could doubt that a serial killer was on the loose in Dawson, just as freeze-up was upon them. Jo also drew Claim 53 at Sourdough Creek into her editorial spotlight with the observation that at least two of the victims were connected to the mine: May Wong had been the owner and Marlo McAdam had been investigating the mine at the time of her death. Jo noted that she herself had received a death threat and a dreaded "blue ticket" after making inquiries about the mine. She added an article on the ecological hazards of placer mining ("Dawson's Silent Killer"). Finally, there was a story ("The Big Freeze") on ferry, road, and airport closures, paired with severe weather forecasts. *Dawson can consider itself warned.*

While Jo did report that the remains of a person thought to be May Wong had been found in the charred wreckage of her SUV, she chose not to mention the parallels to the Surrey Strangler case. It was difficult to say why she'd made this choice. Something about it felt wrong, though Jo was deeply troubled by the similarities to the Strangler's pattern: firstly the strangulation, then the mutilation of the ear and escalating violence to the corpse, and finally, the last body set alight in a vehicle. *Had he come back? Was he in the North?* Jo pushed the thought away.

Rather than writing a memorial to the three victims herself, Jo called on Dawsonites to submit their own photographs and stories about Marlo McAdam, Doug Browning, and May Wong for the next edition of the paper, to help the community mourn the loss of its members. Jo finished updating the content of her blog to match the cover of the *Daily* just as the last page of the print edition slid off the printer. With a slight twinge of guilt, she swung the stack of Doug's version of the *Daily* toward the recycling area. Right next to Marshall-the-guinea-pig's cage.

Jo took a deep breath of winter air as she dropped her stack of newspapers at the General Store. They made a satisfying *shlep* sound on the counter as they were deposited, turning woolly heads. Next, she delivered copies to the Bonanza Market on Second Ave, the Bonanza Esso gas bar, each hotel, the liquor store on Third, and the lounge at Bombay Peggy's. She wound up at the beer parlour called The Snake Pit, at the Westminster Hotel, in time for morning Irish coffee. It was still dark outside.

At The Pit, the stack of newspapers disappeared by the time her coffee was poured, and the smoky room hummed with gossip as people read the paper with astonished expressions. Jo took a sip of her morning cuppa, closed her eyes and tipped her head to her right shoulder to stretch a spasming muscle in her neck. A woman at the far end of the room began sobbing.

Jo looked up. The woman was a brunette in her late thirties with lank hair and cow eyes. Her bottom lip was quivering. The newspaper (such as it was) shook in the woman's hands and she was muttering something that sounded like, "It's too late … it's too late …"

"Shhh … Shhh …" The man next to the crying woman rubbed her back. "It's all right," he said, but he glared at Jo beneath the visor of his baseball cap.

"It's too late to get out," the woman cried. "He'll kill us all, won't he? It's too late."

"Geez, might not be a he," the man said. "Might be a she, eh? Someone who would kill for a good story. Someone who knew just how to leave the victims to tell a particular story." The man in the baseball hat was still staring at Jo.

The Surrey Strangler. The story with no end. It felt to Jo as though she were being forced to repeat the same torturous experience. Prometheus, destined to be devoured by the same winged horror, day after day. Something tightened inside her, but she stood and said, "Sir, if I wanted you dead, you'd know about it." She let a few coins from her pocket clatter to the table.

"That was a death threat!" the woman shrieked. "Did you hear that? She's crazy! Why hasn't she been locked up yet?"

Jo pointed her new North Face boots in the direction of the door.

31

Jo followed the mayor's receptionist into his office and accepted a seat in an over-stuffed chair. "Peter's not in yet, but he's not likely to be long. I'm sure he won't mind if you wait for him here. Help yourself to the biscuits in the tin. God knows Peter doesn't need them." The woman rolled her large eyes. She wore a put-upon expression on her long face.

Inside the tartan tin, Jo discovered a stash of homemade Nanaimo bars, probably the work of Mabel. She glanced around the room as the cloying combination of chocolate and custard cream warmed her mouth. Peter's assistant had left the door ajar, and Jo leaned into the hallway to make sure that no one was around. The corridor was empty.

Peter's desk was home to an archaic computer, a chipped coffee cup full of pens and a letter opener, a plastic in-tray, and an out-tray. Several pieces of mail rested unopened in the tray. Jo flipped through them, glancing at the door for any sign of Peter. A letter from a government office in Whitehorse, something from the Yukon Hunting Association, and what looked like a bill. Jo picked up the bill, with a quick look over her shoulder. She held it up to the light to attempt see through it, but the envelope was too dense. Jo held it in her hand, as though weighing the importance of it, then grabbed the letter opener and slid it under the seal. The tearing sound made her flinch.

The letter expressed concerns that the holder of a credit card in the name of City of Dawson had exceeded his limit. An attached summary detailed cash advances and expenditures that amounted to hundreds of thousands of dollars. The letter was addressed to Peter Wright.

Approaching footsteps rang out in the cold corridor in time for Jo to fold up the letter and return it to the envelope, but there was not enough time to solve the problem of the broken seal on the letter. Jo leaned forward toward the in-tray, then changed her mind and unzipped her shoulder bag. She was just depositing the letter into her bag when the mayor entered the room. Peter froze when he saw the white corner of an envelope disappearing into her bag, then glanced at the in-tray.

"Good morning," Jo said with a joviality that sounded forced.

Peter Wright stood in the doorway for a moment, his massive figure blocking the frame. "Morning," he said with an uneasy smile, his eyes darting back to the tray and then her handbag. There was an awkward pause before he turned and pushed the door heavily shut. "Now then ..." he said. "What can I do you fer? You're up with the birds." In fact, it was after nine, but the sun had become increasingly reluctant to rise above its low bed of flannel clouds each morning. Night was overtaking Dawson City as winter closed in.

Jo cleared her throat. "Well," she said, debating whether to flee with the letter or make certain that she was correct in her theory that both Marlo and May had discovered the mayor's secret. Marlo's office was directly across the hall, so she could have easily stumbled across the information if she, like Jo, had been waiting in Peter's office to see him. *But May?* "Actually, I wondered how well you knew May Wong." Jo wondered again whether the "MC" in May's ledger stood for "Meter Cheater."

Peter blinked, but recovered smoothly. "Do sit down," he gestured toward the cosy visitor's chair and Jo sank slowly back into it, heart thundering so loudly that she was sure the mayor could hear it, too. Peter strode around to the far side of the desk and sat down. He glanced at the door. "May Wong ... Can't say I knew her very well." He offered Jo the biscuit tin but she waved it away. She was about to say that she'd already had one, then decided against it.

"She was at the town meeting on Monday, before she disappeared."

"Yes," the mayor said. "She was."

"She asked you whether the town's budget was balanced, didn't she?"

"Yes," the mayor's smile faltered a little. "She was on the board for Dawson businesses. She owned a shop, you know— The Gold Digger."

"Yes," Jo said, but waited for him to continue.

"She was always very involved in town matters. Shame about what happened." He shook his head. "A great loss to the community." Somehow he managed to look sincere.

Jo shivered. She shoved her hands into her armpits for warmth, then thought the better of it—just in case she needed to seize a weapon. She kept an eye on the letter opener. Peter followed her look. "And were they?"

The slightest flicker of something in the mayor's eyes at this. "What?"

"The books. Were they balanced?"

"Yes, I told her so. At the meeting. We've had a very good year." The mayor shifted a little in his seat.

"I see," said Jo. "Well, that is good news." Peter seemed to relax for a moment. "Did Marlo ask you the same question?"

"What?" The mayor stood up. "What exactly are you driving at, Ms. Silver?" But it was too late. Jo could see that the mayor knew exactly where she was going.

"I'm wondering whether Marlo also asked you about Dawson's books before she died. Whether she questioned any … expenses."

"Of course not. Now, if you'll excuse me, I'm a busy man."

"Yes, of course," said Jo, standing up. Peter Wright was a large man, and in easy reach of the letter opener on his desk. Jo thought of the stab wounds on Doug's body. As Peter picked up the letter opener, Jo began backing away, afraid to take her eyes off of him. "Thank you for your time." She grabbed the door handle and opened the door quickly.

When Jo turned to look back at the mayor, he was sliding the long blade under the seal of one of the envelopes, splitting it open as easily as skin.

32

The day was bright, and the snow outside sparkled and winked. Inside, the waiting area of the RCMP office on Front Street had a lived-in feel, not due solely to the worn furniture, but also owing something to the scent of aftershave and perspiration that permeated the room. The bulletin board was tacked sparsely with posters: Wanted in connection with a hit and run snowmobile incident. Wanted for involvement in brawl at Drunken Goat Taverna; clobbered victim with bar stool. Wanted; suspected of breaking and entering/theft of 26L Canadian Club Whisky (10 year reserve).

Jo left her toque on but unzipped her parka a little. She had not expected or wanted to return so soon, but she had little choice. If Peter Wright had killed three people in town, she had to see Johnny Cariboo.

She barely had time to wipe her new boots before the sandy-haired officer had retrieved Sergeant Cariboo from the depths of the building. Cariboo looked surprised to see her. "Ms. Silver," he said. "C'mon in." Jo wondered whether the formality indicated a coolness toward her, but when he opened a door for her, it was to the casual lounge and not the interview room.

Jo took up her previous position on a tweed chair. "We have to stop meeting like this," she said.

Cariboo smiled a little. "Look, about that. I'm sorry for holding you, but I had no choice. I was just doing my job." He toyed a little with the tape on his knuckles that hid his tattoos, as though he wished he could remove it. "I hope you can understand."

"Yes, well," she said. "I do understand. My dad is a cop."

Cariboo gave her a long look. "Then you should know that you can trust me."

"I do," said Jo. There was something about him that made her wish she wouldn't say what she was about to. "About as much as you trust me." Cariboo looked away.

The silence between them was like a skin of ice forming. Jo broke it first with, "Or about as much as I trust anyone, if you want to know the truth."

He cocked his head a little and ran his hand over dark stubble on his chin. "At some point, you have to trust someone again." Jo looked away.

"There's something I have to talk to you about. Someone, really."

"Okay," said Cariboo. "Can I tape the conversation?"

"I'd rather you didn't. Not yet."

"I see," he said, but didn't object or ask why. Jo was thankful for this.

"Because I can't give you all the information without exposing someone else." Cariboo raised an eyebrow. "I'll get to the point. I think you should look at Peter Wright."

"The mayor," Cariboo said.

"Exactly."

"Might be nice if I had a little more to go on?"

"Town finances. Specifically, the town credit card," Jo said.

"And you can't tell me more …"

"No," she said briskly. "Now you're going to have to trust me." Johnny Cariboo nodded. "Okay."

Jo stood to leave, a little relieved that he wasn't stopping her. She'd worried about this moment. "By the way," Jo said. He lifted his chin. There was something hopeful about his countenance. Jo had planned to ask him about Alice Wolfe, about what had happened to her and whether there could be a connection to what was happening now, but she saw that the timing was all wrong. "No," she said. "It's nothing."

He looked somehow disappointed, and she wondered if she had made a mistake, but the moment passed.

"Josephine!" He called to her when she had a hand on the door handle. Her heart jumped, fearing that he would stop her from leaving. "Ms. Silver," he corrected himself. "I shouldn't tell you this, but …" he licked his lips, thinking. "Off the record. We've just brought someone into custody. Someone else."

Jo thought of Christopher Byrne, and she didn't like how she felt when she thought of him in the same cell she'd just been in. "Who?"

33

A sound like a shotgun startled the patrons of the Sourtoe Saloon in the hotel aptly named "The Downtown Hotel." A woman squealed.

As the bartender poured something sparkling, nervous laughter bubbled over like golden liquid in a spotty rock glass. People were in the mood to celebrate as word spread of the arrest of Jack Grikowsky. It seemed their problems were over.

By the third drink, Jo had almost relaxed, and Sally was well on her way. "But what was May blackmailing Grikowsky for?" Jo said.

"Don't know, but the police must have something on him, or they wouldn't be able to take him in." Sally was in the middle of reattaching a diamond to the top of a precisely manicured nail. She held it up to the light with a gleeful expression as the diamond winked in the light.

"But if the killer were Grikowsky, why did he make the bodies look like victims of the Surrey Strangler?"

"To distract police? Maybe he wanted police to think it was you," Sally said. "And it worked—god knows I don't trust you." Sally gave Jo a suspicious look. "In fact, I still have my eye on you."

"How did he even know about that story? In fact, how did you know about it?"

"Doug told me," Sally said. "I don't know who else he might have told. Can't ask him now." Sally laid down some wrinkled bills on the counter for the two cocktails she'd just ordered. "Anyway, what you need right now is another drink. A cocktail, in fact."

Jo didn't argue. There was something she needed to ask Christopher Byrne, as soon as possible, and a little liquid courage wouldn't hurt. A hand reached over and dropped something—about the size of a big olive—into a glass, making the drink fizz and froth over the top. The glass was passed down the bar, en route to its intended victim. An off-key symphony of slurred voices chanted their dark invocation:

> *You can drink it fast,*
> *you can drink it slow,*
> *but it doesn't count*
> *'til lips touch TOE!*

Jo held the macabre concoction dubiously in her hand and attempted to peer at the thing inside the glass. It looked a little yellowy. It occurred to her that an olive should be more … green … but she'd had quite a bit to drink already. Perhaps her judgement was impaired. The crowd at the bar appeared to be especially interested in her bubbly. *Strange. Had someone just said the word "toe"?*

"Bottoms up!" cried Caveman, a crazed glint in his eye. He chuckled maliciously.

Jo sniffed at the beverage a little. It smelled peculiar … not just champers, then. Something else. She glanced at Sally for a second opinion. Sally, dressed in cancan attire (even though Gertie's had retired its cancan act for the season), raised her glass and flashed a wicked smile. "Cin cin!"

Jo held the cocktail up to her lips. Whisky. Probably something else. Some other base note ... She closed her eyes. "What was that thing they said about a toe?"

"Nothing." Sally's voice. "Go!"

"But it's not a real toe, right?"

The crowd egged her on. "Drink! Drink! Drink!"

"Not a real, *human* toe ..." She said it more to herself than anyone, for no one else was listening. Jo wrinkled her nose and took a little sip.

"Oh please. You can do better than that. Show us some ovaries," Sally said.

Jo looked at Caveman. He only shrugged. As she slugged about half of it back, something cold, wrinkled, and slimy bumped into her lip.

"Hooooorrrrraaay!" The voices shouted. "Welcome to the Sourtoe Cocktail Club!" Someone clapped Jo on the back, handed her a blurry certificate, and offered to sell her a T-shirt. Sally leaned over and snatched the bottle of "Baby Canadian Sparkling" while the Saloon's keep had his back turned, pouring for herself and Caveman too. They raised their glasses.

"To Marlo," Caveman said.

"To Marlo and May. And to getting our man Grikowsky behind bars." Sally held her glass high before taking an inelegant swig.

Jo raised her own, "And to Doug Browning. May they all rest in peace."

"Rest in peace." Sally and Caveman murmured.

Jo took another sip of the vile substance, then peered into the nearly drained glass. "What? Wait a minute ... I think this olive has a toenail."

Sally smiled. "Of course it does. That's why it's called a 'sour-toe cocktail.' Sour. Toe."

Jo clasped her hand over her mouth and made a little sputtering noise. She felt the contents of her stomach churn. "Oh! I find that a little hard to swallow."

They laughed and Caveman looked sympathetic for a moment. "Don't worry. It's completely sterile. Been sitting in alcohol for yearrrs, eh?" His Canadian r's seemed to lengthen as he drank.

Jo grabbed an ice water, which turned out to be vodka on the rocks. The oily liquid carved a path deep inside her chest. "Arrrgh! Whose toe is it? Where do they get the toes?" She took another mouthful of vodka, swished it around, and spit it out in the tumbler. Her imagination was already beginning to get the better of her. She pictured a quick flash of a body on a morgue slab—minus the toe and the accompanying toe tag.

"I have a theory about that …" Caveman began to say.

"Omigod …"

"The Yukon has a real problem with frostbite …"

"Stop!" Jo said, holding up one hand. "Who *are* you people? No civilized culture drinks cocktails full of body parts."

"Please. Nobody here said anything about civilized. Part of our charm," said Sally, winking.

The bartender, who wore a plaid shirt and put the "dirty" in thirty, motioned to Jo. "Call for you," he shouted over the noise, leaning across the bar. He gestured "phone" with his hands. Everyone looked at her.

Sally chimed in, "I had our calls forwarded here so you didn't miss that one you were waiting for." Anyone else would have looked sheepish, but Sally laid it on down like a gauntlet.

"You had my calls forwarded to a *bar*?" In the back of her mind, Jo wondered who the caller might be, imagining Kessler at the *Sun*, or one of her other former colleagues. *What would they think? Then again, what did it matter at this point?* She had already hit rock bottom—right at the bottom of her rock glass. Garnished with a toe.

"Of course I did. No cellular service here, my dear." Sally said, with a patronizing tone of voice that got under Jo's skin. *The only thing worse than being patronized is being patronized by a woman.*

"You can take it in the kitchen, but make it quick," the bartender said, adjusting his trucker cap.

———◦◦◦———

Jo sincerely wished she hadn't seen the kitchen of the Sourtoe Saloon. Between the human toe in her drink and a glimpse of the cooking area, which didn't appear to have seen soap since the gold rush, Jo was certain that she would never order here again. But that didn't matter right now. What mattered was that she obtain a piece of information that might solve at least part of a greater puzzle: why May Wong had been blackmailing Jack Grikowsky. Jo was certain it had to do with the mine. With smuggling. And possibly with uranium smuggling. She picked up the phone, which may once have been white, but had long since been covered in a layer of filth and fingerprints. "Jo Silver ..."

Nothing but staticky breathing for a moment. Jo was about to hang up, when a man's weathered voice said, "What, you *live* at the bar now? Jesus. That's what I call bungee-jumping off the wagon. You do your old man proud." The quality of the call made Frank's voice sound as if it had been imported from a foreign country. And in a way, it had been.

"I *really* hope you're calling me with the results of that water analysis ... You certainly took your sweet time returning my call, Frank."

"No uranium. But I wouldn't brush my teeth with it. Totally polluted with effluents, apparently."

"What?"

The crowd at the bar was shouting and catcalling, making it difficult to hear anything even from the kitchen. Somewhere a glass smashed: a violent, discordant sound. This was followed by a few strains of guitar and a cheer.

"Hello? *Hello?*" Jo heard her father fumble with the phone, accidentally pushing a button against his cheek. "Goddamned things ..."

"No uranium?"

"You sound disappointed. How much of this water have you been drinking, anyway? Are you all right? You're not in any kind of trouble up there, are you?"

Jo didn't answer right away. She was still reeling from the news that the puzzle didn't fit together in the way she thought it would, or should. She had thought that she held some knowledge of the town, of its dark riddles, but yet again that knowledge had evaded her. "No," she said, hoping she sounded convincing. Whoever had broken into her office and murdered Doug hadn't taken the Geiger counter. Whatever was going on at the mine wasn't about uranium, then. She'd lost the thread of what connected three victims in Dawson. Perhaps it wasn't about the mine at all.

"Good. There's something else." Frank was never one for preambles. She listened to the sound of his breath for a moment as it mingled with the wind. The sinking feeling she experienced made her think of the river, of sliding under ice, a calm stillness settling in. "Something we need to talk about." He wasn't cursing or berating her. This was definitely going to be something bad.

"Jesus, Frank, you're scaring me now. What is it?"

"You might want to sit down."

There was nowhere to sit. "Okay," she said. Jo listened to him breathing for a moment and pictured him running one hand through silver, close-cropped hair.

"He's back, Jo." She didn't need to ask the question "who." This was something she'd been dreading for a year. "At least, the VPD thinks he is."

"Where?"

"Washington. A hiking trail southeast of Tacoma."

"Was she ..."

"Strangled. Burned."

"Shit." Jo felt her throat closing up. *My fault.* There it was. It didn't matter what she did in Dawson, the past was always ready to tap her on the shoulder and make her look back. But, if the Strangler was in the Seattle area, then he sure as hell wasn't in Dawson.

"I know," Frank said, and for the first time in a long time, Jo wished she were home. "You okay?"

"Yeah," she lied. They both knew it was a lie. Everything felt different now. Breathing felt different. She tried to focus on just taking the air in and out. She knew that Frank was listening to her laboured breath and shaky voice. Neither of them said anything for a moment.

"You want me to come up there?"

"Thanks, but the airport already closed."

"I'll come anyway. I'll drive up. I can leave tonight."

"You'd have a hell of a time getting through, and if you did, you'd be stuck here all winter in some drafty old brothel."

"Doesn't sound so bad."

"I'll be fine. Thanks for letting me know." She decided not to tell him about recent events just yet. He'd only worry.

"Jo ..."

"I'm fine, Frank. I'll talk to you tomorrow."

"Okay."

A man with bulging eyes and a sizeable head, perhaps exaggerated by the salmon costume he was wearing, had taken to a makeshift stage in Jo's absence. He was belting out such an enthusiastic rendition of "Friends in Low Places" that Garth Brooks himself would have surely stomped his cowboy boots in appreciation. The salmon-man's fishy friend clapped his fins in time to the beat, while a fiddler and guitarist provided raucous backup. As the fish hit the chorus, the entire bar joined in.

The room went crazy. Sally and Caveman had disappeared from their barstools, but it didn't take Jo long to locate Sally, who was climbing onto a table to provide impromptu entertainment with her scarlet cancan costume, while singing several notes flat and at the top of her lungs. Someone called out for beer chasers as Jo began shoving her way through the crowd. The mood of the room was infectious, and Jo wished she could give herself over to it, but she felt now that something was terribly wrong.

The news that Grikowsky had been incarcerated had ripped through the bar like a northern wildfire. A beer-bellied man in a cowboy hat handed Jo a bottle of Gold as the next cacophonous round of the chorus kicked in. He wouldn't allow Jo to pass until she agreed to take a swill of beer with him.

"If you insist," Jo said. "But I draw the line at line dancing." Thankfully, Cowboy Hat moved aside, raising his Yukon Gold in a wordless salute. Jo wiped her mouth with the back of her hand, cursing under her breath as she slid in a pool of liquid. Things were getting messy.

A moment ago, Jo had felt the dizzying effect of too much cheap sparkling wine (and pickled toe), but now she felt disagreeably sober. Or at least, a little more sober. The room seemed to tilt a bit less as she fought to keep control of her faculties and the situation. Jo had gotten it wrong again. And she was very concerned that the RCMP had gotten it wrong too. She had to talk to someone.

The room swayed with the music. Jo made her way over to Sally and tried to attract her attention, but Sally was too busy dancing on a table to notice. Jo reached up and tugged on her skirt. "Sally! Sally!"

Others began to join the chant. "Sal-ly! Sal-ly!" Sally, who had just removed a pair of frilly bloomers and was waving them around her head, motioned for Jo to join her on the table. A throng of men cheered.

"Sal—I need to talk to you. It's serious." Someone in the room was responsible for the deaths of several people, and that person might not have finished their ghoulish work. The pink ruffled bloomers landed on Jo's head. The crowd went wild.

34

Jo waded through the crowd and the opaque fog of cigarette smoke at the Sourtoe Saloon, headed for the door. She'd given up trying to talk to Sally, and left her dirty-dancing with a salmon. Jo was almost at the door when someone grabbed her arm.

He was a young man, probably midtwenties, with black hair and eyes almost as dark. Something about the mouth reminded her of Johnny Cariboo, and Jo guessed that he must be a relation. He also wore a trucker hat that read "Han Construction." A dead giveaway.

"You're not what I expected, eh?" His tone was cheerful.

"Pardon?"

"I'm Johnny's cousin." He grinned suddenly. "I thought you'd be bigger!"

"I work out," she said, shoving her hands into the pockets of her parka with a flash of annoyance. Jo knew that she was scrawny. She tried to compensate for it by wearing heavy, solid boots and bulky black sweaters.

He let go of her, but made no move to leave. "The guy who's too self-sufficient to live in Moosehide with the rest of us."

Jo knew that Moosehide was the First Nations community upriver from Dawson. She'd heard of it, but to date it hovered around the outskirts of her imagination, like everything else off the map of Dawson City proper.

"The only cousin pushing thirty who isn't hitched yet. Hunts his own food—won't take even a rabbit from his aunties."

"Okaaay ..." She had no idea where he was going with this.

"Melted him like snow." He was still smiling, a bemused expression on his face. He glanced at her boots and seemed to find something funny there as well. Jo wondered if he knew that they were a gift from his cousin. "Wait 'til I tell the others ..."

"I didn't melt anyone," Jo said, "I hardly know him."

"If you say so." He coughed and gave her a knowing look, as though Jo should know what he was talking about.

"I didn't catch your name," she said.

"Mike."

As soon as he said the name, it clicked. "Not Cousin Mike who worked at Claim 53," she said, seizing a sleeve of his flannel shirt.

"Yeah! But that was ages ago."

"I've been meaning to talk to you!"

"Me?"

"Yeah. Your friend, Christopher Byrne, said you thought guys at the mine were getting sick."

Mike nodded slowly, giving himself time to remember. "Oh, yeah. There was this rumour going round. We always thought there was something wrong with the water near the mine." He pushed his trucker hat back on his head a bit.

"Why was that?" She felt a little shiver of anticipation.

"Well, a lot of guys who worked there got headaches. Real bad ones, eh? And this one time, my friend Paul found this mutant fish in one of the streams."

"In Sourdough Creek?"

"Yeah, like, a tributary stream, eh? The fish only had one eye."

Jo felt as if she had been slapped. It had been right there, staring her in the face, the entire time. She knew that Jack Grikowsky was up to no good, but she'd assumed that it was *what* he was mining. It wasn't. It was *how*. The inspection reports had asserted that Claim 53's tributary streams didn't support fish. The inspector must have known, so he had to be in on it. Marlo must have discovered the truth about the mine. That's why they killed her. It *was* Grikowsky.

"I'm sorry, I have to go …" She began to back away, still watching Mike for a moment, then turned and hurried for the exit.

A gust of bleak air surged through the room as the door opened, raising the flesh on Jo's arms. Christopher Byrne entered the bar, wearing a fur-trimmed parka, and Jo almost collided with him.

"Easy, tiger," he said.

"Sorry?"

"Where's the fire?"

Jo licked her dry lips. She had been going to find Cariboo, to tell him what she knew about the falsified inspection papers and the fish in the tributary streams at Sourdough Creek. But on second thought she realized that the RCMP offices would be closed, and anyway Grikowsky was already under lock and key. Perhaps it could wait until morning. Besides, five minutes ago she had been sure that they had the wrong man. Maybe she needed to sober up and then process things. "I was just going home," she said.

"Well, I'm wrapped at Gertie's for the season—not enough players for the Hold 'Em tables." He placed one hand lightly on the small of her back, but the heat of it seemed to burn right through her wool sweater. "Snowing pretty hard. You need a lift?"

Jo looked away, at the dizzying red and gold damask wallpaper, trying not to smile as she thought of the statue Byrne had carved. "Yeesss …" she said, wondering how much she had just slurred.

The sound of tires crunching on snow had an air of finality as they pulled up in front of Sally's house. Jo hesitated for a moment. She dreaded the bone-chilling sprint from Byrne's cab to the front door; the wind outside sounded querulous. More than that, Jo was reluctant to raise the subject of what she'd overheard Byrne say to Sally.

Byrne nudged the truck gently into neutral. "Well …" he said. He looked at his lap and did something with his mouth, as though looking for the right words. "Good night, then."

"Wait," she said. He moved the gearshift to park. "We should talk." Byrne turned to her and raised his eyebrows, but said nothing. In the light of the dashboard, his blue-green eyes were extra blue. "About last night … I overheard you and Sally talking …"

"I see," he said, and his expression clouded.

"You were asking Sally whether I suspected."

"Yes." She had expected denial. She hadn't expected his sense of quiet resolve, and it made her less certain. Jo reminded herself that Dawson police had enough evidence to incarcerate Grikowsky, not Byrne. But she needed to know for sure. "What did you think I might suspect?"

He looked away for a moment, watching angry torrents of snow hurtling toward the headlights. "Okay," he said. Another pause. "Sally and I used to date."

It was strange the way Jo's body seemed to tighten and relax both at the same time. Jo laughed. "I thought … I don't know what I thought."

"It was a long time ago," he said. "And if you want to know the truth …"

Jo held up her hand. "Stop! To quote a friend, there are some things I don't need to know that badly." Jo thought of the worn photograph tucked away in the corner of Sally's mirror. The looks on their faces, frozen in time.

He smiled a little, the laugh lines fanning out around his eyes in that familiar way that made her melt every time. "No, you should probably know. That's the reason that Marlo was following me. She couldn't get past the Sally thing."

"And what was it that Marlo saw when she followed you? The thing you fought about?"

"Marlo saw Sally kiss me."

"Oh."

"I'm not proud of it. But it didn't mean anything to me—that was all over for me years ago. And I know it didn't mean anything to Sally. You know what Sally's like."

"Yeah." Jo thought about the look on Sally's face when Jo had asked for directions to Byrne's cabin.

"It was at Gertie's one night, at the end of a shift. Sally'd had a little too much to drink and tried it on. I pushed her away, but a little too late. Marlo saw."

"I see."

"Jo, I'm not into Sally."

"Okay," Jo said. "It isn't really any of my business."

"That's why I didn't want Sally to tell you. But you wanted to know."

"Yes. Well, I'm glad it's all been cleared up now. Good night," she said, clinging to her last thread of sobriety and willpower. She turned away to open the truck door. She'd been mistaken about the uranium. And she'd been mistaken about Christopher Byrne: he was guilty only of dating her housemate a long time ago.

"Hold up," he said. "I have a question for you, too."

"Yes?" Jo leaned back in the seat.

"Do you have a boyfriend back home?"

She hesitated for a moment, thinking about how to classify her relationship with Kessler, then said, honestly, "No. Not really."

"Good." Byrne leaned forward a little. "Why not?"

"I don't know." But she did know. Jo knew exactly what her problem was, but it was too late to do much about it. "Trust issues, maybe." *Not maybe. Also taste issues. A series of self-absorbed and ill-chosen musicians … And then Kessler.* "My father was a cop in Vancouver. He was strict. He saw a lot of things, I guess, so he … worried about me."

"All fathers worry." Byrne's brow was furrowed, but he was smiling sympathetically.

"True, but Frank—that's my father—was a little extreme about it. Once, when I was a teenager and broke curfew, he took me to the morgue. There was a girl there. Well. The remains of a girl." Jo opened the door, allowing a tide of cold air to wash over her skin. She felt she needed the slap of cold to knock some sense into her. Before she did something crazy, like kiss Byrne. Again. "I've just never been good at relationships."

"At some point, you might need to get over that."

"At some point, maybe I will." She smiled at him and hopped down from the cab.

"Good night, Josephine Silver." His voice was husky.

"Good night."

She could feel him watching her as she moved purposefully toward the front door. The porch light was off and she had to feel around numbly for the keyhole, the antique key grating loudly in the icy lock. Success. She turned and waved to signal Byrne that she was all right. He gave a little salute and threw the truck into gear. She heard his truck pulling away as she hit the light at the kitchen entry. Nothing happened. The kitchen remained in darkness.

Jo felt a queasy tide of panic slam into her. She began feeling her way through the blackness toward the living room, where she remembered leaving the candle in the Mason jar, and hoped she might also find some matches. Partway there she began to wonder if it was a new power outage, or whether someone had cut the power to the house. Jo tripped over something on the floor, put out a hand to steady herself, and grabbed onto someone's arm. She screamed.

Jo stumbled backward, turned, and fled, smacking directly into a dark figure blocking the door. She hit him. Hard. In the stomach.

"Uh!" The man said. He doubled over, coughing. "Jo, it's me! Chris!" Byrne's voice.

"I heard you leave!"

"I didn't see any lights come on, so I thought I'd better check … Then I heard you scream."

"Body at the kitchen table!"

"Alive? Or dead?"

"Not staying to find out!" She grabbed him by the parka and pulled him back out through the door.

They left the truck running and the headlights on after they'd found Byrne's emergency kit, just in case. Together, they went back in with a flashlight to reveal the hideous thing seated at Sally and Jo's kitchen table: a heavy parka draped over the back of a chair, a scarf stuffed up one sleeve. Byrne had the good sense not to laugh, and after they'd checked the rest of the house and determined that the power was out on the entire street, Jo agreed to go home with him.

35

A fire crackled behind a glass door in the woodstove. Veils of smoke waved sinuously, while the bright flame hissed and popped.

Jo returned her attention to a Scrabble board on the floor, where Byrne had just formed the word "myopic." "Curse you and your triple word scores," she said. "Maybe it's time for me to get going while I still have my pride ... and the roads are still open."

They'd pushed the table to one side and were stretched out on the floor in front of the stove. Byrne was lying on his side, propped up on one elbow on a well-worn fur. This fact alone made Jo feel uneasy. She was not the kind of person who lounged about on animal skins. Byrne looked relaxed. "Oh, I think you're already trapped here for the night," he said.

"What?"

Byrne laughed, watching her face. "Seriously though, the roads have probably snowed in by now. And in a storm like this, your power will still be out." As if on cue, the wind howled through the beams of Byrne's cabin. Nugget raised his head from his paws and sniffed at something unseen. "You're much safer here, don't you agree?"

"What, in the middle of nowhere with no phone or power? Sure, sure." There was little doubt about what Byrne was suggesting in terms of sleeping arrangements if she chose to stay the night, and Jo wasn't sure how she felt about that. "Besides, the whole town will be talking if I roll in tomorrow morning in your truck."

"You're *cheechako*. A newcomer. People will talk no matter what you do."

Jo shot him a look. "Or don't do." He smiled again.

The warmth of the cabin was undeniably appealing, as was the company. She had a brief, sobering bout of mistrust ... thought of what Frank might say about her holing up in the woods with someone she barely knew. But then, Jo reminded herself, the police already had their man, and they had enough evidence to incarcerate. And she'd just discovered more evidence of Grikowsky's guilt. She would share the information with Cariboo first thing in the morning.

In the meantime, it was probably something like minus thirty and dropping, and Byrne's cabin was as good a place as any to weather the storm. Better. "So, what do you when you're not playing games?" She took a sip of the wine he'd poured for her. He'd poured something suspiciously juice-like for himself.

"I don't play games." He gave her a hard look. One that made her momentarily regret the question.

"No?"

Byrne looked away, the expression on his face cryptic. "To answer your first question; nothing."

"Define nothing."

"Look after Nugget ... keep the fire going ... read."

"Uh huh. Keep the fire going ..."

"And I carve.

Jo stared at him. Christopher Byrne remained a mystery to her, and that made him intriguing. The wind picked up again with a shriek and a moan, sending a draft through the cabin that caused the flame in the hearth to leap. Jo wrapped her arms around herself.

"You're cold. Just a second."

He snatched up a fur throw from the bed and then wrapped it around her shoulders.

"Thanks."

Byrne began rubbing her arms, kneading them like willing clay, radiating warmth and melting the tension from her body. When he stopped, their eyes met. It was the kind of kiss where teeth knock and lips crush, imperfect in every way but for the conviction of the moment.

Byrne hefted Jo up and carried her to the bed, stumbling a little. As he dropped her on the mattress, she bounced inelegantly and then sank into soft folds of blankets, cool to the touch, giving her gooseflesh. This time when he kissed her, he leaned into her, pressing down on her. They fumbled awkwardly with an obstacle course of winter clothing. A clunky North Face boot fell to the floor, along with one woollen sock. Jo grabbed at Byrne's sweater and yanked it over his head, catching in his hair. Byrne unzipped her jeans, tugging hard at the denim until he'd exposed the white, waffled texture of long johns underneath. He laughed, shaking his head.

"Shut up." She kissed him, unbuttoning his flannel shirt, the fabric brushing softly in promise against her fingertips. She clawed the shirt back, revealing a sinewy chest with a long, angry scar running down the length of it. Jo hesitated for a moment, resting her hand on the rise and fall of his chest while she decided whether or not to speak, to ask about the strange road map imprinted onto his skin. The wind waited too, seeming to hold its breath, and the heavy silence permeated the cabin and the woods beyond like the snow bearing down, muffling the world with its gentle insistence. Then, she traced the scar from the top of the line where it began, adding weight as the scar ran south, to the borderline of his belt.

36

It was well after midnight. Jo lay with Byrne in blanketed silence and leaned her head into his chest, inhaling his scent—a pleasing combination of musk and wood smoke. Her fingers traced a circular pattern on his smooth skin. The storm outside made idle threats, but the dim popping of the fire had a calming and hypnotic effect. Her eyelids fluttered, but she fought against the drowsy feeling that was spreading through her body. It wasn't easy. Byrne's four-poster bed was weighted with deep, soft layers of blankets and furs. Jo had the sensation of sinking, drowning, with another swell of exhaustion.

A hanging candelabra made of bone or antler lit the room softly, the branch-like arms casting a forest of flickering shadows. The elegant contours of the piece mirrored the graceful lines of the bed, which appeared at first glance to have been hand-carved. But the bed seemed more organic than that, as though each tree limb had supernaturally grown and twisted together to take on a more functional form. She raised herself on one elbow to look more closely.

"What?" His voice was a soft growl. "What is it?" Byrne turned his face toward hers.

"Nothing. This is a beautiful bed."

"Thanks."

"You made it, didn't you?"

Byrne nodded, then looked at the ceiling, studying the pattern of branches that were not branches. Jo wondered what it would be like if their lives were tangled together like the head of his bed. Roots knotting and curling into one another until they were inseparable. But now she was being ridiculous.

"Can I ask you a personal question?" He didn't turn his face toward her this time.

"Um, okay …"

"What are you doing here?"

"I like you." Jo felt a little unsettled by the question, especially since she had just resolved not to take what had happened between them too seriously.

"No, I mean here in Dawson."

"I got a job here."

"Now who's playing games?"

Jo sighed. "You answer a question first."

"Okay." Byrne rolled toward her, his expression open and attentive. His blue-green eyes were smiling, and now she reached out and touched the laugh lines, gently.

"Where did you get that scar?" Jo surprised herself a little with the question, but Byrne didn't even flinch. He held her look.

"My father."

"Oh …" Something clicked for her. "That's why you don't drink."

"Oh, no. I drank plenty growing up, until I was caught smuggling liquor into a dry town up north."

"What's that?"

"It's a First Nations town that has agreed to alcohol prohibition."

"Ah …" She ran her hand lightly across his chest, across the scar. She felt foolish. Christopher Byrne was a young man who'd made a mistake. Not a uranium smuggler. "What happened?"

"A First Nations court assigned community service in the town I'd supplied, so I could see the devastation I'd caused first-hand."

"Was it …"

"Horrible. I gave up drinking after that. That, and my father. I didn't want to be like him." He smiled at her, and stopped the hand that was tracing the scar.

Jo watched his face. It occurred to her that she could get used to watching this face.

"I'm sorry."

"Don't be. My father taught me other things. Aside from being a bootlegger and an alcoholic, he was also a backcountry guide. I learned how to survive out here."

"And you still watch the northern lights."

"Yes." He leaned forward and kissed her, gently. "I still watch the stars." He was looking at her.

Nugget interrupted their pillow talk with a long, low growl. His attention was focused on something outside the window. The fur down the centre of his back bristled into a thick warning stripe.

"Nugget! Down!" Byrne said. Nugget didn't move. "Down!" The big dog laid back down. "Animals in the woods. Sometimes they spook him a little. He's part-wolf, so he's not the most sociable creature by nature." Indeed, the collarless beast was unusually dark, with but a thin streak of white about the lips, as though it had just eaten something sugary. The dog had a particularly wild look about it that made Jo's injured thigh smart. Without thinking about it, she covered her thigh with her hand.

Nugget dropped chin to paws, but his ears continued to twitch and turn like well-tuned satellite dishes. The wolf-dog lifted its great head again, staring into space as it listened to something presumably beyond human range. Jo felt unnerved by its stare, by the one brown eye and the other ice-blue. Nugget made another deep grumbling sound, the timbre rich in meaning.

Byrne ignored the dog. "Your turn," he said. "Why are you here?"

Jo sighed and stretched, examining the wood grain on the heavy beams above them. The wind whined and wailed at the cabin walls, searching for a point of entry. Jo imagined the drifts stretching, too, spreading long fingers of snow across highways, claiming them. Closing them. "You already know, don't you." It wasn't a question.

Jo pictured her face, then. The dead girl. The smiling eyes and flawless, young skin. In the photograph that all the newspapers ran, you could see a bridge of freckles over her nose.

"We've never talked about it." The comment settled over them like Byrne's thick blankets, filling and warming what remained of the space between their bodies.

She laughed. "We've never talked much about anything, except on that night I don't remember." It was the truth, but Jo regretted it as soon as she'd said it. He'd given her an opening and she'd promptly closed it. Byrne permitted her words to resonate, without refutation. She rushed to say, "I just mean, we don't really know each other. Yet."

"I think I know something about you, Josephine Silver." Byrne traced a line softly down her shoulder and arm, studying her.

Jo sighed. "Her name was Nicole Hoffman. She was a student at Vancouver Community College. Eighteen years old when she died. The worst part is, I'll never know whether I could have made a difference. I have to live with that every day." She thought about this for a moment.

"I'm sorry," Byrne said.

"So am I." Jo didn't make eye contact with him. She couldn't, not without crying in front of him, so instead she permitted herself to feel the hot rush of rage that pulsed through her body. She told herself that the feeling was directed against the officers she'd trusted, but deep down Jo knew that she was furious with herself. Still, better than fear or regret, which made her feel cowardly. Jo's face burned.

"Everybody makes mistakes," he said.

She nodded, curling into him and closing her eyes, breathing the wild scent of him. Byrne massaged the muscles in her back and neck, gently kneading out the anger. Her breathing slowed, until there was nothing but the warmth of skin on skin, the soft fur of his leg, the distant howl of wind, the spit and sputter of the fire.

"Sleep well," Byrne said, kissing her forehead and waking her up. He smiled, fanning the lines around eyes that were the colour of the ocean. Jo's eyelids drooped. She closed her eyes, drifting away from him.

"Sleep well," he'd said in the truck, kissing her cheek with a brush of beard. Her head had rattled a little against the icy window, causing her to move her glove under her head. She'd heard the rattle of the handle, a thin whistle of wind, then the shock of cold metal on metal as the driver's door shut.

Jo's eyes flew open. Byrne was watching her. "What?" he said. "Everything okay?"

Everybody makes mistakes.

"Fine," she said, and closed her eyes to give herself a chance to think, wondering whether he had registered the panic in her eyes, whether her eyes now looked squeezed tightly shut. He'd left her in the truck alone. They weren't looking at the northern lights. He'd lied. And if they weren't kissing, then Byrne was alone on the Bluffs. With Marlo.

The words came to her then. The missing lines of the poem.

I know noble accents
And lucid, inescapable rhythms;
But I know, too,
That the blackbird is involved
In what I know.

She opened her eyes slowly this time. Byrne hadn't moved. His brow was furrowed and a frown twisted his mouth. Jo tried to smile, and then faked a yawn. She closed her eyes and moved her body closer to his, as though preparing to sleep, but now there was a sharp feeling in her stomach and all her muscles felt tense. Byrne stopped massaging her back. Perhaps he could feel the tightness there. She realized that she was breathing too quickly and forced herself to slow her lungs. Jo thought about that night, rattling around in the dark corners of her memory for anything useful. She remembered the sound of their laughter at Sally's, but now his seemed forced. There had been a kiss, but at Sally's. Not in the truck. Not at the Bluffs. And it had tasted of whisky.

He was still watching her.

"Could I use your bathroom?" she said.

"Sure … let me get you a flashlight. And take Nugget with you."

Jo was caught off-guard by both suggestions. Now, doing a second survey of her surroundings, Jo realized that she might have an opportunity to escape. Byrne's cabin was one open living space. No indoor plumbing. She layered on her long johns again, avoiding his eyes.

At the door, Byrne stooped to place a set of bear bells around her ankle. "Here," he said. The bells clanged in warning as they were fastened. "You shouldn't need these. The bears will probably be hibernating." Byrne smiled grimly. "But just in case."

Don't let him know that you know. "It's the word 'probably' that I'm not comfortable with. I read an article that said they don't hibernate at all anymore because of global warming." Jo reached casually for her scarf and toque. She had to be warm if she were going to brave the elements to find help.

Byrne said nothing but the moment hung between them. The wind shrieked, as though in laughter. As though the idea of any kind of warming, given current conditions, was entirely ludicrous. A corner of Byrne's mouth smiled, without committing to completion of the shape.

"Well," she said. In response to nothing he had said. In response to the wind.

"Well." He left a painful pause, exaggerating Jo's own impatience. "Just follow the path. I'll keep the bed warm for you."

37

The wind lashed her face as she stepped out of the cabin, flashlight in hand, blood rushing. Jo took a sharp breath and began tromping through the snow into the distance. The bells jangled in challenge, like spurs. She wished she could have found an excuse to leave them behind.

"Nugget! Go!" Byrne called out after her. The big dog loped toward her, giving her a start as she turned to see its dark wolf shape, tongue lolling and a hungry expression in that one eye the colour of frozen sea. Jo stiffened in preparation for attack, but Nugget bounded by her and rushed ahead down the path. She exhaled a cloud of breath. The air smelled of pine and wood smoke—a familiar and reassuring scent. Jo squinted to see if Byrne were watching, but she didn't dare risk pointing the flashlight at the cabin. She had to keep going.

Jo picked her way through the darkness, following the weak circle of light, ringing as she went. *Ching. Ching. Ching.* The narrow overgrown path, almost obscured by snow, led through the woods toward an outhouse. She stopped at the clearing.

Now that Jo was away from the cabin, she had begun to doubt herself. She had no proof that Byrne had done anything.

Just a feeling. No, more than a feeling. It was the way he looked at her, like he *knew* that she knew. Jo thought she had a few minutes at best. When she didn't come back, he'd come after her. She might have just enough time to make it to the truck. *But would the keys be there?* Jo began walking, slowly at first, looking over her shoulder. Then faster, her boots sinking into the snow past the tops, dampening her shins. Jo cut away from the path at the back of the house, through the woods toward the lane where Byrne parked his pickup.

The timid line of light from her flashlight was no match for such an opaque night. It was possible only to see a few feet in any direction, where branches waved their dark claws and bright flakes of snow lunged and circled. Feeling exposed in the spotlight of her flashlight, Jo hurried forward, against the wind. *Ching. Ching. Ching.* It was difficult to move either quickly or with any stealth, and the bear bells broadcast her location to anything that might be … The word "hunting" came to mind. Hunting her. She stooped to remove the bells, causing strips and patches of ice to crack at the knees of her jeans. Her numb fingers fumbled with the bells, a fury of metal noise, but it was no use. He'd tied the leather strings into a tight knot and now she would have to remove her gloves. She tugged at the first glove, exposing flesh to a rake of icy air just as a flash of movement caught her eye. She dropped the glove. A black figure in the brush. A bear? A man? A dog? Jo didn't know. She half-whispered into the darkness, "Nugget?" She swung her torch.

Jo was startled by the heavy shape in the snow that awaited her. She made a little noise at the back of her throat. Nugget turned his head to look up at her, face placid.

"Oh, for the love of Christ." *Not a bear,* she thought, her whole body rejoicing. *Not a man.* She gasped as the wind kicked in again, feeding on the exposed skin at her face and throat and left hand. Jo tucked her chin into an already icy scarf. "Good boy," she said, stretching out her bare hand toward the dog. The dog ignored her, turning back to look at something in the woods, an animated expression on its face. Then, the animal threw back its head and howled.

"Shhh!" Jo said, fearful that the dog would give her location away. She fumbled to pick up the glove in the snow. The dog stood, the hair rising on the ridge of its back. He began to bark emphatically. "Nugget, no. Quiet ..."

The husky gave her a baleful look, then continued with his loud warning to something unseen in the dark. Jo hesitated for a moment, hating to leave the dog in case it was in any kind of danger. *Stupid dog. Please don't get yourself killed.* She looked back over her shoulder. The dog suddenly darted off into the underbrush, a departing shadow in a tangle of snowy branches.

The wind harangued her as she scanned the capricious shapes of waving trees. She took a deep, needling breath, head turned against the wind, and began jogging away. *Ching. Ching. Ching.* The bear bells rang out in the darkness. Then, in the distance, Jo heard Nugget howl again. She paused, struggling to hear anything else above the wind. Where was the sound coming from? Behind her? Or ahead?

She ran like her life depended on it. The bells clamoured as she rounded a corner. *Ching. Ching. Ching.* Her left hand burned, and she realized with horror that she'd dropped the glove somewhere. No time to go back for it. Snow pelted her cheeks. How long before frostbite set in?

The toe of her right boot caught on something—she tripped, touched bare hand to snow briefly, but did not go down. Her breathing was ragged, each inhalation knifing her lungs. She was almost there. Almost to the truck. *Please let the keys be inside.*

Jo lurched into the glade where she thought Byrne's pickup should be parked. Saw the truck. A warm wave of relief washed over her, then receded. The drifts were halfway to the windows. *Will never get out ... Might be a shovel in the back ... Imagine the state of the roads ... One thing at a time.* As she neared, Jo tried to peer through the window to see the ignition, but the feathered pattern of frost obscured her view. The door handle was frozen, but she was able to jiggle it free. It moved. The door opened. Her heart soared. But no. There was no key in the ignition.

Jo climbed in anyway, closing the door against the juddering cold and locking it. *Think. Think.* Would she be safer here? Could she somehow hotwire the engine? *Not likely.* She checked the driver's mirror, half hoping to find a key, then opened the glove compartment. There was a drawstring leather pouch inside. *Please.* Numb fingers clawed at the string until the bag revealed its treasure. Two fleshy round lumps. Bear balls.

There was no key anywhere to be found.

She was halfway out of the truck when the first shot rang out. A rush of panic gripped Jo, making her hands shake as she clawed at the off switch on the flashlight. For a moment, she couldn't feel the button. Then the ring of light at her feet winked out with a tremor. She hesitated, unsure of which direction to head, then darted helter-skelter toward the shadowy contours of trees. The bells around her ankle trilled like an alarm, echoing across the blowing landscape.

Jo flinched as another shot thundered, propelling her forward as the sound of the explosion faded into the yowl of the wind. She was sprinting back along the path toward the outhouse, but realized with a shock that it would dead-end, and that he'd be able to predict her route. She veered off to the left, into the woods again, knee-deep in snow. Her breath was coming in great crescendos, like waves battering a shoreline during a storm. The grim scent of winter was magnified.

Bullets of hard snow pelted her face and her eyes watered, the tears freezing on her cheeks. Jo followed a less-tangled area in the forest. It might have been another path, It was difficult to tell. Another shot exploded somewhere in the night, and immediately she shifted direction, arms pumping, slicing through the crisp air. Her legs ached with fatigue and cold, and her one bare hand had gone numb. She wondered what it might feel like to die here, with only trees for tombstones, the snow piling up around her body, and wolves to pick the bones clean and white.

Then, she spotted a dark, structural shape not far off. *Please let it be another cabin.*

It was a roughly hewn shack, smaller even than Byrne's. The windows were dark, and the pipe chimney smokeless. Jo banged on the door. There was no answer. Jo rattled at the handle until the front door gave way, swinging inward with a swirl of snow, the darkness swallowing her.

As she plunged inside, it was the smell of the place she noticed first. A raw, spoiled scent like rank meat. She gagged. It felt as though the smell were clinging to her, getting inside her mouth and nose and down her throat. Jo found the switch on her flashlight and lifted the light. A bear snarled at her, fangs bared, just a few feet away. She almost dropped the torch.

Taxidermy. The heads of animals had been mounted everywhere, in silent roars. The glassy, yellow-green eyes of a cougar made Jo think of a child's marble. A small, empty treasure. One table contained bits of bone or antler. Another, a collection of bear paws. Not far away, something howled, expressing the passion of the hunt.

Jo swallowed. She had nowhere to run, and he was coming. She moved to the door, closed it, and bolted it with the heavy, wooden latch. She scoured the one-room shack for something to use. There was a long-bladed knife and some saw-like instruments on the table with the paws. She seized the knife.

Outside, boots crunched on snow like a funeral march. The sound conveyed a dreadful sense of purpose. Motion at the window caught her eye as a man in a balaclava flashed by the window in profile, headed toward the door.

A fresh surge of panic, made worse by the chaotic ringing of bells as she rushed to the window closest to the front door. Frantically, knife in gritted teeth, Jo closed and secured the rough wooden shutters as best she could. They clattered and shook in her numb hands. Then, she backed away, holding the knife in front of her.

The doorknob turned, slowly, then rattled, but the deadbolt held.

Jo glanced around. There was no window on the wall that housed the animal heads but, at the wall opposite the door, her open-mouthed expression was reflected in an inky mirror of glass. She rushed to the other window and closed another set of wooden shutters, a flimsy hook locking them loosely in place. Then Jo stooped down to hack through the twine holding the bells in place around her ankle. They fell to the floor with a dismal clang.

The crack of a rifle tore the arctic air. Across the room, there was now a dime-sized hole in the wooden shutters. Jo scrambled under the work table and listened. Nothing but the fury of the wind for a moment, then the sound of footsteps receding into the storm. Jo exhaled a fog of breath. She quickly leaned into the table with her shoulder, tipping it over in a shower of bone and metal as random animal parts and taxidermy tools rained down. Jo lay flat on the floor behind it, covering her head.

Nearby outside, boots crunched on snow again, growing louder. His step was calm and confident. A crash made her wince, then an icy log skidded across the floor in a wake of glass. A rattling sound at the window. She peered out from behind the table. A gloved hand was reaching in through the splintered shutters, feeling its way toward the deadbolt on the door with outstretched, crab-like fingers. Icicles of glass fell to the floor, playing a melodic tune.

Jo lunged with the taxidermy knife just as the encroaching fingers made contact with the bolt. The long blade disappeared into the meaty bit between the index finger and thumb, pinning the appendage to the door. The person attached to the hand made a horrifying sound. The arm wrenched and the fingers spasmed.

Byrne was screaming, but it wouldn't be long until he was free if the skin tore. Jo darted to the back window and opened the shutters. She snatched up the log and hurled it through, leaving fragments of glass hanging like loose teeth. Grabbing a long taxidermy saw, she smashed the remaining shards out, then began climbing through the window.

She glanced over her shoulder, behind her. The knife still pinned a black glove to the door like some great, horrid spider, but the glove was now empty. Her gaze shifted to the opposite window, to the bullet hole in the shutters, sensing that he was watching her. She barely had time to leap. Something seared through the air just above her head, where she had been a second before. "Hunt," she heard Byrne call out.

She landed in a thick drift of snow, almost up to the window, and the thing was on her, slavering and snapping its jaws. Nugget. Jo swung the saw at the dog, but it leapt away easily and was back at her, crouched and snarling. Each time Jo stabbed with the saw, the husky backed off to evade the blow, but she couldn't escape while it guarded her. Byrne was coming. He would find her here. When the dog lunged again, Jo threw the saw. This time, she found her target. The beast whimpered and fell back. Running up the drift onto the window ledge, she hefted herself up onto the cabin roof. She scrabbled and slipped as she climbed, clutching the icy edge of the shingling while the husky launched itself just below her feet once again, fangs bared.

How many rounds were in a rifle magazine? Five? Ten? She pictured the gunman's arm swinging wildly about, struggling to hold the barrel steady with only one good hand.

"Jo," Byrne called out. "It doesn't have to be this way. Come back and let's talk." His voice was carried away by the wind. Did he think she'd escaped into the woods? Or did he think she'd gone back inside and was cowering behind the work table? *He'll see my tracks if he comes around to look.* Jo inched forward in the snow caking the roof of the hut, trying to reach the peak. Could she go over the top and take him by surprise? Her arms were shaking as she pulled herself up the incline.

For a moment, Jo heard only the rising wind, then the sound of snow under boots. Byrne was moving away from the front of the cabin and down the side, toward the back. He would find her. He would kill her.

38

The frenzied dog hurled itself below Jo's feet. The muscles in her arms burned with the effort of clinging to the roof, some misplaced gargoyle. She strained to hear over the wind, but there was nothing but the yammer of the husky. She couldn't go down, and she didn't know where Byrne had gone. Her only choice was to crawl up and over the small cabin and hope to escape on the other side. Or drop down on Byrne from above if she found him there. She inched her way forward, lying on her belly, the cold soaking into her jeans. She brushed away treacherous snow as she went, gripping the edges of shingles, praying that they would hold her weight. If Byrne sighted her on the roof, he would pick her off with the rifle. She pictured him lying in wait. Stretching forward, she grasped the icy stovepipe chimney and strained to the top. She looked over, squinting into the night and roiling snow. There was no one there.

Jo caught her first strong whiff of gasoline, then. A splashing sound below. He was hunting her, flushing her out. She had to leap now, before he tossed a match, but she hesitated, knowing he'd shoot as she fled. She thought of the girl in the burning car. Jo knew how her own remains would look when they found her.

Wooosh! The shack went up in flames.

Some motion caught her attention in her peripheral vision. Someone was running through the snow, toward the cabin. He was carrying a gun, making a beeline for the door of the cabin below her. At first she thought it was Byrne, but as the figure got closer, she realized with a shock that it was Johnny Cariboo. In the glow of the fire, he looked determined. *Does he think I'm inside?*

Nugget was on Cariboo before Jo could shout a warning. A shot ripped through the fabric of the night sky, and the big dog lay still. Cariboo stooped and reached out to the dead animal. He didn't see Byrne. "Look out!" she screamed. A second shot exploded in the darkness beyond the shack and the fire.

"Johnny!"

He didn't respond. He had a stunned expression on his face. He opened his mouth to say something, before he crumpled into the snow.

Jo rushed to swing her leg up over the roof to the other side. That was when she lost her footing. She scratched and clawed as she slid, plummeting down toward the hungry sound below. Her foot hit a bit of trim at the edge of the roof, slowing her down for a moment. Then she hurtled into nothingness.

She landed hard on her back in front of the cabin, the heat of the flames making her blink. The snow on her cheeks and eyelashes was already melting and running down her damp face. She didn't know where Byrne was. She struggled to her feet and raced toward Cariboo, where he lay sprawled in the snow, his rifle lying abandoned beside him.

There was a thunderous noise like the cracking of ice on a frozen river.

She looked down, trying to see the bloody hole in her chest. She couldn't seem to feel the bullet. *Shock. This is how it feels to die.* She was falling. She hit the ground with her numb, bare hand, landing not far from Cariboo. Close enough to see shallow swirls of his breaths. *Alive*, she thought, and the idea spiraled out inside of her like ink in water.

Next to Cariboo: the gun, a dark promise reaching up out of the snow just a few feet away. She looked down at her chest. Nothing. *Not hit*. She could make it to Cariboo's rifle. Jo jammed her hands into the ice and snow to lift her body, sending a searing lick of pain through her wrist. She used her elbows instead, crawling forward through the snow.

When she looked up, Byrne was bearing down on her with the gun. He was having trouble holding the rifle with only one hand. The blue-green eyes blinked, either in surprise or acknowledgement. It was difficult to know. "Jo," Byrne said. His eyes were locked on hers. "I wish things could be different. I never wanted to hurt you." She was glad he was wearing the ski mask, because even now she felt the pull of him. For a split second, she was tempted to imagine what it would have been like if Marlo hadn't followed him, hadn't discovered his secret, but she pushed the thought away.

"Like you didn't want to hurt Alice?" Cariboo said, his voice a thin whisper.

Jo's mind reeled. *This is about Alice?* Just when she thought she had the puzzle of Dawson put together, the landscape shifted again. She wished Cariboo would say more, but he either couldn't or wouldn't. He'd turned his face toward them, but his eyes were closed and his face was contorted with pain.

Now she felt the despair welling up inside of her. Even if they managed to evade Byrne and escape into the cover of the woods, her damp clothes would quickly freeze. And Cariboo couldn't be moved. She needed time to think. "They'll know we didn't die in the fire."

Byrne shook his head. "They think it's Grikowsky. I planted May's gun in his cabin. They won't be looking for me. Not tonight."

Cariboo's voice was raspy. "We let Grikowsky go. I came to warn Jo because Sally …" Jo never found out what Sally had to do with any of it. Cariboo's voice was lost on the wind.

The gun wavered, swinging back and forth in Byrne's one good hand like a venomous snake about to strike. "Have you ever seen a wild animal in a trap? I see it all the time. They chew their own limbs off to escape. I'm sorry, Jo, but I just can't be locked up again."

She thought about the abusive father and Byrne's one-room cabin. No closets. No cupboards. Nowhere to be locked in. Then she felt the arctic cold in her lungs, felt her insides tightening.

"They won't look for me until tomorrow," he said, "and by then I'll be gone. My partner is coming for me with a ski plane." Byrne lifted the gun again, with a gesture of resolve.

There was another explosion, and this time Jo squeezed her eyes tightly shut. When she opened them, the back part of Byrne's head was missing, and he was face down, the snow painted crimson around him.

The cold had permeated every part of her now. Her entire body seemed to be vibrating with it. A wave of nausea passed over her. She looked away from the piteous thing in the snow, peering into the night to see who the shooter was, but could see nothing. Jo rolled over onto her side, cradling the injured wrist, and staggered to her feet. She lurched over to Johnny. His face was pale. "Johnny?" His eyelids flickered open, but he said nothing. His breathing was rapid. She removed her scarf.

Then he said, "I have to know about Alice—is he …?"

"Gone." She folded up the scarf, placed it over the hole in the shoulder of his parka and pressed down, making him cry out between gritted teeth. "I'm sorry!"

Something or someone moved in her peripheral vision. Jo froze, thinking immediately of the second person: Byrne's partner, the person with the ski plane. Another member of the smuggling ring, some kind of vengeful accomplice who had double-crossed Byrne. A malicious, unknown entity still lurking in the woods with a shotgun or rifle. Jo squinted though the smoke. The flames had engulfed the cabin and lit up the surrounding area, making the approaching form a black silhouette.

The shadowy figure stepped forward, walking in a peculiar manner. The little mincing steps sounded like the crackling of tiny spines as boot heels broke a thin crust of snow. She stepped into the flickering light cast by the fire like a demon from the underworld, a flash of fur and fiery skirts. She was holding a long rifle.

Their eyes met. For a second, Jo thought of seizing Cariboo's gun. She thought of the gleeful look on Sally's face when she'd discovered the animal parts in May's house. But Sally lowered the barrel, hands shaking, cheeks streaked with frozen tears.

"What are you doing here?" Jo said.

"They released Jack Grikowsky. I had to warn you. You weren't at home, so I told Johnny I thought you'd be here." Sally's gaze shifted to the thing in the snow. "It's where I would have gone." The look on her face was horrible to see.

"But how did you get through? Is there anyone else here?"

"There are certain advantages in taking the occasional tumble with a snowplough driver. When we heard shots, we called Johnny on the two-way radio on his snowmobile. He called for backup."

"So where is it?"

In the distance, the urgent wail of a siren hit a high note, in harmony with the wind. Through the blowing snow and trees, a pulsing light appeared, first bright blue and then red. An RCMP snowmobile, yellow and black like a hornet, emerged from the forest path, bounced over a hill and into the clearing, toward the fire. Surrounded by trees and nearly obscured by snow, the snowmobile looked small and insect-like, an impossibility in a frozen landscape. And still it came.

39

Marshall the guinea pig sniffed the air as though checking for trouble, whiskers twitching anxiously. He'd been quite skittish since Doug's death.

"It's all right," Jo whispered. "They're not angry with you."

At the sound of Jo's voice, Marshall started nervously and buried himself in a pile of wood chips and headlines.

"Go ahead, hide. Wish I could do the same." Jo deleted the message she'd been listening to and skipped to the next heated opinion sounding from the speakerphone on her desk. She had received countless calls and letters in the weeks since the death of Christopher Byrne and, subsequently, the arrest of Jack Grikowsky and a DFO inspector for bribery, fraud, and environmental crimes.

The town had taken on a theatrical atmosphere, where political sideshows were the order of the day and blame was handed out like popcorn. Candidate hopefuls jostled for position to replace the disgraced mayor and made impassioned speeches about the decaying moral fibre of the community. In all things, a deep sense of shame permeated the town, as well as fear. Fear, in the wake of Christopher Byrne, that you could never really trust your neighbour again, in a place where survival depended on trusting your neighbour. Fear that Dawson, now known to be badly in the red, might lose its right to self-governance and be gobbled up by the territorial government. Often, this particular problem was attributed to the revelations Jo had made about the mayor and the mine. Many asserted that her dedication to publicizing the truth had damned the lot of them. Others left messages at the *Daily* to say that Dawson City without self-governance would cease to be Dawson City. Dawson's particular brand of charm, it was widely felt, was due to its fierce sense of political independence, die-hard do-it-yourself attitude, and strong sense of local community. And Dawson without Claim 53 would not be able to support the miners and their families. Jo couldn't win. *Damned if you do, damned if you don't.*

Frustrated, she picked up a copy of the story that she'd had published in a glossy American newsmagazine, an article that had garnered international attention. The headline read, "A Tale of Two Cities," in a gilded Western font, and featured a huge photograph of Christopher Byrne, dressed in his turn-of-the-century poker attire, his smile enigmatic. The opposite page pictured Peter Wright being led into custody. Jo hadn't written about Doug, although she suspected that he'd known about the mine and been paid off by Grikowsky to keep his silence. She had no proof that Doug had gone back to the office that night to read her article, to find out whether she'd pointed her finger at him too. Most likely he'd encountered Byrne there, doing something similar. Jo turned her thoughts away from Byrne. Her feelings about him were still too complicated. She ripped out the page, allowing Byrne's face to tear in half so that he was like the city itself: part one thing, part something else. A page in a story that was constantly fabricated, told, and reinvented again. Jo passed the torn paper to Marshall. "There you go, furball. All the news that's fit to eat."

Since publishing the article, Jo had been offered a crime column with the *Toronto Star* in the new year. The big time. She would have a regular paycheque, access to the city's biggest stories, and a chance to make a new name for herself in a national publication. It was what she'd been hoping for. She'd be a fool not to take it —once spring came and freeze-up relinquished its hold on her.

The answering machine beeped. Jo let the next caller go to voice mail. She was done caring about what anyone thought. She stood, stretched, and reached for her parka.

The wallpaper that adorned the Jack London Grill was crimson with a silver flock pattern that looked like smoke. In places, the paper was eclipsed by old movie posters: Charles Bickford and Irene Rich starring in Jack London's *Queen of the Yukon. Sign of the Wolf. Wolf Call.* The heroines of these stories were cruel-lipped and poised, raising their thin, arched eyebrows in expressions of challenge while they clutched poker hands and pistols. Jo searched the details of these images for some hidden truth, some parallel to her own character. Finding nothing, she returned her attention to her cup of coffee. The room smelled of gravy and reheated pastry—a warm, comforting scent that almost relaxed Jo's permanently tensed shoulders. She'd slept the previous night, six hours straight, without dreaming. Or rather, if she had dreamed, she had no memory of it, and was happy for that small blessing. *Simple pleasures.* She wondered if her present quietude was an illusion, like the flickering half-truths of the films made about the Yukon in the early decades of the last century. Somewhere just below the calm surface of her subconscious, something menacing floated yet, threatening to breach the still waters and emerge at any time to point a bony finger in accusation. Jo consoled herself with the notion that this particular ghost might not haunt her quite so often.

She cupped her hands around the porcelain "Call of the Wild" mug, letting the warmth leach into her flesh. The irony of the moment did not escape her: now that she had the luxury and the time to enjoy her morning ritual, she was almost two thousand miles away from a café that prided itself on its coffee, unless it were laced with booze. She wondered how different life would be if she accepted the position in Toronto.

Everything would change. Of course it would. She pictured herself, jostling into line for a paper cup from a faceless server whose fingers had never graced a piano at a turn-of-the-century gambling hall. Jo would be looking at her watch, feeling the squeeze of the day's time constraints already. She thought of Johnny Cariboo, of his particular stillness.

He'd been airlifted to hospital in Whitehorse, but was now recuperating at his mother's cabin in Mooshide. Jo had visited him. She'd intended to ask him if the RCMP had located the ski plane yet and whether the pilot might be able to use the frozen river as a runway. Instead, she found herself asking about Alice Wolfe.

His face had clouded over. "I looked for Alice for eight years." He'd left one of his long silences, but it was not uncomfortable, somehow. "But that's the thing about winter. Even a Dawson winter doesn't last forever. You'll see." He'd reached out his hand then and she'd taken it. Perhaps he'd meant the gesture as some kind of reassurance, but it felt more like a bridge. "At a certain point, you just have to let go of the past." She'd smiled, not trusting herself to speak, but she'd let the moment settle over her, softly.

Now she turned her face toward the café window. It was snowing again. Thick, lazy snowflakes that stuck to one another and crystallized on windowpanes. Jo closed her eyes and cleared her mind, allowing the sounds of the room to wash over her: the bright tinkle of cutlery, the clink of porcelain cups on tables, the low conversations of those around her.

It was Jo's particular curse, she thought, that she was a shameless eavesdropper. Any sort of meditative process was doomed to failure if she were in close proximity to other human beings. Much easier to eavesdrop on the conversations of others than to think about what might lie ahead, or the decision she would have to make. Toronto wouldn't wait forever.

A high-pitched voice from a table behind her: "Jim come up yesterrrdee to help chop firewood. Wish I could say the same for them ones next door. You know who I mean."

"Goddamned huskies won't shut up, neither."

Jo allowed the voices in the hotel lounge to wash over her with nuances of language that were still largely unfamiliar.

"My cousin's on disability in Whitehorse and he just sunk all his money into a claim. I tried to tell him."

"You can't reason with 'em once they git like that. Only interested in pay dirt, eh?"

"Won't be hitting pay dirt now. Have to wait until thaw."

"Geez, hope they've got enough in the shed to last until then."

A woman made a sound that suggested some doubt.

"Hey, did you hear about May? Not only was she blackmailing half the town, she'd also been exporting illegal animal parts to China with Christopher Byrne. They reckon he killed Marlo because she found out. Then he killed May, too."

"Well, I heard somebody else has taken over the racket now."

"Somebody told me was that dancer. The one that shot Byrne."

"He was going to kill both of them … she had to shoot."

"Hmm. I heard they were partners. Maybe she wanted to keep him quiet, like."

"That's bull and you know it."

"Yeah? Then where did she get the cash to buy out Bombay Peggy's?"

"No!" A pause. "Well, who cares where she got the money, as long as Peggy's stays. And better a local owns it. Anyways, keep your voice down in here."

"Jerry's kid just had another ATV accident."

"No! Again?"

When she opened her eyes, the world looked a little different to her. Jo stared out the window, gently cupping the drip brew. The dawn light illuminated thin streaks of bone-coloured cloud that feathered across the horizon, curling into the distance like a hollow rib cage. On the boardwalk, a woman was using her husky to tow a snowsuited child atop a scarlet sled.

From a distance, the town of Dawson City had the idyllic quality of a postcard. The quaint Victorian houses splashed in colourful pastel relief against a white landscape. The solemn appearance of the fir trees. The jaunty stovepipe chimneys that threw soft spirals of smoke into the air like ticker tape, suggesting an atmosphere of celebration. And the snow, the snow falling silently over everything.

Burying all of the town's secrets.

Acknowledgements

This book has been a long journey for me, which could not have been completed without the support of many helpers along the way.

I would therefore like to acknowledge the kind support of both The Canada Council for the Arts and the Klondike Institute for Art and Culture (KIAK), which aided in the development of the story by enabling me to travel to Dawson City and live there for a time as an Artist in Residence.

This project would not exist in book form without the efforts of two people in particular: Carolyn Forde, my lovely and good-humoured agent at Westwood Creative Artists (thank you for the late night conversations across multiple time zones), and Diane Young, who has earned a special place in my heart during the editing of this story. Thanks also to copy editor Laurie Miller for his enthusiasm and attention to detail.

I consider myself fortunate to have had a swat team of advance readers who are also professional writers: Kat Rooney, Phyllis Smallman, and Lucie Wilk. All three were tireless and unwavering in their dedication to providing feedback on rewrites.

The project also owes a lot to the mentorship of Gail Anderson-Dargatz, my instructor while I was a student in the University of British Columbia's Masters Program in Creative Writing. The story also received the support of the Crime Writers of Canada (CWC), via their New Writers Mentorship Program. The CWC paired me with Donna Carrick of Carrick Publishing, who provided invaluable feedback and encouragement at a crucial time in the process.

Thank you in advance to the team of good people at Dundurn Press for taking this story on and seeing it through to book form.

I also owe a big thank you to those members of the community in Dawson who helped with early research, especially the Dawson RCMP and the Trondek Hwech'in via KIAK. Later Chris Coulter of the RCMP on Bowen Island fielded procedural questions (and taught me how to preserve footprints in snow).

Muchos gracias to my son's nanny, Rosie Perez: the only person my toddler deemed worthy of minding him two mornings a week so that I could write and the person who taught us the words to "La Bomba."

Finally, thank you to my family for supporting the project, and still managing to dredge up enthusiasm for this book even on days when it took me away from you. This story is especially for you.